VEGAS SKIN

THE VEGAS TRILOGY
BOOK 2

DALLAS BARNES

ROUGH EDGES PRESS

Vegas Skin
Paperback Edition
Copyright © 2025 Dallas Barnes

Rough Edges Press
An Imprint of Wolfpack Publishing
1707 E. Diana Street
Tampa, FL 33610

roughedgespress.com

Paperback ISBN 978-1-68549-723-1
eBook ISBN 978-1-68549-618-0
LCCN 2024952436

AUTHOR'S NOTE

Although based on the writer's experience as Director of Security & Surveillance in Resort & Casino operations, the characters, locations, and events herein are the product of the writer's imagination and used fictitiously.

Any resemblance to real persons, living or dead, is purely coincidental. All references to Resort & Casino operations, locations, protocols, and procedures are fictional presentations in an effort to protect the integrity of actual operations, the safety of staff, support personnel, and those who make Las Vegas real, our guests.

THE CHARACTERS

Luke Mitchel - Director of Security at the Silver Palace

Greg Larson - General Manager of the Silver Palace

Charlotte Johnson - Director of Rooms at the Cosmo Resort & Casino

Tom Roberts - Card Room Manager

Gayle Turner — Surveillance (OIC)

Barbara Nichols - F&B Wild River Resort

Jackie Fallon - Executive Assistant

Mario Lopez - Security Supervisor (Day Watch)

KC King Security — Supervisor (AM Watch)

Anakoni Stone - Security Supervisor (PM Watch)

Candice Harmon - Surveillance (PM)

The Strip - Las Vegas, Nevada

This book is dedicated to the men and women you don't see. Serving behind the scenes in Resort & Casino operations, they protect the lives, property and safety of guests and employees, as well as the integrity of gaming. Their qualifications and standards are set by State Gaming Commissions.

*The security challenges are not an easy task in an environment where emotions, money, alcohol, and nudity seem the norm. Many times, the money is mixed with blood. It takes more than luck to protect **Vegas Skin**.*

VEGAS SKIN

ONE

WHAT HAPPENS IN VEGAS

HER NAME WAS TAMMY. She had just turned eighteen. There was no party. She had slept most of the day thanks to a combination of fentanyl and meth. Now she was strolling, looking, searching on the crowded Fremont Street in downtown Las Vegas. It was almost eleven o'clock, but darkness and time were fleeting on Fremont Street. A canopy above, arched over the crowded street displaying brilliant, colorful videos, turning the faces of the young and old as well as a sea of cell phones, skyward.

Among them, Tammy was looking for a man. No, more accurately, she was looking for money. She had three dollars and thirty-six cents in her purse, and she needed at least a buck fifty for an eight-ball of meth. Most men in Vegas carried money. Tammy wanted a man with money. Fremont Street had many. She was looking for one. Ironically, Tammy thought, there were men there looking for her. All she had to do was make eye contact with the right one and they would both recognize their wants. The wants were different, but the shared need was real.

Suede boots reaching almost to her knees, a short leather skirt and a snug unbuttoned blouse with nipples pushing out, made sure the eighteen-year-old with too much makeup and a swaggered walk did not go without attention from the crowd. Most looks were coming from men with women. Young and old alike. Most tried to mask their lustful looks, but those who didn't get away with it, got a stiff elbow, or a look, warning it was going to be costly.

Tammy was a prostitute, and all knew it. Especially the cops, but Las Vegas had more whores than cops. Soliciting sex or sex for sale in Las Vegas was illegal, but the Vegas Telephone Book had nineteen yellow pages listing escort services, massages, and female companions. Business cards advertising sex could be found in restrooms, on the windshields of parked cars, lamp posts, and everywhere else a crack would hold a card. Those making prostitution a profession in Vegas, those turning heads, looking like escapees from the Playboy Mansion, earned on average $72,000 dollars a month, cash, or give or take, about $1600.00 per client. All this before pimps got their commission or cops got in the way. Most, but not all, casinos and resorts in Las Vegas barred whores. Why? Because in addition to fees, whores stole cash, wallets, credit cards, wedding rings, and anything else of value. The majority went unreported. Thus, Las Vegas was rightfully tagged *Sin City*.

In addition to the women making prostitution their profession in Las Vegas, there were the uncounted free-lancers. The women who, for whatever reason, were desperate for cash. Among them was eighteen-year-old Tammy whose hunger for meth could not go ignored.

She finally exchanged a look with what she guessed was a fifty-year-old man. He was alone and his unshaven face gave him sort of a *Fort Wayne* look. He was wearing a plaid shirt and jeans. His rolled-up sleeves assured her he wasn't from Vegas. After an exchange of friendly glances and a smile, Tammy paused to glance at the colorful video on the overhead canopy. The bearded man moved closer to her. She had him.

"It's a real show, isn't it?" the Beard said, moving even closer. He now stood at her shoulder.

Tammy granted him a smile. "I like it."

The Beard looked her up and down. Boots to hairline. "I'm surprised they don't charge anything. A good show usually costs money."

"And you're looking for a good show?"

"I think I may have found one. You are one good-looking girl."

"Thank you. If I were in a show, I think I might charge, say, three hundred."

"This is your lucky day, girl. I won four hundred dollars from a slot at the Golden Nugget." He dug in a pocket to pull out a wad of folded currency. "I'll gladly pay three hundred for a show. If it could be a private one, you know, an hour or so?"

"It's your lucky day. I like privacy, too. You staying in town?"

"Four Queens. Sixth floor." The Beard smiled with the money clasped in hand, glancing toward the resort.

"And you're here alone?" Her heart was racing.

"Do I look lonely or what?" an eager smile answered.

"I can fix lonely," Tammy answered. "But we're talking three hundred. And it's due before we pass go."

The Beard discreetly counted twenty-dollar bills from the wad of money in hand. The crowd around them showed little interest. Somehow, Tammy felt lost in it. The man finished counting. He held some and returned the other bills to a pocket. "This show we're talking about," the Beard said, looking at the crowd around them as if to assure no one was listening. Satisfied, he returned his look to Tammy. In a quieter tone, holding up the cash, he added, "Includes you naked and me getting satisfied top to bottom. You know, like sex?"

Tammy's mind raced ahead thinking where she could buy meth. She raised an open hand, eager for the money in the Beard's hand. "No one has ever complained about my show."

The Beard pushed the folded twenties into her hand. Tammy quickly pushed the bills into the top of her skirt. "The queens it is. My name is Tammy." She was wishing it was over. The shakes from her last hit were beginning in her feet.

The Beard reached into a back pocket to pull out what looked like a wallet. A man and a woman, both dressed casually, moved from the crowd to either side of Tammy. The Beard raised the wallet to her face and flipped it open to reveal a polished gold badge. "Metropolitan police, you're under arrest for prostitution."

TWO
AFTER SHOCKS

THE THREE VICE officers surrounded the shaken eighteen-year-old Tammy Larson in the crowd on Fremont Street. "As long as you do what you're told," the bearded officer said quietly to Tammy's bowed face. "They'll be no handcuffs. Do you understand?"

Tammy managed a nod without looking up. Tears dropped from her chin.

"Okay," the Beard said. "Follow me." The Beard turned and began moving through the heavy crowd. The crowd on Las Vegas's Fremont Street was thick, pushy, and noisy. Most attention was on the light and color playing on the arched video screen covering the street from one side to the other high above them. Tammy, as instructed, followed the Beard with plain clothes officer at each of her shoulders. As they neared intersecting Fourth Street, the crush of cigarette smoke, spilled drinks, and laughter faded behind them.

An unmarked police car waited at the curb. The Beard opened the rear door of the police car when the trio reached it. He pulled a set of chromed handcuffs from the rear of his waistline.

"Policy says I have to handcuff you in the car."

Tammy's head was still bowed. Her hair hung over her face. She was sobbing. The Beard took one of her wrists, snapped the handcuff on her and then reached for her other arm. Her sobbing became louder.

"Watch your head," the Beard cautioned as, holding Tammy's handcuffed wrists, he guided her into the rear seat of the unmarked car.

She welcomed the air conditioning, but the car was filled with the scent of men's cologne. The Beard closed the car door with a thud. Tammy lowered her head onto the back of the front seat. She wished she could die. Her sobbing mixed with the country music the driver of the car was playing. Outside, the Beard spoke with the other two Vice officers. Tammy could hear the voices but not the words. A moment later, the door opened across from her as the Beard climbed into the back seat. The driver silenced the music.

"Take us to Clark Detention," the Beard told the driver.

He nodded and pulled the car into gear. Tammy rode in silence as the car found its way through the evening traffic. After several blocks, she took a deliberate deep breath in an effort to calm herself. The handcuffs were painful on her wrists. She moved, trying to ease the pressure. It did little to help. She sniffed and forced herself to raise her head from the seatback and look at the Beard.

"Please, listen to me," she said with effort between sobs that filled her choppy voice with emotion. "My dad, he has lots of...money. He's powerful. He'll give you whatever you want."

"I don't know who *Dad* is," the Beard answered

soberly as the car slowed for a red light. "But we don't care. You're going to Clark County Jail. You're going to be booked for prostitution. Tell that to Dad."

The ride was short. The unmarked car pulled into the walled and gated court where prisoners were unloaded. There was a black and white police car ahead of them. A Black handcuffed prisoner being pulled out of the car was screaming profanities and kicking at the officers. He was quickly surrounded by a foursome of uniformed police officers who choked, twisted, and forced him to the pavement. Held there, the man continued his struggle as another officer, a jailer, arrived with a heavy-wheeled plastic chair with multiple straps. The profanities from the handcuffed man continued as he was lifted into the chair. One of the uniformed officers forced a nylon mask over the man's head. The straps were wrapped tight around him. He was wheeled off toward a broad doorway.

The patrol car pulled away, and the unmarked car pulled forward into its space. The car door beside Tammy was opened. She tensed as warm night air reached in.

"Is this one looking for a fight?" an overweight jailer spat at Tammy. The Beard was quickly out his side and around the car to join the jailer and two other uniforms.

"Young one for prostitution," the Beard announced. "No resistance."

"Nice weather for whores." The jailer smiled as he looked Tammy up and down.

Tammy was escorted inside and turned over to an attractive, uniformed female officer in her forties. She was ordered to stand against a wall while yet another female officer searched her for weapons. Tammy's sobs yielded to fear. The booking area was filled with loud voices, buzzing slamming metal doors and an army of cops, but more than the police officers was the sea of arrestees. Shaved heads, tattoos on necks, arms, hands, legs. The well-dressed, young and old, the tattered, weeping, crying, joking. A mix of males and females, most repeaters, others crying, pleading for help. Tammy was examined by a nurse, photo'd, fingerprinted electronically. Private property, including her purse and everything in it, like her earrings and watch, were all seized. She was formally booked as a prisoner of Clark County on a charge of prostitution. When the processing was over, she was given an opportunity to use one of several age-worn-looking wall telephones.

She had no money for the telephone.

"Make it a collect call," an attractive Black woman in a short black skirt and high heels said beside her at another telephone.

Tammy sniffed, dialed an operator and told her it was a collect call. She gave the operator her mother's telephone number. It was twelve forty a.m.

After three rings, a sober, mature female voice answered, "Hello."

"Mom, it's me. I need help."

"Tammy, what's wrong? Where are you?" The noise from the booking area, the cursing, the shouting of warnings and commands, metal doors slamming, telephones ringing. It was an alarming mix for the mother awaking from her sleep.

Tammy gripped the telephone tightly as she pressed it to her ear and mouth. "Mom, I'm, I'm in jail."

"Jail! My god, Tammy, what have you done?"

Tammy cried, "Mom, I need help. Please."

"Where are you?"

"In the, in the Clark County Jail."

"What have you done?"

Tears ran down Tammy's cheeks. She twisted, cried, bent with the heavy grief.

"Come on. Get off the phone," a male prisoner with a snake tattoo on his neck waiting behind Tammy complained.

"I've been arrested," Tammy wept into the receiver. "They're calling me a prostitute." Her voice was a harsh whisper.

"Oh god," Naomi Larson answered emotionally. She could almost feel her daughter's pain. "I'll call your father. He'll know what to do. Are you all right?"

The waiting man with the snake on his neck reached over Tammy's shoulder and pushed the black button on the receiver's base. A dial tone sang in Tammy's ear.

"Your time's up," the Snake warned.

———

GREG LARSON, the general manager of the Silver Palace, one of the three *big dog* resort casinos on the Las Vegas Strip, was asleep. He was separated from his wife Naomi. Their divorce proceedings were in process. They had not spoken since Greg moved out. They had been separated for five months. It had been a bitter fight. Money mostly.

Charlotte Johnson, an attractive Black woman, lay asleep at Greg Larson's side. She was the former head of human resources at the Silver Place and the current Director of Rooms at the Cosmo. The affair between the two, which started while Charlotte was still employed at the Silver Palace, became public and big news after Greg Larson unexpectedly kissed Charlotte at a VIP management meeting on the Strip. Also adding to the stress of the Larson divorce was a shooting in the GM's office at the Silver Palace when Greg Larson shot and killed a former employee. The police investigated and found the shooting justified. Greg Larson became a bit of a hero. At least to most. Not so much with Naomi Larson. She was the one calling. It was now almost one a.m.

The cell phone on the nightstand beside the sleeping Greg Larson began to hum and vibrate on the table's glass surface. It awoke him. He was reaching for the telephone in the room's darkness when Charlotte, annoyed with what she was certain was another annoying call from the Silver Palace, rolled away and pulled the sheet up to cover her head. Larson looked at the caller ID on his cell.

"Oh shit," he whispered, swinging his bare feet to the floor.

"This better be goddamned important," Larson growled into his cell.

"Greg," Naomi answered. "Tammy's been arrested."

"What!" Larson blurted. "Arrested. For what?"

The alarm in Larson's voice reached the sheet-covered Charlotte. She pushed the sheet aside and sat up, revealing she was nude.

"She called me," Naomi continued, her voice was also full of distress. "She said she was in the Clark County Jail."

"Jail!" Larson blurted in disbelief. He switched on a table lamp beside the bed as if the light would somehow soften the stress. Behind him, Charlotte sat up and pulled the sheet up over her breasts. She was listening. "What the hell is she in jail for?"

"Prostitution," Naomi answered soberly in his ear.

"How the hell could you let this happen, Naomi?"

"Don't start with me, Greg, or I'll hang up and you can go to hell."

"Okay, okay," Larson answered as he pushed off the bed to pace in his shorts while talking on the cell. "What do you want me to do?"

"I want you to act like a father and go get her."

"And once again, I'm picking up the pieces for your mistakes."

"You bastard. Could you, for once in your life, just act like a father and go get her?"

"When did she call?"

"About ten minutes ago. I called my attorney, but he didn't answer."

"The prick is probably busy filing a new action against me."

Charlotte connected the dots from what she had heard. She pushed out of bed and walked into the bathroom in her panties. She slammed the door shut.

"Greg, listen to me please," Naomi pleaded from where she sat on the edge of her king-size bed eight miles away in the hills of Las Vegas's Lake District. "This isn't about our divorce. It's about our daughter. Can you, will you, help get her out of jail?"

Larson looked at the light beneath the closed bathroom door. "Yeah, okay," he answered. "I'll do what I can."

The sound of a toilet flushing reached out from the closed bathroom as the panty-clad, sober Charlotte Johnson opened the door to lean a shoulder on the doorframe and glare at Larson as he paced in his shorts, cell phone in hand.

"Greg, please, promise me you'll call."

"Yeah, okay, I'll call," Larson answered as his thoughts raced ahead.

He knew the streets of Vegas were paved with gossip. Especially when the talk was about those wielding power, and Greg Larson was among them. In Vegas, power was called *juice*. And those with *juice* paid a price for it. In Larson's case, he knew the arrest of his daughter for prostitution would be news. Not only news but talk, gossip, lies. The Silver Palace, where Larson sat on the throne, had over ten thousand employees. Has word of Tammy's arrest already reached them? Larson knew he had to act quickly before the fire reached him.

Larson punched a button on his cell, ending the call from his wife and looked to the panty-clad Charlotte who moved to sit down on the unmade bed. "That was your wife."

"My soon-to-be ex-wife," Larson answered.

"Don't make me ask," Charlotte cautioned, playing with the edge of the wrinkled sheet.

"My daughter's been arrested," Larson answered, returning the cell phone to the table beside the bed. He reached for a pair of pants draped over a nearby chair.

"So, your wife calls and now you're going to do what she wants?" Charlotte said soberly.

"Charlotte, I'm Tammy's father. It doesn't have shit to do with my ex. I've got to help." He sat on his side of the bed and pushed his legs into his pants.

"And when does it stop?" Charlotte questioned soberly. "Your ex just found her way into our bedroom. What's next?"

————

IT WAS LATE, dark on most of the West Coast but not on the Las Vegas Strip. The digital lighting and illuminated billboards erased the darkness. The sidewalks were busy, and the streets were crowded with cabs, buses, and cars. In the bowels of the towering Silver Palace,

Luke Mitchel, the director of security at the Silver Palace, was in the resort's sprawling busy kitchen with the uniformed security AM watch commander, KC King. The kitchen was alive with a mix of noise and activity as the crew prepared work on a pending breakfast buffet. The two men had just finished counting hundreds of boxes of frozen shrimp unloaded from a vendor's refrigerated truck into a large and vapor-filled freezer.

KC King, the uniformed watch commander, a dark-haired iconic fit forty-year-old, slammed the big heavy door on the refrigerator. He shook off a chill and looked to Luke. "Six hundred and forty-eight boxes."

Luke Mitchel, dressed in a tan sports coat over a black tee shirt, looked at the clipboard he carried. On it was an invoice prepared by the vendor. Signing the document would confirm delivery. "We're short two boxes."

"I'd say we got a thief somewhere," KC King suggested.

The two men walked across the kitchen to the face of overheard doors where an unshaven fifty-year-old driver wearing a faded wide-brimmed hat, sat with a paper cup of coffee in one hand and a smoldering cigarette in the other.

"Don't get up," Luke said as the driver started to. KC King grabbed two more chairs and brought them to Luke. The two men sit down with the driver, who continued drinking his coffee. He looked worried.

"Is there a problem?"

"Let's start with you putting your cigarette out," Luke ordered as he glanced at the invoice. "Says here you delivered six hundred and fifty boxes of frozen shrimp. We counted every box, twice, and all we got is six hundred and forty-eight. Before anybody signs this, you need to change the invoice. We're short two boxes."

"Maybe a miscount when they loaded your truck?" KC King suggested.

"Whatever," Luke added, aiming the clipboard and invoice to the driver. "We need you to change the invoice before it can be signed."

The driver ground out his cigarette with a boot and sat his coffee on the floor before looking at the invoice. "What's the deal. This hasn't been a problem in the past."

"Box of frozen shrimp cost a couple bucks," Luke suggested soberly. "Delivery has to be accurate."

"Maybe you should talk to the chef." The driver stalled after a glance at the invoice.

"Why would we do that?" Luke asked.

The driver looked at the invoice again and then to Luke. "This is a Vegas thing, you know. One of those things that doesn't show on paper."

"When two boxes of frozen shrimp disappear," Luke answered. "It's not a Vegas thing, it's a theft."

"I got nothing to do with theft," the driver defended, adjusting his hat nervously.

"Then change the invoice," Luke suggested.

"I made my delivery like I do every time I wheel in here. You two must know what's going on," the driver pleaded.

"You're right," Luke cautioned. "We know what's going on. We paid for six hundred and fifty boxes of shrimp, but two boxes got lost. Disappeared. Could be theft."

The driver raised an open hand in protest. "Don't be talking theft to me. I drove up here with a full load."

"Then where's our shrimp?"

"Like I said," the driver argued. "You know how business is done in Vegas. Talk to your top man. You know, the chef with the big hat."

"Why should we talk to him?"

"Okay," the driver said, offering the clipboard back to Luke. "It was a tip, you know. A courtesy. We want the business, so we call it a tip."

Luke and KC King exchanged a look before Luke added the question. "Who got tipped?"

The driver rubbed his hands on his pant legs. He looked stressed. He looked to both men before he answered. "The chef, you know, top dog, Jack Howard. He got the tip."

"You mean he got the two boxes of shrimp?"

"Yeah, that's the deal. His house was my first stop. That's our agreement."

"How many times have you made this tip trip?" Luke pressed.

"Chef phones his order in. Manager tells me if the chef wants a tip."

"And tonight, before you came here, you dropped two boxes at the chef's house."

"Come on, this is Vegas," the driver said, rubbing the back of his neck.

"Right," Luke said, pushing the clipboard back to him. "This is Vegas, and you lose. Now, if you want a delivery signature, change the number, and next time, no, every time, no more tips."

The driver looked stressed, but he pulled a pen from a shirt pocket and changed the numbers on the invoice. When he finished, he offered the clipboard back to Luke who added his signature. "You're out of here. Drive carefully."

The driver pushed out of his chair, looked at the two and walked away.

Luke looked at the invoice, then at KC King. "Sort of explains the missing steaks, meatballs, bacon, and who knows what else."

"So, do we get a new chef?" KC King asked with a smile.

The cell phone clipped on Luke's belt beneath his jacket began chirping. He reached for it. "This is Luke Mitchel."

"Luke, Greg Larson here. Sorry to wake you but I need your help."

Luke gave KC King a look that said the call was private. King got the message and moved away, taking his chair with him. Luke pushed out of his. "I was awake. You're going to have to look for a new chef."

"Right now, I need to talk about something else," Larson answered. It was a near plea, and Luke could hear the stress in Larson's words.

"How can I help?" Luke questioned.

"You were a police officer once, right? You know about arrests. People going to jail, bail, stuff like that," Larson asked.

"Yeah, I've been there, why," Luke said, reading where the words lead.

"My wife called. She said Tammy, our eighteen-year-old daughter, is in jail at Clark County. She was arrested for prostitution, Luke, I don't know what the fuck to do. I can't go to the county jail. I can't call our attorneys. If the press gets a hold of this, I'm screwed. GM of the Silver Palace, Father of the Year. You gotta help me."

"Got it. Tammy. Clark County. We can get her bail. It might take a couple hours. Where can we meet?"

"Meet! Luke, I can't be part of this."

"She's going to need a ride. Where do I take her?"

"Up on the hill. Her mother's place. You've been there. Tammy still lives there."

"Okay, I'm on it." Luke felt the growing buzzing in his ears.

He knew what was coming. He reached to the fresh jagged scar of his left temple where he had been hit with a glass pitcher. He massaged the scar gently. It was still painful and sensitive. He stepped to the closed overhead door and leaned against it for balance. Wanting out of the hospital, he lied and hid the dizzy, near fainting spells haunting him after he had been hit with a heavy glass water pitcher by a hostile ex-employee and hospitalized two weeks. The attack had taken place in the GM's office. Greg Larson, the Silver Palace GM, had a CCW permit. He had drawn his pistol and shot Luke's attacker to death. Luke, as well as the rest of the world, credited Larson with saving Luke's life. Luke closed his eyes as the kitchen spun before him.

"Luke, did you hear me? You still there?"

"Yeah, boss, I'm on it."

"Give me a call when you have her. I'll meet you at my wife's home."

"Will do," Luke said, taking a deep breath with effort. He ended the call and snapped the phone back on his belt. He pushed away from the door he was leaning on to make sure the dizziness and ringing in his ears were fading. They were nearly gone. He steadied himself as the uniformed KC King returned.

The lieutenant gave Luke a look of concern. "Everything okay, Chief?"

"Yeah, everything's good," Luke answered.

Luke's first call was to a bondsman. He found the telephone number on the Silver Palace's Internal Net under human resources. Goodfellas bail bonds on Main

Street. A friendly female voice answered on the third ring. Luke was surprised it was almost one thirty a.m.

"Good morning, Goodfellas Bonds, this is Rockie. How can I help you?"

"Rockie, this is Luke Mitchel. I'm the director of security at the Silver Palace. I need bail for an eighteen-year-old arrestee. She's in Clark County. Her name is Tammy Larson. The charge is prostitution."

"Clark County Detention posts their in-custodies online. Let me have a look. May I have her name again?

"Tammy Larson."

"One moment, please." The line was quiet for a moment and then Rickie's voice returned. "Okay, I've found her. Bail is set at one thousand. No prior offenses. The Silver Palace has an active account with us. Would you like me to post bail?"

"Yes, please."

"Okay, your name was?"

"Luke Michell, Director of Security."

"Okay, I see you in our corporate profile of the Palace. I'll text you a copy of the bond I set, and I'll include a copy of the bill I'll forward to Cash Ops. I'm going to need maybe forty minutes or so to get everything done. When done, I'll text you. You'll need to take a copy of the bond with you to Clark County. There, go to the Release Window, next to booking, and present the bond. The Sheriffs will do the rest."

"You've made all this very user-friendly, miss."

"Thank you," Rockie answered. "Unfortunately, bail is usually just the beginning of a story."

Forty minutes. There wasn't enough time to go down to the employee cafeteria or do anything other than wait. Luke's thoughts took him to Greg Larson, the GM. He was waiting too, and then there was his wife. They were separated. A divorce in the works. The GM had been caught in an affair with the head of HR. It had to be tough for all of them. Their daughter was in jail. In the city where most were forgetting the problems they left at home, ironically Luke was finding he was becoming part of a problem that wasn't going to go away with a smile or a drink. Like the others. He would wait. He put his feet up on his desk and fought off a yawn. Damn, it was well on its way to two a.m. The fact he had forgotten what time it was proved he was becoming a native. He looked at the watch on his wrist. Could he get through a day without caring what time it was? No, meetings, reports, and meals all needed a time, and soon it would be time to go pick up Tammy Larson, the GM's eighteen-year-old daughter, arrested for prostitution. Other than that, it had been a quiet night. They had plugged an expensive hole in kitchen operations by discovering where the frozen shrimp, missing streaks, and hamburgers were going. The chef was probably asleep at this hour. Luke knew the man. He was a loud and sober German. A German who slept through the end of his Vegas career. A German Luke pitted. A German who would soon be looking for a job. The thought made Luke look at his inner being. Damn, everything he did seemed to put a rope around someone's neck. No, Luke reasoned, refusing the thought. He wasn't putting a rope around anyone's neck. They were putting it there themselves. He was simply the man who turned on the light. He was thinking about all that when his cell phone buzzed. He reached for his cell. It was a text from Rockie at Goodfellas Bonds.

Copy of Bond being sent to your email. Luke had no sooner read the text when then the printer behind his desk began printing out the bond release.

They needed copies folded and in a pocket, Luke headed for one of the company cars in the basement. He advised his AM watch commander by radio that he would be off property and drove onto the nighttime Strip. The wide, usually crowded street was quiet. More cabs than cars. Although traffic was light with even fewer *peds*, the Strip was basking in a wash of digital and video lighting that washed away the night. Luke drove into downtown Vegas to the cluster of towering County Buildings with the detention center in its midst. The detention center had a better-known title. It was the county jail.

Luke was pleased to find a visitor parking space vacant outside the jail. A sign on the outside of the door marked *Visitors* read, *Possession of concealed weapons of any kind as well as possession of controlled Substances in this facility is strictly prohibited. Violators will be prosecuted.* Luke reached the door, read the sign, and returned to his car. There, he took out the loaded Glock 23 concealed on his belt beneath his jacket and pushed it under the driver's front seat.

Inside, Luke found his way to a worn counter divided by a heavy wire mesh. He could see the booking area where a male arrestee was being spread eagle on a wall while a uniformed jailer patted him down for weapons. A uniformed female deputy appeared behind the wire mesh. Luke was surprised at how attractive she looked.

"How may I help you?" Even her teeth were perfect. She was fulfilling the Vegas myth. Luke's eight years with the LAPD now seemed very distant. Even though he enjoyed the *juice* his true title at the Silver Palace brought him as director of security, it wasn't much help on his side of the protective mesh. The cops were on one side, and he was on the other, without his gun. Hoping, some-

how, the attractive thirty-year-old on the other side of
the wire would see he was once one of them, Luke
pushed the bond release paper through a gap on the
countertop.

"Her name is Tammy Larson," Luke said in his best
cop voice.

The deputy picked up the paper and read. Then with
a look at Luke, she questioned, "Who are you?"

"Luke Mitchel. I'm the director of security at the
Silver Palace."

The deputy nodded, offering Luke a glance. "Have a
seat, Mr. Mitchel. It will be a couple of minutes." She
turned and walked away.

Luke eyed the reception area. It was small, and the
lighting was dim. An empty trash can sat beside a worn,
long bench attached to the wall. Luke sat down in the
middle of it. He didn't feel an attachment to any of it. He
thought about the number of arrestees in the jail. A smile
comforted him. He was sure they had more guests at the
Silver Palace than they had prisoners in cells.

At the Silver Palace Luke was juiced and seldom had
to wait on anything. The many faces of Vegas. Most of
the real faces were hidden. Most had more than one life,
one face to show. He sat on the bench and listened. He
could hear telephones ringing, iron cell doors rolling
closed with dull metallic thuds, deputies' voices—sharp
with authority, cries from the arrestees, muffled radio
and loudspeaker voices joining to get lost in the drama
of the sound.

His wait was short. Luke saw the female deputy
returning with an arm holding Tammy Larson. Luke
pushed to his feet as the deputy paused on the other side
of a heavily wired mesh gate. She offered a paper bag to
Tammy.

"The bag contains your personal property, a copy of your bail release and the date of your arraignment. Do you have any questions?"

Luke and the deputy both waited for Tammy to speak. She didn't. Her chin was lowered. She stared at the floor. Luke studied Tammy. With her chin lowered, her long dark hair masked her face, but she was as tall as the deputy. Her eighteen-year-old body looked younger than her escort. Younger and shapelier. Her high heels, short leather skirt and snug blouse completed the look. In Vegas, even a glance at her said, *Whore*. Luke hoped his bias wouldn't show. He hoped it wasn't real. This was the daughter of the man that saved his life. He owed her and her father. The deputy brought all three of them back to the moment by pushing a button inside the heavy door. The electronic lock buzzed, and the deputy swung the gated door open.

"You're free to go."

Tammy glanced up at Luke as she stepped through the door which closed with a thud behind them. Too much makeup, Luke decided as their eyes met. Hers were dark. He gestured toward the door leading outside and then turned to lead the way. Tammy followed. She stayed quiet as they reached the car where Luke opened the door for her. He closed the door, rounded the car and gathered his gun from beneath the car seat. Tammy watched as he holstered the automatic pistol beneath his jacket.

Inside the detention center, the female deputy sat down at a desk inside the booking & release area to update the status on the release. The balding older deputy with the weight problem walked to stand and looked over her shoulder. He watched quietly for a moment before he spoke. "You know whose kid that was who just walked out?"

The deputy paused from her typing on the keyboard and glanced at the man. "Yeah, says right here. Tammy Larson."

The heavy deputy crossed his arms in a confident manner and smiled. "Tammy Larson, huh. Look there on her booking slip. You'll see her old man, Daddy with a capital D, is Greg Larson. He's a big dog on the Strip. General manager of the Silver Palace. I might know a few people that would enjoy learning she was in here."

The female deputy ignored the comment and resumed her typing. The heavy deputy unfolded his arms and walked away. He was looking for a telephone.

THREE
THE GOOD, THE BAD AND THE...

LUKE DROVE AWAY from the detention center looking for East Sierra which would take him into the hills above the Strip. Tammy's presence in the car was one that could not be ignored. Luke was guessing it was Versace, but it, like the lipstick and rouge, was too much. He knew he had to speak to the kid, offer some assurance she was safe, soon to be with those who loved her.

"We're going to your mother's house. Your dad said he'd meet us there." Luke hoped the words would somehow bring her some comfort.

Tammy raised her head, nodded acknowledgment, and looked at Luke. "Who are you?" The question sounded childlike although the words were from a young woman.

"My name's Luke Marshal. I work for your dad at the Silver Palace."

"And you carry a gun?" Tammy's voice was anxious.

"I'm the head of security. You've seen the guys in uniform at the hotel."

"Is my dad angry?" Again, her anxiety showed.

"I'm sure he's worried."

"My mother will be pissed," Tammy said to the street ahead.

"You don't want this to happen again," Luke cautioned as he slowed for a traffic signal with a cab beside them. "First time you'll come away low bail and probation. Next time it's a felony and the bail goes up. Probation becomes jail time."

"You think I don't know that? I'm the one who was locked up."

"On your booking slip. I've got a copy and so do you," Luke cautioned as they moved on with the traffic. "In addition to the charge of prostitution, they also say you were under the influence of an illegal substance." Luke looked at her. "I'm guessing meth."

Tammy returned Luke's look. "So in addition to carrying a gun, you go around accusing people of using drugs."

Luke was surprised at the tone. It was because the jail was now further behind them. She was no longer a frightened child. Now, she was more a victim than an arrestee with a court date. Luke knew who he was talking to.

"I didn't say you were under the influence of drugs," Luke defended. "The Metropolitan police who arrested you for an act of prostitution are the ones saying you were under the influence. Save your sarcasm for them."

Luke's words were heavy. Tammy, who was erect and poised, now sank into her seat as if in surrender. Luke glanced at her. He could see the want to be whore had become a child again. He was quiet as the street became steeper. The lights of the city were yielding to the darkness ahead. Luke knew he had to say more. The girl needed help. "Your parents are going to hug you, cry, but that's going to pass. They're going to want answers. Why did this happen? Why are you using drugs? It's going to be tough. Don't say much tonight. Wait until morning. Get the story ready. And no bullshit. We're talking truth. You gotta sell and you gotta tell the truth. Mom wants it. Dad wants it. The courts are going to demand it. Find the truth and use it. Tell it. Follow it and find a way out of this. You're a rich kid. Oh, you might think you have to have meth, but you can't. You know that. It was easier to try and be a whore than it was to ask mom or dad for money. Why? Because it's wrong. You were wrong. You gotta accept that. You with me?"

"But I'm scared," Tammy confessed, wiping tears from her face.

"I've been scared too," Luke confessed. "Scared just means you can't find the answers. It also means you need help. Accept that. Let them in. They love you."

Tammy's crying grew. She knew they were now just minutes away from her mother's house. She covered her face as the sobbing increased.

"Tammy," Luke said. "Listen to me. We'll soon be there. I'll have to leave, but I want you to know this. No one's going to hear what we talked about. It's just ours. No one else is allowed in, okay? You ever need help with anything, call me. Just dial the Palace and ask for Luke. They'll find me." He dug in a jacket pocket as they approached the closed gate to the Lakes. As they slowed to a stop, Luke pulled out a business card. He pushed the card into Tammy's hands. "That's got my cell number on it. You call me when you need help. You got that?"

Without a look to Luke, Tammy pushed the card beneath the fold at the top of her skirt. Luke allowed the car to drift to the edge of an illuminated box displaying rows of keys with numbers imprinted on them. Once again, he looked to Tammy. "What's the combo?"

———

GREG LARSON, as the general manager of the Silver Palace, was in charge of ten thousand two hundred and six employees. He was a powerful man when in his role as GM. It was proving far different in the confines of the condo he shared with Charlotte Johnson, the handsome Black woman he claimed as his love. She had listened after Naomi Larson's call came late in the night with the news Tammy had been arrested. Her sympathies and attitude were far different than Greg Larson's.

"You had to know she was going to call," Charlotte told Larson as he dressed to leave. "If it wasn't Tammy being arrested, it would be the dog dying again or the car wouldn't start, or the garage door won't go down. Greg, they're just fucking excuses. She's pulling the string and you're reacting. She's no longer your wife."

"You're right," Larson agreed, sitting on the edge of the bed to push his shoes on. "She's no longer my wife. I don't give a shit about her, but I am Tammy's father, and she needs me."

"Greg," Charlotte pleaded, holding the front of her robe together. "You already helped. You found someone to get her out of jail. The rest, the *come help me*, is just Naomi bullshit. I thought you had decided. What will it be the next time? She's manipulating you. Don't go. Don't leave me alone."

Larson pushed off the bed and tucked his shirt into his pants. "Charlotte, goddamn it, I have to go."

"Why can't you call Luke Mitchel and have him bring Tammy here? We've got an extra bedroom. Why is it you have to go there? Greg, she's pushing herself between us."

Larson grabbed his suit jacket from an open closet. "Listen to me," he said as he pushed his arms into the jacket. "This isn't about her." He stepped closer to Charlotte. "It's my little girl. My baby, my daughter. I'm going."

"Okay, fucking go, but I'm done with this. You claim you love me. You promise everything, but when she says jump. You jump. You've made your choice. I have, too. You go out that door and you'll be coming back to nothing but a room full of memories. I'm done, gone, outta here. Outta everything."

Larson glared at Charlotte, but he said nothing. Was she being serious? Why the hell couldn't she understand? He turned, gathered his keys from a tray on the nightstand. "Do whatever the hell you want," Larson said, moving for the door.

———

Naomi Larson was dressed in a robe, too. She was standing outside her front door looking for headlamps. She had turned on all the outside lights. The garage and driveway were illuminated. Her dog sat at her feet. It had read the apprehension filling the air. The night air was more than cool, it was cold. The desert was hot during the day and surprisingly different at night. The chill was getting to Naomi, but she wouldn't go in. She had to see Tammy when she arrived. She would hold her, assure her it was all right, although she knew their lives were never going to be the same. She thought the betrayal and divorce by her husband was the worst life could bring, but now, somehow, it was even darker. How could she tell her family, her friends, anyone.

Who would understand, who could understand, an eighteen-year-old being arrested for prostitution? It was ugly, it was bitterly cold, and it wasn't the night that was making her shiver. She wiped at the tears tracing down her cheeks and then she saw the headlamps. Tammy was coming.

The car pulled into the driveway and stopped. Naomi rushed toward it. The passenger door opened, and Tammy the whore climbed out. She looked very much like one of the young whores found on the Strip. She swung the car door shut, and it backed away.

Naomi reached Tammy and pulled her into her arms. Tammy buried her head on her mother's shoulder as they wept. The two women clung to each other.

Luke Mitchel allowed himself a final look at the two. He offered a fleeting prayer that together they might find a path out of the storm they were in but then he wondered if God really paid attention to those who paid so much attention to him. He shifted gears and backed out of the driveway quietly. Tammy, and the talk about her age, took Luke's thoughts to his daughter. How old was she? Eight, came the answer. He thought about the last time he'd seen her. A little over two years. It wasn't that he neglected her. Luke sent child support every month and his ex knew she could call on him when and if there was ever a need. Need, did she need to see him? Wasn't her stepdad filling in the blank for him? Why make an issue out of seeing the kid and rock the cart, and what would he do, what could he do? Go there and bring the kid to Vegas. What would an eight-year-old do in Vegas? He had never even seen where she lived. His ex had married another LAPD police officer so that helped with knowing the kid was safe and comfortable, but life had to be more than safe. Luke made himself yet another promise. Now that he had a home, a condo, he might invite the kid up. Maybe he'd fly her up from LA. Las Vegas was surrounded with beauty. Red Rock Canyon, a great zoo, and more. He reminded himself he needed to send his ex a check as he slowed for the gate leading out of the complex.

As Luke waited at the gate, allowing it to open, a set of headlamps approached. The car was traveling fast. It slowed at the gate but flashed by with a roar with it partially open. Luke recognized the driver. It was the GM, Greg Larson.

Greg Larson parked in front of the garage and scrambled out of his Lamborghini. The lights were on all over the house. Inside and out. It was as if someone hoped to wash away the darkness. *Irony*, Larson thought as he hurried toward the kitchen door.

He was eager and in a rush to see one of the women inside. He loved one of them. There was nothing he wouldn't do for his daughter. His love for her had no conditions. The other woman. His thoughts for her, his heart-felt feelings were bitter and defensive. After twenty-two years of marriage, seemingly all she wanted was his money. She didn't earn it, it had nothing to do with her role as his wife, it was a persona of greed. He thought about it, but seldom, because she was no longer fit. The once shapely loving, caring companion had become a woman who wanted to destroy him.

Their sexual relationship had died long ago. Soon after that, the trophy wife became a distant near stranger whose love seemed reserved only for her dog. He had lost his wife to a dog. Larson forced himself to take a deep breath as he neared the back door. He wished he knew what to say. What to do.

Naomi and her daughter Tammy were sitting at the kitchen table. Tammy had a glass of orange juice sitting in front of her. Naomi was dressed in a robe she had pulled tight around her neck as if she were cold. She looked exhausted. Her big dog lay at her feet. Larson was surprised at Tammy's appearance. He was used to seeing her in casual jeans and sneakers, with a smile and captivating green eyes. The woman he saw shocked him. She looked like a Vegas whore. Teased hair, too much face makeup, boots almost to the knees, a short leather skirt, a tight form-fitting blouse that accented her breasts. Larson forced himself to her.

He hugged her neck. "I'm relieved you're home, baby. How are you?"

"I'm okay, Dad. I'm sorry." Her breath was less than pleasant. She snaked an arm around her father's back without getting out of her chair. Naomi's expression remained sober as she watched the two.

Larson pulled out a chair and sat down between the two women. His attention was on Tammy. He reached and took her hand in his. "I'll get you an attorney. We'll get this cleared up, dismissed."

Tammy's hand was in her father's, but her eyes were fixed on the glass of orange juice. "Dad, I don't want to talk about it."

"I understand. You need some rest. Come home with me for a while."

"She lives here," Naomi cautioned, reaching to brush a sweep of hair from her daughter's face. Larson read it as a challenge. His eyes went to Naomi's. Tammy withdrew her hand from her father's.

"She did live here," Larson said in a sober masculine

tone, "and look what happened. She's coming home with me."

"She's eighteen now," Naomi answered with a quick warning. "You can no longer tell her what to do. I think she's had enough of your choices."

"And whose choice was tonight? Where did she get those clothes?" Larson questioned. "Do you know what time she went out? Where were you? In the bedroom watching television, maybe brushing your dog, having a drink or two, maybe more."

"You're her father. Where were you? Shacked downtown with that Black…"

"Don't say it, Naomi," Larson warned, burning her with a threatening look.

"I'll say it because it's true," Naomi barked in reply.

Tammy raised her hands to her parents. "Mom, Dad, please. Don't do this."

Naomi and Larson fell silent as their eyes continued the bitterness filling the space between them. Tammy lowered her hands. Larson noticed they were trembling.

"Let's allow Tammy to decide," Larson said in a quiet tone, holding Naomi's look.

"She's not going anywhere," Naomi warned.

A tense silence followed as the two waited on Tammy to speak. The girl lowered her chin and laced her fingers together in front of her. Larson silently marveled at his daughter's appearance. He could have passed her on the street and not recognized her. Guilt tensed him. He wanted his little girl back. The teen who loved horseback riding, the senior on the honor roll, the sixteen-year-old he taught to drive. They seemingly had been captured by darkness and the street. He reached for Tammy's hand again, but this time she pulled it away. Larson fought an urge to ask how she got to where she was, but his guilt kept him silent.

Finally, Tammy took an audible breath and looked up at her mother. "Mom, Dad's right," she said, digging at a thumbnail. "This hasn't worked. All we do is argue and fight. Maybe if I..."

"Don't say that," Naomi answered, pushing her robe even higher on her neck. "I do everything I can to make you happy. Is this what I get?"

"Yeah, like when I brought Doug out here," Tammy answered. "You treated him really great."

"He smoked marijuana in your bedroom," Naomi defended.

"Maybe you haven't heard, Mom. Weed's now legal in Nevada."

"I'm not letting anybody smoke anything in my house."

Larson was surprised at his daughter's attitude. She was sounding adult, mature, and responsible. He chose to add to his suggestion. "It might be best for both of you if Tammy came downtown for a while."

Tammy gave her father a quick look of agreement. Naomi saw it. She reached and petted her Rottweiler's ears as the dog sat up. "I'm not joining in this game," she said, warning both Larson and her daughter. "You choose to go down with your father and that woman he's shacking with, it's going to be a one-way trip. You're not coming back here."

Larson tried to mask his enthusiasm. "Tammy, go get what you need. It's late. Let's get going."

Tammy pushed up out of her chair. The sober Naomi suddenly stood up. She looked first at Tammy and then at Larson. "You can both go to hell." Naomi turned, pushed the chair aside and marched from the room. Her dog followed with its head low.

"I'll go get some things," Tammy said to her father, but her thoughts were racing ahead.

On the Strip, she'd be able to find meth. She'd find some dealer on the street. That was if she could get money from her father, and asking him before had never failed. Here, take the money and go away. She needed relief. Tammy followed after her mother.

Larson sat and waited in the quiet kitchen. A pendulum clock ticked on the wall beside the refrigerator. He looked around the familiar room. It felt comfortable, familiar. He remembered buying the house, when they moved in, excited with their ten-year-old daughter, the big party Naomi put together, the feel of the sun out near the pool. Somehow, it all faded, slipped away, and turned dark. Sparky, the Rottweiler, came into the room. He wagged his tail as he crossed to Larson and pushed his big head between Larson's legs. Larson smiled and petted the dog's head.

———

ELEVEN MILES away and six blocks off the Vegas Strip near Angel Park at the Desert Flower Condominiums, Charlotte Johnson had pulled her SUV from the covered off-street parking to the front of the complex. There, after putting on jeans and sneakers, she raised the back hatch and began the task of carrying her belongings. It wasn't packing, it was an unexpected, unanticipated unpleasant move, and she wasn't packing, she was throwing things into the SUV. An older woman walking a dog paused to watch. Charlotte ignored her. All she wanted was out, away, gone. Greg Larson had committed the unforgivable sin of going home. It wasn't that he went home, it was that his wife called, and he jumped through the hoop. She needed help, she called, and he went. She cried out in need, and he chose to answer it. It was clear to Charlotte where Greg Larson's heart was, and it wasn't with her. The sonofabitch hadn't even asked her to go along. In six trips back and forth, her two closets were empty, now she was gathering what was hers from the master bath. Thank God she still had her apartment on Sahara Avenue. It was on the third floor but unpacking and carrying the shit upstairs could wait until daylight. She would find help and Greg Larson, the man who had betrayed her, could go to hell.

When she had everything out, Charlotte paused in the living room, where she worked a key off of her keyring. She looked at the key and then tossed it onto the glass top of a cocktail table in the living room of the condo. She was leaving more than one key behind. The key to her heart was also being left behind. It was over. Charlotte turned and walked out, closing—slamming— the door behind her.

FOUR
SEX AND THE CITY

LUKE MITCHEL WAS DRIVING HOME. Home had six thousand, nine hundred and eight guestrooms, three indoor pools, a waterfall with a river, a spa, seventeen restaurants, nine bars and a shopping arcade. Home was the Silver Palace, one of the *big dog* casinos on the Strip, and Luke was its director of security. Driving down the hill from the Lakes, he could see the glow from the lights on the Strip. It was almost bright enough to declare darkness prohibited. The distant Sphere lit up the darkness with a seemingly endless string of colors and images that could not be imagined or ignored.

Occupancy at the Silver Palace when Luke drove away was at eighty percent plus. That meant over ten thousand guests were in-house, and unknowingly, they relied on Luke and his team of security officers to keep them safe. In addition to the Silver Palace's two wings and sixty-two floors, there was only one resort casino larger. Three blocks away stood the mother of them all, the Park MGM Grand. Although Greg Larson, the Silver

Palace's GM, claimed, *The Grand might be bigger, but the Palace is better.*

Luke turned onto the Strip from East Sierra. As he made the turn, he noticed a woman in high heels on the corner. He guessed her age at thirty-plus. She wore a tight blouse and a short skirt. Attractive, she didn't go unnoticed. The car in front of him slowed for a look. Ironically, Luke remembered he was returning from dropping off an eighteen-year-old wannabe prostitute. And here was another. His action hadn't turned the tide. Sin City! Say the words and what city came to mind? Las Vegas. He decided Vegas may, in fact, be the skin capital of the world. Rather than a topless chorus line at the Grand or a naked twenty-year-old from Pittsburgh, dancing at a Gentleman's Club, sex was an integral part of the Vegas experience. Skin city! The fact was Las Vegas had more prostitutes than police officers.

Compounding that was the fact prostitution in Clark County was a crime. Although selling sex was illegal, there was a vast number of legal escort services providing curved beauties for up-close and comfortable companionship. Luke had learned escort services in Vegas, as well as freelancing pimps and whores, wanted the same thing from the Silver Palace that its guests wanted—money. In addition to a significant service fee to get laid, pimps and whores alike were skilled at stealing cash, rings, watches, credit cards and anything else they could get their hands on. How could a guest from Columbus explain to his wife what happened to his watch and wedding ring?

Another blurred line for Luke, as an ex-cop from the LAPD where he learned there was right and wrong, guilt or innocence, although in Vegas, the difference between the experienced, skilled dancers at the Hard Rock and the twenty-year-old from Bakersfield who had lost it all and needed money to get home or buy the pants she saw at the Old Navy, was a faint one. Casinos in Vegas were governed by the Nevada State Gaming Commission. Prostitution, a crime in Clark County, was prohibited. Every casino has a variation on the prohibition of prostitution. Most posted security personnel at their elevators leading to guest rooms. That minimized the freelancers as well as thieves from access to the guest room floors.

Luke Mitchel's policy at the Silver Palace was zero tolerance of prostitution. It was a crime, and together with his skilled security force, they fought it. They didn't stop, but they tried. Facial recognition provided by surveillance helped turn away many, but then there was the reality of the big spenders, those who gambled with millions, usually not their own, who after gambling, often turned their suites into pleasure palaces. Luke's interference with supply and demand often put him in conflict with GM Greg Larson. Their conflict was rooted in the ageless battle between money and privilege. Luke wondered if the arrest of Tammy Larson, the GM's daughter, for prostitution, was going to affect his thinking. Luke reminded himself of the cliché, "What Happens in Vegas stays in Vegas." Although an iconic cliché, secrets had their way of finding light. Luke hoped the GM's daughter wasn't going to become another mountain he had to climb.

As Luke drove up the Strip toward the towering, glittering Silver Palace, he counted six more whores. Vegas and skin—a complex mix of good, bad, and ugly. The story was ageless. Sex and gambling seemed inseparable. Vegas proved that. The untold story of Vegas was what went on behind closed doors. The events of the night had proven it true for Luke Mitchel.

The GM's policy at the Silver Palace dictated the director of security, as well as all department heads, had to be on property when occupancy was above seventy-five percent. Seventy-five percent meant when the hotel had over five thousand rooms booked, there were likely ten thousand guests in-house. The thousands coming in for headliner shows, shopping, drinking, dining, or gambling were valued, but those who paid to stay at the Palace were considered family. The ten thousand-plus employees at the Palace were taught that every day. With occupancy high, Luke was staying in a guest room on the third floor. That kept him close to his office, the security briefing room, and the surveillance complex. The surveillance complex was where two thousand seven hundred and thirty-three cameras were monitored. The big dog in the camera mix was the facial recognition system. Its covert cameras were located at every entrance. Facial Recognition cameras scanned from one face to another as they entered the casino. If Mandalay Bay identified a cheat, they would distribute a photo on the casino network. The image would be programmed into the system and the next time the bad guy walked through the front door, he would be politely or otherwise, turned away.

Another camera system in surveillance proving invaluable was Alf. Alf was AI, Artificial Intelligence. An AI algorithm was linked to the surveillance system. Alf looked at everyone and anything that came through the doors. Alf read body language, dress, tattoos, scars, hair, eye color and more. When Alf saw something it found suspicious, alarms went off.

All twenty-seven hundred and thirty-three cameras recorded their images onto CDs. The majority of the cameras in gaming, on the casino floor, were covered by

PTZ, pan, tilt, and zoom. Every elevator, guest or employee was seen by camera. Guest floors had fixed images of hallways from every angle, although guest privacy was never violated. The back of the house, including all corridors, hallways, kitchen, and parking decks were covered. Cameras also covered all exterior doors, the river, the waterfall, the pools, and every cash point in the house. If it happened at the Silver Palace it was going to be seen and recorded.

In addition to the network of primary cameras, a variety of special ops hardware was used. Electronic sweeps of the GM's office and other department heads were made routinely, looking for hidden listening devices and cameras. Sweeps were also made of the Silver Palace's private aircraft, a plush upgraded Bombardier—Seventy-Five hundred, before each flight.

Covert cameras were also a vital part of the inventory. A fire extinguisher in a back hallway concealed a camera after reports of employee drug use. A concealable camera could become a button on a jacket, or a clock on the wall. In short, just about anywhere. Cameras could provide both video and audio. Reinforcing all this was a fleet of drones. The drones could stay airborne for seventy minutes. The surveillance staff had all been to drone piloting school.

In spite of the small army of uniformed security officers at Luke's command and the vast array of electronics supporting them, the Silver Palace, like every casino, still had losses. The thieves, like ants on a piece of candy, in spite of all the efforts to keep them out, found a way in. They stole money, food supplies, television sets, silverware, light bulbs, lamps, dishware, towels, blankets, pillows, sheets, rugs, and everything else that wasn't nailed down or had a security officer standing guard over it. Not only did thieves come through the front door they came in the employee entrance. Luke was never able to put a number on it, but the reality was most of the really good thieves were those the casino hired.

The Silver Palace, with all of its glamour and allure, was like a lighthouse on a dark night. It attracted bugs. Only these bugs wanted more than light, they wanted money, and the Silver Palace had millions. The Palace cost billions to build but its turnaround had come quickly, and it was now generating billions in profit. The casino floor with its table games, flanked by thousands of slots with comfortable seating and alcohol, reinforced by the sports book and on-screen betting in guest rooms, generated more money, in cash, than most of the countries in the civilized world. Luke Mitchel, as director of security, had many responsibilities, but protecting the casino's cash flow was number one.

————

It was nearly two a.m. when Luke pulled into employee parking in the underbelly of the Palace. He reached out to the on-duty security watch commander, KC King, by radio to advise him he was back on property. That done, he climbed out of his car, waved at the on-duty surveillance officer who he knew would be watching and headed for his room. The back of the house was quiet as Luke rode an employee elevator to the third floor. Alone on the elevator, Luke thought about the path that led him to the Silver Palace. He was a runaway from the shooting death of his partner in LA while working narcotics. He wore the badge of the LAPD for eight years. The loss of his partner, like combat service with the Marine Corps in Afghanistan, had its heavy price. Most called it PTSD—Post-Traumatic Syndrome Depression. Luke called it by other names—insomnia, isolation, rage, and nightmares. It had many names, and Luke added another—divorce. Luke's wife, having lost the man she married, left him. Luke came home early from a job he could no longer stand to find an empty house. Not only was his wife gone. She took their infant daughter with her. A dead partner and a divorce put a painful end to Luke's career with the LAPD. He simply ran away.

It wasn't so much an intent to drive into California's desert than it was to get away from his pain in Los Angeles. Luke drove aimlessly until both he and his car gave up in Rio Vista, Arizona. There, as Luke called it, in the middle of fucking nowhere, he found the Mojave Indians had built an impressive casino. Desperate for food and cash, Luke took a job in security. It was gun work, a fit. Over the next three years, he was mentored by a refugee from Las Vegas who knew the nuance of gaming. As months turned to years, Luke learned it too. He not only found refuge in the Rio Vista Casino he found the Mojaves were much more friends than they were Indians.

A getaway from Rio Vista, better known as a wide spot in Highway Ninety-Five, took Luke to the Silver Palace in Las Vegas. He and Barbara Nichols, a close female companion at the Wild River Casino, planned to see Lady Gaga's show. A getaway, a retreat, a quiet weekend, with no cell phones, just Las Vegas in the raw. That's what they both wanted, but life got in the way. Barbara went shopping in the Silver Palace's arcade while Luke relaxed watching the NFL on a widescreen, at least that was his intent. Annoying crowd noise drew Luke onto his balcony. He was shocked at what he saw. One floor beneath him, a naked woman stood balancing on the railing of her balcony, ready to jump to her death as the crowd gathered below, phones and fingers pointing into the air.

Luke knew what he had to do, even though it meant his life would be in jeopardy. He backed away from the balcony into this room. His heart pounded in his ears. "Shit!" he muttered. He knew the woman was going to jump. He took a deep breath, wiped his face, and bolted barefoot and shirtless for the open balcony door.

A collective hush fell over the crowd gathered below near the main entrance. Faces and cell phones watched as the bare-chested Luke leaped over the railing of the balcony directly above the naked woman. He grabbed the metal railing, swinging his weight up and over. It took only seconds, swinging in a downward arch, as Luke glanced at the crowd and the cement far below. Luke released his grip. Momentum carried his one hundred and seventy-seven pounds down, slamming into the nude. He grabbed the woman as they crashed onto the balcony floor. Luke's foot slammed the sliding door shattering the glass as they rolled to a halt.

Luke saved the woman's life. Minutes after his daring rescue, the first images began appearing on social media. TikTok, Facebook, Instagram, and more, followed shortly by CNN and then a glut of network television. He became a hero. A hero recognized by the GM of the Silver Palace. The GM learned Luke had been a police officer in Los Angeles, and perhaps even more importantly, he was the acting head of security at the Wild River Casino run by the Mojaves in Rio Vista. Luke was shocked when he was offered the job as head of security at the Silver Palace. He was even more shocked when he learned what they were willing to pay him. Luke took the offer.

Along with his title and money, Luke found that the two-tower Silver Palace with its six thousand-plus rooms and ten thousand employees was a challenge. His days became twelve-hour-plus marathons, usually seven days a week. Wanting to feel like Vegas was home, he had recently bought a plush three-bedroom condo in nearby Green Valley, but even owning a home, he found he spent as many nights sleeping at the Palace than he did at his condo. Much like this night.

Along with his title and salary came the responsibility of supervising nearly a hundred security officers whose job it was to police the transient population of their vertical city while safe guarding nearly a billion dollars in cash. Along with his impressive title and salary, Luke found himself dealing with a relentless army of cheats, whores, thieves, dishonest employees, corrupt managers, drugs, domestic disputes, dead or dying guests, naturals as well as ODs, and the ever-changing policies and rules coming from the throne, better known as the GM, but he loved it.

The still-healing scar on Luke's left temple was the result of one of his investigations. Gold was missing from the Palace and the arrows of guilt were pointing at a former security supervisor. A hearing was held in the GM's office as a result of the man protesting his termination. During the hearing, the man attacked Luke with a heavy glass pitcher of ice and water. Knocked unconscious, the man went after Luke's gun. The GM surprised everyone when he drew a concealed gun and shot the man to death. Luke went to the hospital while the GM went on GMA and then Inside Addition. He was a bonified hero, who just happened to have a CCW permit—Carrying Concealed Weapon, from the state of Nevada. The bond of trust that existed between the two men before the shooting grew even tighter. Luke now owed his life to the GM of the Silver Palace, and he had a scar to prove it.

Luke was almost to his third-floor room at the Palace when KC King, his AM watch commander, asked him what his *twenty* was. *Twenty*, on their radio protocols, meant location. Luke answered and suggested they meet at the elevators on the third floor. KC King, looking his usual iconic model self in uniform, appeared from the elevator where Luke waited. "We've got a problem in the penthouse with Frank Holland."

"The big-money guy that owns a tractor factory in India." Luke nodded. He had dealt with Holland before.

"We've had four calls from adjoining rooms," KC explained. "They're big money too, and they're tired of the noise. I've been up there. I talked to Frank at the door. The music was deafening. He has two guys in there playing a sax and trumpet. I think they're from Lady Gaga's band. I told Holland we had complaints about the noise, and he had to quiet it down. He wasn't happy to see me. Third time I was up there, a whore I've seen before answered the door. There were three other girls inside. None wearing very much. It looked like a strip show."

"How'd they get in?" Luke questioned.

"Front door. Escorts. Holland's invitation," KC answered. "They cheered him on while he played poker. He lost eight hundred grand tonight. The card room manager popped in while he was playing. Patted him on the back."

"Shit," Luke complained. He was tired, but he knew they had to find an option to another door knock and warning. The reality was Frank Holland had spent over a million dollars for the night when his poker losses and penthouse costs were combined. Thinking about the math gave Luke the idea. "Who's the host on duty tonight?" he asked with a look at KC King.

The on-duty host was the individual responsible for accommodating the wishes of the in-house high rollers. The high rollers were pampered from check-in until check-out. The hosts were responsible for the high rollers' care and comfort as far as policy allowed and was all about how much money they spent.

"Darlene Burns," KC answered. "Last I saw her, she was with some Canadian having a late-night dinner in the Lotus Blossom."

"They're closed at this hour," Luke said after a glance at his watch.

"Not if your Canadian dollars are already on deposit in our cash cage." KC smiled.

"Okay, go find Darlene. Have her get a bottle of Suntory Royal from the bar. I'll wait for you up at the penthouse."

"Got it," KC answered, heading for the elevator.

There were only two elevators that went to the penthouse level. A private non-stop elevator for whomever the guest was and another hidden behind closed doors for employee service. Luke had to ride down to the casino level to reach the elevators that serviced the penthouse. As he stepped out into the casino, the noise reached him. It was a mix of electronic chimes from the slots mixing with music and voices. He noticed the uniformed count team pushing their four-wheeled cart, table to table, through the card room, which surprisingly was still busy. Luke wondered how many millions they were collecting. He'd find out later when he got to the office. The daily drop, showing the total from every cash point in the belly of the Silver Palace, would be posted on his computer. Luke also noticed the uniformed officer, a young Hispanic assigned to monitor the traffic for the bank of elevators, was standing too far away and his back turned to the elevators. He seemingly hadn't noticed Luke's arrival. Luke made a mental note to talk with KC King later about the officer's oversight. King would get in the kid's face more than Luke would. He turned his attention to the bank of elevators when the one reserved for the penthouse reached the lobby. A chime sounded as the car arrived and the doors parted. Luke was surprised. Two attractive women, both dressed in nothing short of head-turning attire, stepped out. Luke greeted them with an approving smile. The two, one a short-haired Black brunette and the other a long-haired blonde, both carrying bags, returned his look and his smile. Luke knew the two, both in their early thirties, were in the business of returning smiles.

"Good evening, ladies," Luke offered, adding bait. "You getting away from the party early. I was just going up."

"Up is a good thing," the blonde said, evaluating Luke in his black tee shirt and sports jacket. She granted him a smile with her glossy red lips and white, even teeth.

"We prefer being together." The brunette exchanged a quick glance with the blonde and then looked to Luke. "You looking for the company of two?"

"Damn, that sounds exciting," Luke suggested with a grin and a southern accent he hoped didn't sound too phony.

"We're on our way to work, but if you wanted to pay for overtime." The blonde smiled. "We could say hang with you for a while."

"Overtime. Sounds like folding money maybe?" Luke answered, pretending to look around them as if someone might hear.

The brunette shifted her shoulder bag and leaned toward Luke to speak softly. He could smell her rich perfumed scent. "I've heard you can sometimes have it all for three hundred an hour."

Luke had heard enough. He pushed his unbuttoned jacket open and unclipped his gold and silver security badge from his belt near his holstered Glock automatic pistol and held it up in the faces of the two women. Their smiles disappeared.

"You're on camera, ladies. You may have been invited in this evening, but the party is over," Luke warned soberly. "We now not only know who you are, we know what you are." Luke pushed his badge back onto his belt. "You're going to walk straight to the front door and out. You're not only going out, you're staying out. Your business here in the Silver Palace is over. We understand one another."

"You're a real prick," the blonde snarled.

"No," Luke answered. "Not yet, but I can be. Now get out and tell whoever you work for we got pictures of you."

The two women gave Luke a go-to-hell look and hurried away. The officer assigned to watch the elevators noticed them. He looked at the two as they hurried by him and then turned his attention to Luke who he recognized as the director of security. He moved to Luke, sensing he screwed up.

"I saw those two when they went up to the penthouse with the high roller," the young Hispanic volunteered, hoping to save his ass. "He had about five women and two guys with him. I called surveillance to give them a heads-up."

"Okay," Luke said, watching the two women as they crossed near the long front desk heading for the front entrance, "but I don't want anybody getting off this elevator to see the back of your uniform. I want everybody going up and down to see your face. Got that?"

"Yes, sir."

Luke used his black access card for the employee elevator accommodating the penthouse. When he reached the penthouse level, it was easy to understand the noise complaints coming from the neighboring suites. The amplified sound of rap music mixing with shouts of male encouragement and girlish laughter came from behind the ornate double doors of the penthouse, filling the plush hallway with noise and vibration. Frank Holland was obviously enjoying his night. Frank Holland was in his early thirties. Luke had met him on an early visit. The circumstances were much the same. Holland was a wealthy playboy. Fort Wayne was his home, but it didn't have quite the same atmosphere as Vegas. Here, money had rules, but not many.

KC and the on-duty host arrived minutes after Luke. Darlene Burns was an attractive thirty-two-year-old Vegas-looking beauty who Luke had met casually but didn't really know well. She was dressed in slacks and a jacket, and she carried the bottle of Suntory Whiskey. At first glance, Luke understood why she hosted high rollers. He was suddenly aware he was unshaven and tired. Pushing aside thoughts about how he looked, Luke shared his plan. "First, we're going to the adjoining rooms. That's where the complaints are coming from."

KC glanced at the penthouse doors and raised his

voice over the noise. "We had another call while I was downstairs."

"KC," Luke added. "You and I will go to the adjoining suites. We apologize for the noise. Give them some phony reason for why it's going on, then we tell them tonight's stay is on the house. So is dinner tomorrow. Their choice of restaurant. After we talk to them, Darlene, you, and I will go to the door of the penthouse. KC, I want you out of sight. I don't want them seeing another uniform. Darlene, if Holland doesn't answer the door, we say we need to talk with him. When he appears, you'll present him with the bottle of Suntory and tell him we're sorry about all the interruptions, but if he can quiet it down, and because he's a valued guest, his stay in the penthouse is on us."

"That's a big one," KC suggested.

"So's what he lost downstairs tonight," Luke said. "Odds are he'll lose that much again tomorrow night."

"Would you like to become a host?" Darlene Burns smiled at Luke.

———

MILES from the nighttime Strip in the quiet Angel Park neighborhood of Vegas, Greg Larson and his eighteen-year-old daughter arrived at the at the Desert Flower Condominiums. Their drive from the hills had been painful for both. Larson was leaving behind a soon-to-be ex-wife and Tammy Larson, on bail for her prostitution arrest, was abandoning her mother. Larson's Maserati was jammed with a collection of his daughter's clothes and possessions which had been hastily thrown into the car, "Let's leave your things in the car until daylight,"

Larson suggested as they pulled into the covered parking behind his second-floor condominium.

Tammy didn't answer. She just opened the passenger door and climbed out with her bag over her shoulder. She was doing her best, which wasn't going well, in dealing with her meth withdrawal. Her skin was crawling, and she was having chills. She followed her father into the building without comment. After a short ride on an elevator, they were on the second floor. Larson forced a smile, leading the way to his door.

"I think you'll like Charlotte." He glanced at the near stranger with him. Tammy was his daughter, but she was no longer the child he once knew.

Larson was surprised when he pushed a key into the door and found it unlocked. He pulled the key out and opened the door wide. "Welcome home," he said, gesturing Tammy inside.

"Where's the bathroom?" She pushed by him with her arms folded.

"Down the hall on the right," Larson answered, stepping in to close the door with a quick look around the living room. The lights were on, and it was quiet. Tammy disappeared down the hallway.

The quiet unnerved Larson. "Charlotte, we're home," he called with a forced nervous smile.

There was no answer to his call. Worried, Larson followed the hallway, passing Tammy who was now behind a closed door of the bathroom. The door to the master bedroom stood open. Larson paused in the doorway. The lights on both sides of the unmade king-size bed were illuminating the open door of a walk-in closet. It was nearly empty. Charlotte's clothing was gone. A single sock and a pair of panties lay on the carpet beside the bed. Larson's clothes hung pushed to the side. They looked lonely.

"Where is she?" Tammy asked from behind her father.

Larson turned to her. He wasn't sure what to say. His heart raced. So were the frightening thoughts filling his head. He decided to lie. Tammy had no need-to-know Charlotte's reaction to her mother's call. Charlotte's words came back loud and clear in Larson's mind. *I'm done with this. You claim you love me. You promise every-thing, but when she says jump. You jump. You've made your choice. I have, too. You go out that door you'll be coming back to a room full of memories.* Larson felt his breath leaving him. He deliberately stepped away from the door, hoping Tammy hadn't seen the near-empty closet.

"Let's sit in the living room," he suggested, guiding Tammy away from the bedroom. "I'll give Charlotte's cell a call. She must have gone out for something."

Tammy wanted out too, she needed out. She bit at a thumbnail as they walked into the living room. "Dad, listen I…"

Larson cut Tammy short. He was on the edge of panic. What the hell did Charlotte do? Why? How could she do this? He gathered his cell phone from a jacket pocket. "I'll call her." He glanced at Tammy who paced, arms folded. He found Charlotte in his contacts and called her number. Tammy came back to him. She was desperate.

"Dad, please. It's a girl thing. You know, cycles. I need to go out and buy some things." It was an emotional plea but also a lie. Tammy's face was a mask of desperation as Larson listened to Charlotte's number ringing in the cell phone he held pressed to an ear, praying.

"Dad, please."

Desperate, annoyed, angry Larson dug into a back pocket and pulled out his wallet. He shoved it at Tammy. "Here, take what you need."

Tammy grabbed the wallet and turned away from her father. Her hands shook as she opened it, looking for currency. She found several twenties and then hundred-dollar bills. One, two, three, four. She took it all and jammed it into her handbag before she turned and handed the wallet back to her father.

"Goddamn it, Charlotte," Larson muttered in frustration as his call went to voice mail. "Maybe she got a call from the Cosmo," he said as Tammy offered him the wallet. He took it, jamming it into a pocket as he searched for another number on his cell.

"Dad, I'll use my cell. I'll call an Uber," Tammy said, picking up her bag and heading for the door.

"Wait," Larson called with the cell still pressed to his ear.

"I won't be long," Tammy assured, opening the door. "It's okay. Do what you have to do." She was out the door, pulling it closed behind her.

"Son of a bitch," Larson growled, gritting his teeth as again a voicemail answered his call.

Tammy walked a block in quiet streetlight from her father's condominium before she moved from the sidewalk to the edge of the traffic lane, where she put out her thumb to passing headlamps hoping to hitch a ride. She had the money to buy, now all she needed was to get there.

FIVE

TAMMY AND THE BACHELOR

LUKE MITCHEL WAS glad he had a room reserved at the Silver Palace. It was almost three a.m. when he reached it. With occupancy high, policy dictated he stayed in the casino. His newly purchased condo was only ten miles away in Green Valley, but he was glad he didn't have to make the drive. The room was small compared to others, although it had a bed and a lock on the door. He needed little else. He told KC King, his AM watch security supervisor, when they parted after their visit to the penthouse nuisance, that he needed sleep. No phone calls unless, well, no phone calls. KC King understood, he knew the night.

Luke tossed his jacket on a chair, pulled his Glock automatic pistol from his holster, and unloaded it. Then, pulling the badge from his belt, he sat both on a nightstand beside the bed. Collapsing into a soft chair, he pushed his shoes off. If he had learned anything about Vegas it was that daylight was the time for arrivals and the night, like this night, belonged to the dreamers. And there were many. There were those who came to Vegas dreaming of winning, those who came dreaming of seeing their favorite star, those who came dreaming of dressing like they never would anywhere but Vegas with the hope they might turn a head, and those who dreamed of starting a new life by marrying for the first time, or the second, or the third, and then there were those who dared to dream of living in Vegas, making a life, living the dream. Luke smiled at the thought. He was a dreamer, and he knew he wasn't alone. Likely, of the ten thousand-plus employees at the Silver Palace, not many were natives who were born in Vegas. Odds were, most came as dreamers. Vegas was a town where you seldom felt alone. Even if you were a dreamer.

Thoughts of Greg Larson, the GM, found their way into Luke's thoughts about dreamers. Larson was the man who saved Luke's life. Ironically, Luke had found his path to Vegas by saving a life. He was a guest, a dreamer who had come to Vegas to see a star, or was it more than that? Luke believed it was more. He hoped picking up Larson's daughter from the county jail would help. An eighteen-year-old arrested for prostitution under the influence of meth was a problem for any parent. He hoped what he did helped. He owed Larson. If the man needed anything, Luke was ready to provide it.

Luke considered turning on the flat-screen to watch CNN with the hope of relaxing. Picking up Tammy Larson from the Clark County Detention Center, dealing with the multimillion-dollar dick in the penthouse and meeting the two whores from the elevator made the night typical, but that didn't mean sleep was going to come easily. A steady stream of whores were finding their way into the bowls of his hotel. The worst-case scenario would be the Silver Palace getting a reputation for being *whore city*. He needed to find their source. The two women from the elevator weren't streetwalkers. They were clean, well groomed, and in their own words, expensive. Someone knew who to call to have them delivered. It wasn't DoorDash. It was someone who knew rich men needed trophies. Someone was taking a percentage out of what the girls earned, and they weren't cheap. Luke knew if he could find that person, he could keep the Silver Palace safe. Maybe a look at the escort services would provide a clue. Luke thought of the blonde. He smiled, remembering she called him a prick. He was still thinking of her when he fell asleep in the chair.

———————

NAOMI LARSON WASN'T SLEEPING. She was in the master bath of her six-million-dollar house, taking two more tablets of Xanax, following the two she had taken after her son-of-a-bitch husband drove away with their daughter. Naomi had never felt so alone. Sparky, her black Rottweiler, was at her side, leaning his weight against her leg as if he shared the anxiety filling the air, but it did little to change the horror filling the night. Naomi was angry. She wanted revenge. The bastard had to pay. His moving away had come as no surprise. She made excuses to comfort herself and to answer the unwelcome questions from others.

Greg needs to be close to the casino, she told all. Yes, he has a condo, and it's only minutes from the Silver Palace. What Naomi didn't tell the world was the fact Greg Larson was living with some Black woman. The reality stung at her being. Her husband had chosen a nigger over her. Money and her daughter got her through the reality of it. Now, her daughter had abandoned her. She, too, had gone to live with the nigger. They could both go to hell. Naomi petted the dog and walked to check all the locks again. The house seemingly had doors everywhere. It was a sprawling five-bedroom ranch with a pool setting behind the gates of the Lakes in the foothills of Charleston Mountain Northeast of the Strip. When Naomi reached the double glass sliders in the living room, she paused to look at the glow from the distant Strip. Somewhere down there were her ex and the daughter who betrayed her. The little bitch. She wished she had left her in jail. What to tell the girls at the club was going to be a challenge. Naomi decided she'd blame it all on Tammy's drug habits. Hell, every parent understood that challenge. When she finished checking all the doors, Naomi returned to the living room. She was feeling better. The Xanax was working. She decided to sit and have a cigarette before taking any more drugs. She had a prescription vial of Provanax she stole from a purse at the club's gym. Naomi looked it up on the net. It was for anxiety and depression. She decided she'd take two of them when her Newport Menthol was gone. Sparky came and laid down at her feet. Naomi patted the dog's head. Looking at the distant sprawl of the city's lights, she wondered if Tammy was sleeping. The little bitch. Just like her father.

————

TAMMY LARSON DIDN'T HAVE to walk far after she started hitchhiking on Westcliff Street. The hour was late, the street was dark, and traffic was almost nonexistent. Tammy decided after two more cars she would call Uber. She had the money. Four hundred dollars from her father's wallet but she didn't want to spend it on a fucking cab or Uber. A set of headlamps appeared in the distance. Tammy stepped even further into the traffic lane. This prick wasn't going to pass by without seeing her.

The driver of the silver Lexus, forty-eight-year-old Fred Goss, a blackjack dealer from the Flamingo, saw the girl. He was surprised. He also decided what he saw was attractive. He slowed and pulled to the curb. He could see the girl approaching in a rush in his rearview mirror. Fred's shift at the Flamingo had ended four hours earlier. He drove home, fed the parakeet, and tried watching television. There wasn't much. The Seven Hundred Club, headlines on Fox News, and nothing of interest streaming. Alone since his wife died three years earlier, Fred decided he'd do what he loved best: gamble. Twenty-one at the Hard Rock and then maybe a drive over to the Luxor for breakfast. Hell, he was good at counting cards. None of the dealers at Hard Rock knew him so he'd make a few bucks, then breakfast, then maybe home again when it got daylight. The girl hitch-hiking changed all that. She reached the car. Fred unlocked the doors.

Tammy opened the passenger's door and climbed in. "Thanks for stopping." She smiled, rubbing her hands together as if to warm them. "It's cold out there." Her chills were not from the night.

Fred looked at the shapely legs, the boots. The girl's skirt only covered them to midthigh. She was young and attractive. Tammy saw his look. It was more than a look, it was interest. "I'm headed for the Strip. How about you?" She was out of breath from rushing to the car. It added to her allure.

He could smell her scent. It had been a long time since Fred had a woman in his car, "Headed for the Hard

Rock," Fred answered as they picked up speed. "You're out late tonight, aren't you?" Fred questioned with another admiring glance.

"Yeah," Tammy answered. "It's Vegas. I just couldn't sleep. You know?"

"I know the feeling," Fred agreed as he slowed for a traffic signal. There were no other cars. "You live in the area?"

Tammy pulled at the open neck of her blouse as the light changed, and Fred drove on.

"My dad has a condo near where you picked me up. He's in bed, I was bored. You know?"

"Yeah, same thing brought me out."

Tammy saw a cluster of lights ahead. A mix of color and then a sign came into view. Liquor & More flashed its neon message into the night. Her idea took form. "Hey, would you mind stopping at the liquor store? I'd love to have some Newports."

"Sure." Fred was quick to agree as he slowed for the approaching neon. He slowed the Lexus to a stop after pulling into a space in front of the illuminated store.

Tammy began digging in her purse. "Can I get you anything?" she asked with a quick glance at Fred.

"No, allow me," Fred suggested, pushing the car into park. "You stay in here and get warm. I'll get the Newports for you."

"That's very kind of you." Tammy smiled. She reached over and touched Fred's arm. He smiled and climbed out of the car, hoping his generation would get him more than a pack of cigarettes.

A door chime sounded when Fred entered the liquor store. A bearded older man in a turban pushed to his feet behind the counter. Fred walked to him, digging out his wallet. "Pack of Newports…to go."

The Turbin turned to a glass-covered shelf, lined with a variety of popular cigarettes. He pulled a pack and pushed them toward Fred. "Would you like a bag?"

Fred pushed a twenty-dollar bill onto the counter while holding up another for the turban to see. "Pass on the bag, but if you got condoms…"

The turban reached down below the counter to lift a small box lined with rows of condoms packed in plastic. Fred studied them.

"The ones at the back," the turban explained with an accent. "They have a few expandable bumps on them. Top of the line, called the Bull's Horn. Eighteen dollars."

Fred pushed his second twenty-dollar bill toward the turban. He was feeling generous. "Keep the change." He smiled, collecting the wrapped condo from the back of the box.

With the Bull's Horn pushed deep into a pocket and the pack of Newports in hand, Fred Goss headed for the front door. He was smiling. Seemed maybe life was turning a corner. Maybe he wasn't so old after all. Maybe she'd want to go to the Hard Rock with him? Fred's dreaming ended abruptly as he pushed through the door to the spot where the Lexus was parked. The car and the girl were both gone. Fred grabbed his chest as he stood staring, mouth open.

Tammy turned the radio on before she reached the Strip in the Lexus. Didn't take her long to find her favorite station. Hell, this Lexus was the same year as the one her mother drove. She rolled down both front windows as she turned onto the Strip from Harmon Avenue. She was headed for Fremont Street. She had scored there before. There was this guy, Polly, who hung near Seventeenth and Fremont. He always had shit. She'd park the Lexus somewhere, or Polly would see it and want even more cash. She'd find a spot near Seventeenth. She was almost to the Wynne, moving slow for a signal when the SUV with three smiling, tanned, intoxicated young Californians pulled up beside her. One of the young men hung his arm and head out the window behind the driver to stare at Tammy in the Lexus.

"Wow," the tanned Californian yelled. "Look at the tits on her."

The window in the Lexus was down. Tammy heard the remark. She was pleased she had drawn attention. She looked and granted the man a quick smile. He surprised her by pushing himself up into the window of the SUV to grab at his crotch.

"Hey, bitch, you want a bite of this?"

Tammy's smile faded as she raised her right arm and extended her middle finger at the laughing threesome in the SUV. "Fuck you," she snarled.

The trio of smiling faces were all looking at Tammy, obviously enjoying their cleverness, when at thirty-one miles an hour, they crashed into the towering back of an RTC Transit bus, sending chrome and glass flying.

In an instant Tammy was looking at the big bus in her rearview mirror. She smiled as she drove on casually, enjoying the comfort of the stolen Lexus.

Tammy parked on Seventeen Street and walked to the corner where she knew the Snow Man usually hung out with a couple of his lessors. Her near-knee-high-heeled boots clicked on the sidewalk as she walked to the Snowman. Hands in his jacket pockets, the Snowman was standing in place beneath the glow of a streetlamp on the sidewalk. The Snowman was a Black dope dealer. He had three court cases pending. All were for possession with the intent to sell. Knowing that he was going to jail, the Snowman was trying to put together cash money for his two wives and six kids. The Snowman got his name from his gray snow-white hair. He was a muscular Black man wearing dark sunglasses with baggy jeans and a Super Bowl jacket.

"Hey, Snowman," Tammy said as she approached. "You got a forecast for tomorrow?"

The Snowman continued his looking up and down the street, looking for shadows, headlamps, anything that moved. He had seen Tammy's approach, and he knew her. Not as an eighteen-year-old girl but as an addict. After a glance at his two cover men standing with their backs against the wall of the Desert Flooring building, he looked to Tammy. "I heard you got a free ride last night, girl."

Tammy dug out her wad of hundred-dollar bills. The Snowman was watching. Her hands shook as she unfolded the bills. "Two eight balls to go," Tammy answered.

The Snowman smiled, revealing a gold tooth. His eyes went to one of his cover men. "Jimmy, bring us two eights to go." Then he extended an open hand to Tammy. She understood. She pushed two of the hundred-dollar bills into his palm, pocketing the others. "You wanna push another Franklin at me? You know, money in the bank for next time."

One of the two cover men reached Tammy. He paused and looked to the Snowman. The Snowman nodded approval. The man extended a hand to Tammy. She took the folded baggies without looking at them and pushed them into her blouse between the buttons. She turned to walk away without comment.

"Nice seeing you, Tammy," the Snowman called. "Tell Daddy over at the Silver Palace that the Snowman says hi."

Tammy stopped and turned around to look at the Snowman. "How do you know who I am?" she questioned.

"Look on the net, girl." The Snowman smiled. "They gave up your booking picture and bio. Somebody made a couple bucks. Daddy's gonna be pissed when he sees that."

Tammy turned and hurried away. When she was in the darkness nearly a half block away from the Snowman and the duo with him, she stopped and leaned against a cool cement wall and dug at the baggies hidden beneath her blouse. She selected one and pushed the others back. Unfolding the baggie carefully, Tammy raised it and pressed it against her left nostril.

She sniffed hard. Her sinus cavity felt the cool powder as it spilled into her throat. Her heart raced, and she felt as though her feet were lifting off the ground. Tammy smiled and walked on toward the Lexus. Damn, she was tired. She would go back to her dad's condominium and get some sleep. Fuck him and her mother. Fuck them both, she giggled. She reached the Lexus and climbed in behind the wheel. She thought about the Snowman's comment about her picture being on the net. She dug in her purse for her phone. She turned it on and punched into the internet. She dialed up Instagram. Thumbed through it. Nothing. Next, she tried Facebook. Again nothing. X came next. She thumbed through the postings and then it appeared. Her heart rose into her throat as her breath left her. It was her. A sober-colored booking photo. Below the picture was the date, time, and a booking number as well as a label reading Las Vegas Metropolitan Police. Tammy pushed the phone into her purse. Then she dug in her blouse for another packet of meth. She unfolded it, being careful not to spill any but she did.

"Son of a bitch," she growled as powder and dust fell onto a knee and her short skirt.

She raised the unfolded packet to her nose and inhaled hard. First one nostril, then the other. The snort sent her head back.

"Fuck 'im all." She smiled, dropping the wrapper onto the floor of the car as she started the engine. The car roared. "Oops!" Tammy said, pushing the car into gear.

A tire squealed as the Lexus surged backward and slammed into a pickup truck parked behind it. Glass and chrome fell to the pavement.

"Goddamn it," Tammy mumbled.

She avoided the Strip, driving back to Angel Park. Halfway there, a police car passed her, going in the opposite direction. The sight of it made her heart race. She avoided looking at the lights, passing cars or people on the sidewalks. She gripped the steering wheel with both hands and studied the streets ahead, hoping she'd recognize her father's. The thought gave birth to the idea. Tammy slowed and punched the screen on the dash for the car's navigation system. It chimed and lit up. She looked at the commands beneath the illuminated digital street map. She saw the button. *Previous destinations*. She punched the button, and *Home* appeared on the screen, followed by a street address. Tammy smiled and followed the commands on the screen.

————

FRED GOSS's walk home after his Lexus and the girl disappeared took him almost forty minutes. He wasn't sure what his story was going to be, but he knew he had to call the police. His parakeet seemed happy to see him.

He turned on the television in the living room but sat in the kitchen, pitting himself and thinking about the story he would tell the police. He decided a drink would help. He took a bottle of Jack Daniels from a cabinet and poured himself a straight shot. He gulped it down and decided on another. "Fucking girl." He coughed after the second drink. No, he decided it wasn't her fault. Who could he tell about picking up a young girl hitchhiking at night. No one! No one that wouldn't think he was a fucking idiot. He decided on a third drink. Just to calm his nerves.

After his third drink of liquor, Fred decided he needed to piss. He would call the police officers afterward. His story would be that his Lexus was stolen from the curb in front of his condo. Coming out of the bathroom, Fred noticed an episode of *Love It or List It* was ending on HGTV. He was a fan of Hillary and David. He decided to watch the reveal portion of the show. He sat down in his recliner in the living room. The combination of the hour, the stress of the night and the liquor got him.

Four minutes later, after a commercial for HIV prescription drugs, then another for upset stomachs and a third for leasing an EV, he fell asleep with his chin on his chest.

———

Twenty-eight-year-old Dawn Wilder was in the bathroom of a Luxury Suite on the fifty-eight floor of the Silver Palace. She found a small bottle of sealed mouthwash on a nearby shelf. She twisted the bottle open and rinsed her mouth time and time again as if trying to wash away the night. It all started with meeting Lance Sherman, a graying sixty-two-year-old property manager from Fort Worth in the sidewalk Starbucks café outside the Silver Palace. She had the man's description but the fact he would be wearing a carnation on his lapel made finding him easy. The carnation was Pamela Carson's idea. The evening went well with dinner at the Mandalay, the floor show at the Mirage, gambling at the Flamingo and Caesar's, where Sherman won five hundred dollars in slots. He gave Dawn a hundred dollars of it because he allowed her to pull the handle. Then it was back to the Silver Palace.

Being a prostitute made strolling into any casino on the Strip hazardous, but on the arm of Lance Sherman, a registered guest at the Silver Palace, their entry through the front door drew little if any attention. Escorts were allowed. There was a uniformed officer at the bank of guest elevators but all he did was say goodnight to them after Sherman flashed his room key. Once in the room, remembering it made Dawn shiver with a chill.

"I want you to strip," Lance Sherman ordered, taking off his watch and a gold ring. He crossed to an open bottle of liquor sitting on the bar and poured himself a drink. "And as you take them off, give them to me."

Dawn waited. "You know stripping wasn't mentioned in the agreement. It will cost extra."

Sherman dug in a back pocket, pulled out his wallet and shoved it in the drawer of the nightstand. Smiling, he gathered two one-hundred chips from Caesar's Palace and laid them atop the stand. Dawn nodded a smile and took off her jacket, offering it to Sherman. He took it, returned her smile and tossed it to the bed.

Moving to a comfortable chair, Sherman sat down

and pulled off one boot and then the other. Dawn followed and stepped out of her heels. She was surprised when he unbuttoned his shirt and tossed it onto the bed. His age showed with a heavy stomach and sagging hairy breasts, but Dawn shadowed his move by unbuttoning her blouse. Sherman unbuckled his belt with its Texas star and pushed his pants to the floor. Drink in hand, he kicked away the pants. The Texan now wore only loose-fitting underwear and over-the-calf socks. Dawn noticed he had no sign of an erection. She pulled her arms out of her blouse and tossed it to him. Sherman caught it with a free hand and smelled the blouse over and over. Dawn had seen her dog do the same with its empty dish.

Dawn's short skirt followed. Now she was dressed only in a netted bra and a pair of dark ornate pantyhose. Sherman seemed lost in smelling the skirt. When finished with his repetitive smelling, he downed his drink and raised the glass to Dawn.

"Get me another."

Dawn took the glass and went to the bar to pour, noticing Sherman was now massaging his hidden dick as he resumed sniffing her skirt. Dawn deliberately poured a heavy drink. Drink in hand, she returned to Sherman. After sampling it, Sherman looked to her.

"Get rid of the bra."

Dawn forced a smile. She'd been down this path before with older men who couldn't get it up. Damn, didn't they have Viagra in Texas? She skillfully unhooked her bra and tossed it to Sherman, and making the move, showed off her ample thirty-six. Sherman grabbed the bra like a hungry dog and began smelling it. He paused, downed his drink in two heavy swallows and held up the empty glass. Dawn took it and went again to the bar. She poured it even heavier. When she returned, Sherman smiled.

"Now I've seen your tits, nipples and all, lemme see what's south of there."

He was paying two hundred extra for the strip, so Dawn began her best swaying pull down as she snaked her fingers into the top of the pantyhose and pushed them down slowly, down until they fell to her feet.

"Give them to me," Sherman growled.

Dawn worked a toe into the pantyhose and lifted them to Sherman. He grabbed at them, finding the crotch, then he buried his face in the pantyhose, sniffing repeatedly.

Dawn wished the freak would hurry, but he was paying, so with hands on her bare hips like the model she once wished she could be, she waited. Done sniffing, Sherman downed his drink in three heavy swallows and tossed the pantyhose aside before looking to Dawn.

"Damned, you're beautiful, girl."

"Thank you." Dawn smiled as she walked slowly around the bed naked to pull down the bedspread. That done, breasts swinging, she crawled onto the bed on her hands and knees just as Pam Carson instructed at the Hyatt when the eight girls gathered to meet and learn the protocols of being a Vegas escort. Dawn really clung to the title *escort*. She didn't want to be a whore. She offered an inviting smile to Sherman. "Come on, Lance. Let's play boy meets girl."

"Me on the bottom," Sherman said, pushing out of his chair with effort. He shoved his baggy underwear to the floor, exposing a thick limp dick.

Oh, shit, Dawn told herself as Sherman moved to the bed and crawled onto it. Centering himself on the bed, Sherman laid down on his back. His dick looked much like a spoiled sausage. "Would you like the lights out?" Dawn questioned, hoping it might help his condition.

"No, I want to see you," Sherman answered. "Come on, get me hard."

Dawn did her best. She spit lightly on her two hands, rubbing them together as if getting ready for a heavy task before she spread her legs over Sherman's and reached to take his limp penis in hand. Sherman closed his eyes and moaned as he pushed his head back into the pillows. Dawn continued her gentle stroking with no effect. Sherman's moaning assured her he was enjoying it, but there was no sign of an erection. Dawn tried massing his testicles as she continued stroking.

"Come on," Sherman said without opening his eyes. "I want to feel me inside you."

Dawn leaned forward until she could feel the hair on his chest against her nipples. She continued with the grip on his penis, pushing its limp form into her pubic hair. She pushed her crotch against his. Nothing. She tried swaying back and forth. Nothing changed. Dawn continued until she was tiring. Out of breath, she pushed up and lifted herself off the naked Sherman. "Baby, I tried. You're not ready."

"Okay, okay," Sherman said, pushing up on his elbows. "I know what will do it." He rolled off the bed and went to the chair where he sat down to spread his legs, taking his limp penis in hand. "Do me," he said, motioning Dawn to him.

Dawn climbed off the bed and ran a hand back through her long blonde hair. "Sorry, I did my part. The agreement was...well, you know."

"Okay," Sherman answered quickly as he massaged himself. "Okay, I've got four more of those hundred-dollar chips. They're yours...if?"

Dawn hesitated, drawing in a deep breath. She wanted, needed the money. Her boyfriend, Casey, had been trying to find a job. Their rent was three days late, and he kept failing every fucking drug test he took, but she loved him. She'd pretend he was Casey. That would help, that would make it okay.

"All right," Dawn said, moving naked to him. She kneeled close in front of Sherman and moved in between his hairy, heavy legs and to take his penis in her hands. She opened her mouth and closed her eyes as she leaned to the head of his penis when he shivered and ejaculated into her mouth. Dawn pushed away, spitting repeatedly, wiping her face and coughing.

"Baby," Sherman said, letting his head fall back. "That was great." His hands fell to the sides of the chair.

Dawn spit again as she bolted to the bathroom. She washed her hands and face repeatedly until the imagined taste and scent were gone. Finished, she looked at herself in the mirror. Damn, it has been a long night. She wanted away, she wanted out, she wanted to be home. Casey would be watching some streaming shit on TV, but all she wanted was to go to bed. She dried her hands and turned to the door. Pam said they always had to say thanks to whoever and however it went. Dawn readied herself and opened the door. Sherman was still in his chair, naked with his legs spread, limp dick hanging and his head back with his mouth open. He was snoring. Dawn was pleased the man was asleep. She quickly put on her clothes. Sherman never moved. When dressed, Dawn collected the two-hundred-dollar Ceasars tokens from the nightstand for her stripping. She saw Sherman's gold ring and wristwatch laying nearby. She looked to Sherman. He was still snoring with his head back and mouth open.

Dawn quietly opened the drawer of the nightstand. Inside were six more tokens from New York, New York, three folded twenty-dollar bills and Sherman's wallet. She gathered all but the wallet, stuffing it into her handbag. She looked again to Sherman. He hadn't moved. The old prick. Dawn gathered the watch and ring pushed them into a jacket pocket.

Moving quietly, Dawn opened the hall door and stepped out to leave the sleeping nude Lance Sherman alone in his deluxe suite. She closed the door carefully. The lighting in the long-carpeted hallway was friendly and quiet. Dawn walked quickly to the elevators and pushed a down button. She waited and waited as her heart raced. All she wanted was away from the limp dick Texan. Finally, the elevator arrived. Dawn was glad to see it was empty. She stepped in, and the door closed. An instrumental version of Moon River was playing as the elevator descended. Dawn tried to mentally encourage the elevator to hurry, but it didn't. She watched the floor lights as they winked on and off until the car slowed to a gentle stop and the doors parted. Dawn's mouth fell open in shock.

There were three of them. The uniformed watch commander, Lieutenant KC King, a sober Hispanic sergeant, and a uniformed female officer.

"You just left Lance Sherman's suite up on fifty-eight," KC King said soberly, reaching into the elevator to push the hold button. "He called, said a blonde wearing a short leather skirt just stole his watch and ring. That would be you."

Dawn stared in shock. She hadn't moved. "Step out of the elevator," KC King ordered. "Everything I told you has been recorded by surveillance. The Gaming

Commission of Nevada gives us the authority to detain you."

KC's order was not to be ignored. He took Dawn by the arm and guided her off the elevator. "We're going to take you to a private room where you will be searched. Either you come quietly, or you can try on our handcuffs."

Dawn's face showed the fear gripping her. She was still speechless. KC King took her by the arm to guide her away. The other two officers followed.

SIX

NIGHT UNTIL DAWN

TAMMY WAS PLEASED to park the Lexus after its navigation system took it to its home destination. She was even more pleased with how she was feeling. After walking away from the car, she paused to sniff what remained of her first hit of meth. She was even more pleased when she recognized she was only several blocks from her father's condo, and damn, it was a beautiful night.

Greg Larson was frantic. It was a mix of anger over Charlotte's moving out and Tammy's missing in the night. He considered calling the police, but he knew that had too many risks, so he made the call. It was his only choice.

Luke Mitchel, ironically, was sleeping in a chair in his room at the Silver Palace when his private cell phone began its electronic chirping, repeatedly. Luke awoke, blinking open his eyes, and he was surprised to find himself still in the chair with all the lights on. He reached for the cell phone on the table beside his chair. "This is Luke."

"Luke, it's Greg Larson. Sorry to bother you, but Tammy is missing. I don't know where the hell she is, or what the hell to do."

"Did she run away or what?" Luke questioned, pushing out of his chair.

"Naw, she gave me some bullshit about needing some ladies' hygiene crap and took four hundred dollars from my wallet. That was over three hours ago."

Luke paced, trying to think of how he could help, something to recommend. "Was she angry? Did she say anything about when she'd be back?" It was lame, and Luke knew it, but he didn't know what else to say.

"Maybe I should just bite it and call the police."

Luke shook his head in disagreement as he pressed the cell phone to his ear. "The police will listen. They may even take a report, but not likely. This is Vegas, an eighteen-year-old missing for three hours isn't big news."

"I thought about going out and..." Larson's words stopped as the front door of the condo opened, and Tammy walked in. "Holy shit," Larson said in shock. "She came back." A dial tone told Luke the call was over. He moved for his bathroom.

Greg Larson dropped his cell phone onto a couch and moved to take Tammy in his arms. He held her tight. "Jesus, Tammy, you scared the shit out of me," he said into a tangle of her hair.

"Dad, I told you where I was going."

Larson released his hug and took Tammy by the shoulders to look directly into her face. "You took money from my wallet."

"You told me too," Tammy said with an attempt at innocence. She was still mellow and high.

Larson saw it but didn't want to make her return a

challenge for either of them. "How about we talk later? Get some rest. I got your things out of the car. Put them in the guest room. Come on I'll show you." He led the way into the hallway, hoping Tammy wasn't going to ask about Charlotte. The reality was Tammy wasn't thinking much about anything other than the idea of lying down to float away in total comfort. Being arrested as a whore was no longer a big fucking deal. Driving a Lexus on the Strip, now that was a big fucking deal.

————

THE SOUND of the doorbell told Fred Goss the police had finally arrived. He was annoyed. He had called them almost two hours earlier. He opened the door to find a young, fit, uniformed officer from the Las Vegas Metropolitan Police.

"You called about your car being missing?" the officer questioned.

"It's not missing," Fred said, opening the door wider while gesturing the officer inside, "Someone stole it. I parked it at the curb out front and some sonofabitch stole it." Fred was doing his best to make his lie sound authentic.

The officer was carrying a clipboard. "What kind of car are we talking about?"

"A silver Lexus. I've only had the car a couple months. Bastards."

"Any idea who may have taken the car? A friend, maybe someone you know."

"Not a chance. I parked it out front and…"

The officer interrupted him. "Did you leave your keys in the car?"

"No, definitely not."

"Can you show me the keys?"

"Oh," Fred stalled. "They're around somewhere." He faked a look around the room.

"Come with me, sir," the officer said, stepping out the open door, and led Fred toward the curb with his flashlight. As they neared the curb, the officer raised his flashlight to illuminate a silver Lexus. Fred's heart raised up into his throat. He felt as if he were in a bad dream. The officer stepped closer to the Lexus and shined his flashlight inside the car to light the dash and the ignition where a set of keys hung in place. "Was it a car like this?" the officer pressed soberly.

"I don't understand. I, I...the car was gone, she..." Fred caught himself and fell silent.

"Is this your car?" the officer said, shining his flashlight into Fred's confused-looking face.

Fred looked inside the car. An empty drink cup sat on the center console. It had the Flamingo logo on its side. Fred knew, although stunned and worried, that it was his car. He offered a nod of confession to the young officer.

"Next time, don't give her the keys," the officer said, turning toward the police car which was parked directly behind the Lexus.

Fred Goss stared at his car in silence as the police car pulled away. He no longer felt young or fortunate.

———

LUKE WAS COMING out of his bathroom when his cell phone began ringing a second time. Larson was calling back with an apology, an explanation or maybe another plea for some kind of help. "This is Luke," he said, picking up his phone.

"Boss, it's KC King. Sorry about the hour, but I could use your help. I'm in the surveillance office. I've got an escort in custody I need guidance on."

"I'll be down," Luke answered ."Only be a couple minutes." Luke was glad he had slept, no, napped was a better word for it. Whatever, he was glad he had some rest, and he was relieved it wasn't the GM calling back with another problem with his daughter. Luke gathered his holstered Glock automatic and clipped it on his belt and then gathered his badge. He grabbed his jacket and headed for the door.

————

CANDICE HARMON, an attractive, busty blonde surveillance supervisor, was on duty when Luke reached the surveillance complex. KC King was with her in the glass-walled supervisor's office overlooking the maze of large video screens on the other side as they switched automatically through programmed sequences and images. Candice, in addition to being a surveillance supervisor, was a licensed realtor in Clark County. She had helped Luke find his condominium and walked him through the buying process. They had shared a celebratory dinner, and the flirtation between the two continued, but they kept it quiet in the Silver Palace.

"Let's do a show and tell," KC King said after the three said hello to one another. They sat facing each other near Candice's desk. "Lance Sherman up on fifty-eight, calls the hotel operator in a panic. He says he heard his door close when a blonde escort by the name of Dawn left while he was sleeping."

Luke and Candice both listened carefully. KC continued. "Sherman says she stole a gold ring, his watch, and a bunch of tokens from Caesar's, and some cash."

"Hotel operator alerts us, and we greet her when the elevator reaches the first floor. I had Pauline Lane with me. When we got to the interview room, Pauline searched her. We recovered the gold ring, a man's wristwatch, seven hundred dollars in tokens, and some cash." KC paused to empty a large envelope on Candice's desk. The items described fell onto the desktop. "Candice recorded all that for us."

"I also pulled the tapes on her leaving Sherman's room and getting on the elevator," Candice offered. "I've got a team looking for the images of Sherman and her arriving and going up to his room."

"So, we got her cold. Is she talking?" Luke asked.

"Not yet," KC added. "She's emotional. No priors. You were our first call. Question is, do we handle it or turn her over to Metro?"

Luke considered their options. He glanced at the watch, the ring and the tokens laying on the table. "It would seem this guy Sherman is the real victim. She didn't steal anything from us. That means he's driving. Have you talked to him?"

"Not yet," KC answered.

"Okay," Luke suggested. "KC, you go up and see what Sherman wants to do. We can return his property to him, or we can call the police and have her arrested. His call. In the meantime, I'll talk to the girl. Candice, you cover it. KC, you find out from Sherman who set up the escort. There's a piece of the puzzle missing. We need to find it."

Dawn was recovering from shock. She knew she was in serious trouble. Shit happens. Especially when you steal things. Her regret was soul-deep. Only if she hadn't.

Maybe if she told them she was really sorry, they might let her go, but she knew reality wasn't going to grant that. Pam Carson had talked about situations like this. Her advice was if you were detained for any reason, call, and don't talk to anyone. Pam had a burner, a throwaway cell phone that was difficult to trace. All the girls had to do was remember four numbers. They didn't have to remember the area code or the first three digits of the number. They would always be the same. Dawn did her best to remember the four numbers Pam gave her when she got the call to go meet the Texan, but she couldn't. Fuck!

The ship was sinking because she couldn't remember four fucking numbers. It was thirty-three something, but close didn't count with telephone numbers. She wiped tears from her face as Luke opened the door and stepped in. He closed the door behind him and sat down across the table from Dawn. He deliberately stalled speaking. It was an interrogation technic he had learned with the LAPD. Dawn took the bait.

"Am I going to jail?" she asked carefully, clasping her hands tight beneath the table.

Luke followed his tactic by not answering the question. "I'm the director of security, what is your name?" His tone was as sober as his expression.

"Dawn...Dawn Wilder," she answered hesitantly. The man frightened her.

Luke put his hands together on top of the table. Psychologically, he was declaring he was in charge and Dawn's response assured him he was. "I told you who I work for, now tell me who you work for."

Dawn's eyes went to the tabletop and Luke's hands before she allowed her eyes to find his," I'm sorry. I'll apologize to the man. I'm not a thief. I'm an escort."

"My question was who do you work for?" Luke repeated soberly.

Dawn looked around the room as if she was looking for a way out. When she returned her look to Luke, she could see the man wanted an answer. She was breathing hard. She adjusted her weight in the chair as if it might relieve her anxiety. It didn't. She took a deep breath before speaking," I work for Cloud Nine Escorts."

"And who made the arrangements for tonight?" Luke pressed.

"Her name is Pam. Pam someone. Her name wasn't important to me."

"And this Pam someone called you to set up tonight's date?"

"Yes."

"Where is Pam's office?"

"I don't know. I only met her twice. Once in front of Paris when she hired me and again at some casino. I'm not sure which one it was. It was on the Strip."

"Why did you meet in the casino?"

"Sort of training. You know, the do's and don'ts of being an escort. There were other girls there."

"How many?"

"Six, eight, I'm not sure."

Luke knew he was getting close to learning the source of a challenging escort service, better known in security as, *Dial a Whore*. "How do you get in touch with Pam?"

Dawn sniffed. She was finding the more she talked the better she felt. It was as if it made the guilt fade, and it was true. "She said she'd call me in the morning. And I'd get paid."

"How much?"

"Three, five hundred. I'm not sure."

"Do you know what she charges her clients?"

Dawn shook her head. "No, but working for her beats walking the street."

"How many escorts do you provide in a week?"

"Five, maybe six," Dawn answered.

"What do you earn in a week?"

Dawn considered the question. "Twelve hundred from Pam. Another six in tips," she answered in a confident tone.

"All cash?"

"Yes."

A knock sounded on the closed door. "It's open," Luke called.

KC King opened the door. "Chief, can we talk?"

Luke pushed out of his chair and stepped out of the room to join KC. He closed the door.

"I talked to Lance Sherman. The guy up on fifty-eight. He's not interested in having the girl arrested. He's from Texas. Doesn't want, what he calls, the pain in the ass of having to come back here for her trial. All he wants is his property back."

"No surprise," Luke suggested. "Ten to one he's got a wife and family who would ask questions."

KC nodded in agreement. "Bet on it. He said the girl can keep four hundred from the tokens."

"Screw him," Luke suggested. "We don't make payments to whores for guests. If he wants her to have a tip, he can do it."

"Got it," KC agreed.

"Has she been searched?" Luke questioned.

"Yeah," KC assured. "I had Lane do it. She looks in all the hideouts. We got everything the Texan says the girl took."

"Okay," Luke ordered. "Take pictures of it and give it

back to the guest. Along with his signature on our release."

"Will do. He's in a hurry to check out."

"Remind him they do have whores in Texas."

Luke returned to the interview room where Dawn sat waiting. He sat down across from her. He could see she was regaining her composure. "Here's what we're going to do. We're going to take your picture. Your picture will go out to every casino in Vegas as well as the Metropolitan police. They're all going to know you're a prostitute and all of them won't allow you on their property."

Dawn's eyes filled with tears. Her hands were now in her lap. She lowered her chin. Luke's words were cutting deep.

"You committed a crime, Dawn. A crime that could put you in prison. First, you willingly acted as a prostitute. Then you stole from your client. It gets worse. You obviously joined in a conspiracy with Pam, whoever she is, to commit your act of prostitution. One, or all, could send you to prison."

"Please," Dawn said with a plea, her eyes went to Luke's. "I've never done anything. I don't want to go to jail. Please." A tear ran down her cheek. Dawn wiped it away.

"There is something you could do," Luke suggested.

"Anything," Dawn sobbed. "Just tell me."

"If you agree to get me Pam's telephone number, or her address, you can walk out of here tonight."

"I'll do it," Dawn answered as she wiped away another tear.

"I'll give you twenty-four hours. If I don't hear from you, your world is going to get a lot smaller. You understand?"

"Yes, yes, I'll do it," Dawn sobbed.

"Twenty-four hours," Luke repeated, pushing out of his chair. He took a final look at Dawn. She had lowered her head. She muffled sobs with both hands pressed over her face. Luke opened the door and stepped out. The hallway, off a wing of surveillance, was quiet. He was alone and glad of it. He felt he had somehow just raped a whore. It wasn't a physical rape, but he wondered, as weeks turned to months and then years, what would this twenty-eight-year-old remember. The Texan or the director of security. Both men, although they hadn't met, would agree Dawn Wilder was attractive. It was her beauty that brought her into their lives. Both made demands, for different reasons, but their demands would likely never be forgotten by this young woman. Luke wondered how old a man the Texan was. He thought about his own age, and Dawn's. He was approaching midforties, and she was twenty-eight. There was almost twenty years separating them. They had grown up in two different worlds. The two worlds had just collided. Luke saw his as just and Dawn's as criminal. He wondered why he didn't feel just. Being an officer with the LAPD provided a sense of pride and justice. Being a director of security at the Silver Palace in Las Vegas was making a sense of pride and justice far more elusive. Maybe it was their difference in age, Luke decided. Growing up in two different worlds put a mountain of reason between them which was amplified by the fact Dawn Wilder was a young woman and he was a middle-aged man. The reality of his age made Luke look at his hands. He turned both hands palms up and studied them.

"Maybe you should go wash them," Candice Harmon said as she approached, bringing Luke back to the moment. Luke wiped his hands on his pant legs. He wasn't sure why, but he was glad to see Candice. She was blonde, smart, attractive and he knew she was only two years younger than he was.

"I might just do that." Luke smiled. He was glad to leave his serious thoughts behind.

"KC said you want another picture of the girl," Candice questioned, leaning a shoulder to the wall a few feet from Luke.

"Yeah, in case her spirit of cooperation fades."

"Will do," Candice assured. "How long has it been since you've been home to visit that new condo?"

"Too long." Luke smiled in reply.

———

EIGHT MILES from the Silver Palace on the Strip the world was vastly different. The Angel Park neighborhood, lined with custom towering apartments, condos and tall palms was quiet. Palm trees and parked cars lined the shadowed streets. In the Desert Flower Condominiums, Tammy Larson was sleeping in the guest room of her father's second-floor condo. She had hidden what remained of her meth in one of her boots. Greg Larson, the GM of the Silver Palace was sitting in a living room recliner. He wasn't sleeping. Nor was he feeling like the GM of one of Las Vegas's major resorts. He was a man with his life in crisis. He was separated from a wife he was divorcing, Charlotte Johnson, his Black companion, as well as the cause of his divorce, had abandoned him when he needed her the most, and his daughter, whom he hadn't seen in three months, was asleep in his guest room after being arrested for prostitution. He wasn't sure what he would tell the kid after she woke up. Kid! Hell, she was no longer a child. Her arrest proved that.

And Charlotte, he had called every number she had. No answer. Where the hell was she? Would she come back? Should he allow her to come back? Was what they thought was love just fleeting lust? Larson found himself envying men like Luke Mitchel, head of security at the Silver Palace. Mitchel was single, confident, and happy. No matter what, Larson found himself wishing reality was bringing a new day. Daylight was beginning to erase the night. Larson's immediate concern was wrapped in a blanket, sleeping in the guest room, and she wasn't a guest. She was his daughter. He had a resort to run. A place he had to be at in less than three hours. What would become of Tammy? Could he, should he, leave her alone? What would he tell her about Charlotte's absence? Should he call the attorney that represented the Silver Palace and tell him about his daughter's arrest? Maybe he should call Mayor Bray. He had *juice*. Maybe this thing with Tammy could be buried in some Vegas dump. Larson felt as if he were drowning in a sea of maybes, and the clock was running.

————

LUKE DID what he did best. Passed the responsibility and the line work to subordinates. After he was done with his interview with Dawn Wilder, he turned the case over to KC King, the AM watch commander, and Candice Harmon, the on-duty surveillance supervisor. They would tie up all the loose ends while Luke went to his office to get ready for the GM's bi-weekly staff meeting. In preparation, he scanned security logs for events and instances he knew would be beneficial to the GM as well as other department heads. There had been reports of three bathtub slips and falls. Two had been found fraudulent, and a third, where the guest suffered a compound fracture of an arm, had been sent to the resort's attorney for settlement. There had been three in-house deaths. One, an accidental drug OD in the guests' room, another in the Silver Place River, where a guest thought drowned was found to have suffered a fatal heart attack during the subsequent autopsy, and the third, a guest suicide, where a man was found hanging in his bathroom shower after a single bet loss in roulette for thirty-seven thousand dollars.

In-house, housekeeping reported the loss of six clocks, two flat-screens, eleven pillows and sixteen blankets. Engineering reported an assault by a guest when an engineer was called to a guest room, where the naked guest grabbed the engineer's crotch. The assaulting guest was expelled. The cash cage received eight thousand dollars in counterfeit bills. A surveillance review disclosed the same individual, dressed in four different wardrobes, hats, and glasses, making five different requests for change over a ten-hour period. He was identified by surveillance and arrested on his last attempt. The currency scanner in the cash cage was found faulty and replaced. Eight employees failed random drug testing and were terminated. Three were janitorial, one from security, two twenty-one dealers and two pastry chefs. Two guests from the Luxor were ejected and banned after they were discovered using an electronic flash device in slots. Three known prostitutes were recognized and ejected. Five more females exiting guest floor elevators were intercepted by security and identified as escorts. Surveillance monitored the escorts until they left the property. A housekeeper found an unmarked envelope holding six thousand four hundred and nineteen dollars in cash on the floor of guest elevator #9. Surveillance was reviewing tapes. If the money was not legitimately claimed, it will be returned to the twenty-eight-year-old Hispanic housekeeper in thirty days. Security and the AI system in surveillance had detected and recovered eleven handguns and one long rifle from guests entering the front entrance. The card room and surveillance had detected two card counters and three cheats. All were banned.

Luke made notes for the meeting. The information would be beneficial to managers. He was concerned that nine prostitutes and or escorts were identified on property in the last seven-day period. He would not mention the theft from the Texan by Dawn Wilder. The matter was still under investigation he told himself. Nor would he talk of his encounter with two prostitutes coming down from the party in the penthouse. Whores in Vegas were a reality. It was more than a reality for Luke. It was an issue. A sensitive issue to be discussed with the GM. The escorts were licensed and allegedly monitored by Clark County, but in reality, what went on when guest room doors closed was no one's business. Guest privacy was a priority, but ironically it was guests creating the issue with escorts and prostitutes. The line between the two was thin, and Vegas was filled with beautiful women. In Las Vegas, sex was the color of money, and Vegas had lots of both.

SEVEN

CATCH ME IF YOU...

TIME WAS BECOMING AN ISSUE. As the general manager of one of the top-of-the-line casinos on the Strip, Greg Larson had a reputation for arriving early, staying late, or staying all night. He had planned on arriving early to prepare for the bi-weekly staff meeting where he would announce bottom-line figures, goals for the next quarter, and guest relation issues. The staff meetings would also include comments from department heads. The meetings often became round table discussion, leading to face-to-face arguments where the GM became an important referee. Greg Larson had learned over the arch of his career that the path to success in hospitality was built on teamwork, and he was the coach of the team. That was if he arrived on time.

Larson had been into the bedroom three times, hoping he would find Tammy awake. No such luck. She was not only asleep, she was snoring. He decided after waiting another thirty minutes that he was out of choices. He made noise, showering, shaving, and getting dressed with the TV on, hoping it might wake her. No such luck. He had to wake her before leaving. After Tammy's disappearance last night, Charlotte's absence made talk a must before he left, and after another glance at his watch, he knew he was already late.

He cursed fate and headed for the guest room, determined to wake his daughter. He found Tammy covered and still asleep. He opened a blind to allow light in and then pulled away the spread covering Tammy that she had pulled over her face and head. She moved but didn't seem awake. Larson carefully shook her shoulder. "Tammy, wake up, we need to talk."

Tammy responded by turning her face away and pulling the spread back over her head. Larson shook her again. He was torn with a mix of anger and worry. He pulled the spread away again.

"Tammy, wake up." He was louder this time.

She answered with another snore. Larson gave up and marched from the room.

In the living room, Larson paced and loosened his tie. He glanced at his watch again, shit, he was late. He'd be lucky if he made it in time for the staff meeting. If this was an issue at the Silver Palace, Larson asked himself, what would he do? The answer came quickly. Send in Housekeeping. Housekeeping got stuck with all the shit. His idea grew. He'd call Senora Perez, the head of housekeeping at the Silver Palace. He found his cell phone after a frantic search. He'd left it in the bathroom after his ninth attempt to reach Charlotte. He grabbed it and dialed the corporate cell he knew Senora carried. She answered on the third ring.

"Halo," the familiar Spanish voice answered.

"Senora, Greg Larson here. I'm calling from home. I need this call to be private. Very private."

"Si, lemma close my door."

Larson waited. He heard a door closing.

"Thank you, Senor Larson. Is now private."

"Senora, I need someone we can trust. Someone *you* trust. I need them to come here, to my home, to be with my eighteen-year-old daughter. She's sleeping, and I can't leave her alone. I need someone to watch her...you know what I mean?"

"Si, I understand. Eighteen. I have a son. He was once eighteen."

"I'll pay whoever you send. I'll pay them overtime."

"Yes, that is good," Senora answered. "I think of Dede Garcia. She's forty. A little heavy, but I trust her with anything."

"Can she come right away?"

"Si, are you at the condo we clean?"

"Yes, yes," Larson urged. "I'll wait until Dede arrives."

"I have to go upstairs to find her, I will send her pronto."

Larson sighed with relief. "Thank you, Senora. I owe you."

"Dad, what's going on?" Tammy said behind him. Shocked, Larson turned to her. Tammy was leaning on the open door of the bedroom. She was dressed the same as when arrested, minus the boots, but her clothes had a slept-in look. "Where's Charlotte?"

Larson didn't know what to say. He threw his cell phone at the couch and cursed, "Fuck."

LEAVING HIS OFFICE, Luke went to the guest room he was staying in. There, he found a packet of Fig Newtons in the fridge. He added a Diet Coke. He took both into the bathroom while he shaved. After changing into a fresh black tee shirt, he grabbed his jacket and headed for the security briefing room on the third floor. He arrived just as Mario Lopez, the day watch security commander, was finishing post assignments. "Matthews, you're guest parking with Howard." Lopez had seen Luke enter the back of the briefing room. "Chief, you have anything for us?"

"Thanks, Mario," Luke said, walking up the center aisle dividing the uniformed security officers, both men and women, sitting in rows on both sides of the room. He knew some by name. Others looked familiar. There were over fifty of them.

They all knew who Luke was. "I was going over security incidents this morning. I found something that's happening too often and it's happening on every watch." Reaching the front of the room, he turned to scan the faces. "The problem emerging is a problem we can't ignore. I'm talking about whores, Vegas Skin."

A splatter of laughter came from the ranks. Luke had learned the slang *Vegas Skin* from the men and women in front of him. Luke leaned against the watch commander's desk. "They go by a lot of names, escorts, female companions, prostitutes, hookers. Whatever they're called, they're not welcome in the Silver Palace. In the past week, we've encountered eleven of them. Eleven." Luke repeated the number to stress his point. "The most recent was last night. A call girl, an escort, stole three grand after she serviced one of our guests. She stole his watch, a gold ring, five hundred in tokens, plus cash. This time, we caught her. I wonder how many we don't catch. How many guests are too embarrassed to report what has happened. How do we solve this? You know what they look like. You know a working girl when you see one. Rather, they're dressed in a miniskirt, heels, or a plaid shirt with jeans, you know them. They claim to be professionals. Well, so are you."

Luke paced as he continued. "When these women come in on the arm of a guest policy dictates we don't interfere. Some present no problem, but this is the Silver Palace, not the Silver Whore House. Prostitution in Clark County is a crime. A crime not to be ignored. Policy may dictate we don't get in the way when they're with a guest, but once they leave that guest, we own them. You have the authority to question them. Once you establish they're not a guest, get them out. You have a radio, give surveillance a heads-up so they can be identified the next time."

Luke looked to Lopez. "Lieutenant, pick two officers. One male, one female. Alternate them every day, give everyone a chance. Make it plain clothes, I want them dressed like a guest. The challenge is to find, identify, and notify, every time you spot an escort, a working girl or a prostitute." Luke searched the faces. He sensed enthusiasm. "If you can, follow them. Then we'll know what room they're in so we can introduce ourselves when they come out."

Again, there was laughter among the ranks.

Luke moved up the center aisle. "Word will get out among the escort services, the pimps, and the free-lancers, that the Silver Palace is a place they don't want to be. In plain clothes, you own the place. You don't have a post, you have a mission. We'll start this today. With that, I'll give it back to the lieutenant. Thank you, and as they say down in the card room, good luck."

AFTER SIGNING a statement and having her picture taken, much like a mug shot, Dawn Wilder was escorted to the rear entrance of the casino by two uniformed officers. One was a young Black woman, and the other was a Hispanic male. Dawn had never been to the back of the casino. A shapely blonde in a short skirt and high heels with two uniformed officers drew curious looks as they walked down the side of the card room. Only a few blackjack tables and roulette were busy, but the chimes and electronic beeps from slots filled the air. Dawn was shaken and worried. No one told her where she was going. She expected jail, but the head of security had told her if she cooperated she could walk.

The morning air was warm, and daylight was on its way when the two officers pushed open the double glass doors. "Where we going?" Dawn asked with a look at the uniformed Black woman.

"You can go anywhere you want," the officer holding the door open answered soberly. "Just don't come back here."

A wave of relief swept over Dawn. "I'm free. I can go?" she said, raising a hand to her chest. Excitement swept away her worry.

"We're not releasing you." The Hispanic officer added, "We're throwing you out."

Dawn was too shocked to catch the insult. She gave the two officers a look, turned and bolted away, heels clicking on the walkway. She was free but lost and worried. Security had taken the money the Texan paid her to strip and go down on him. In Dawn's mind the Texan was the problem. He was a real freak. A freak with a limp dick. He had caused it all. She guessed the Strip was at the front of the building. Her high heels echoed as she walked toward the corner of the towering building.

She was still in the shadows while the upper levels of the Silver Palace basked in the morning sun.

Rummaging in her bag, Dawn walked as fast as her heels would allow. She found her RTC bus pass. The bastards inside had taken every dime from her purse. It wasn't fair, thirty-six dollars of it was hers. They were going to give it all to the prick Texan. She hoped his dick would fall off. Insult turned to injury. Dawn found the bus stop at the front corner of the Silver Palace.

There were three Hispanic housekeepers in sweaters and hoodies. They all carried bulging handbags. Dawn had no idea their bags were filled with food from the casino's cafeteria. There was also an older woman sitting beneath the bus bench canopy with a cane. Dawn joined the group to wait on a bus. She knew what they were, and they knew what she was. She saw their looks and heard the whispered Spanish as they spoke. Dawn moved to the edge of the curd in front of all of them to avoid more looks.

Dawn had only been at the curb a few minutes when a polished Tesla with California plates stopped in front of her. The bearded forty-year-old ran his window down and leaned toward it from behind the wheel. He smiled at Dawn. "You shouldn't have to wait for a bus." He pushed open the passenger door. Those waiting had their eyes on Dawn.

"Fuck off," Dawn growled, kicking the car door. The Tesla's tires yelped as it bolted away with its door slamming.

Dawn backed away from the curb, choosing to stand behind the housekeepers. She was flushed with anger and embarrassment. She wished she had a cigarette. The pricks in security took her Marlboros and tore them up, looking for dope.

The RTC bus arrived. Dawn was last on, behind the woman with the cane. She went to the back of the bus to avoid looks. Two young Black men admired her as she passed them. Fuck you too, Dawn told them silently as she pushed by.

The morning sun was bright when Dawn got off the bus, three blocks from her apartment. It was not their apartment, it was hers. Casey never paid any rent. Eighteen hundred and fifty a month on the second floor with two bedrooms, one bath and a toilet that leaked. Did he care how many tricks she had to turn to pay the rent? She wished she hadn't invited him to move in. They met playing Pickleball. Casey Lynch was from South Carolina. He was all charm with a soft southern drawl, and he helped fill her days, but he became nothing short of a costly burden. Anyone looking for a job in Vegas could have one in ten minutes. High-paying jobs were few, but if you were willing to work, Vegas was the place to be.

Casey was still sleeping when Dawn arrived. She looked in the bedroom. He was snoring. The room smelled of weed. He was a worthless dick. When she returned to the kitchen the cell phone on the table was vibrating and rattling in a circle. Pam suggested the girls not carry cell phones on their dates. "Your date is the center of the universe. He's bought and paid for," she cautioned.

Dawn gathered the cell and looked at caller ID. It showed a number, but no name. It was Pam. "This is Dawn."

"Morning, sunshine. You're late," Pam's voice said. "You spending extra time in Texas?"

"It went all right," Dawn lied, hoping her lies would never be known.

"I called earlier. Figured you were still having fun. You send Tex away a happy man."

"It was exciting for him," Dawn added.

"I'll deposit five in the BOA account you gave me. Get some rest, girl. I'm putting things together for tonight. You interested?"

Dawn remembered what the chief of security at the Silver Palace said. Get him a number where he could find Pam, or her pictures were going to become a wanted poster all over town, maybe even on the Sphere. Dawn understood. It was her, or Pam. The guy told her Pam would never know who gave her up. Dawn took a breath before she spoke, she hoped it was a convincing tone. "Pam, when I got to Starbucks at the Silver Palace there were two guys with carnations. I didn't know what to do. How can I reach you without a number."

Pam seemed ready for the question. "Okay, if something like that happens again. Call me. You ready?"

Dawn went to a notepad on the face of her refrigerator and gathered a pen. "Ready."

"Two-three-two, two-three-two, nine-four, four one. That's private. Don't use it, unless…"

"Got it," Dawn assured.

"I'll call after six. Get some rest."

Dawn laid the cell on the table and stared at it. Now, she had insurance. Now, she had a number to give the asshole at the Silver Palace. Now, she was safe as long as Pam didn't send her back to the Silver Palace.

Tammy finally woke up after the sun moved around the room to find her face and become an annoyance. She sat up. She had to pee. She climbed from the bed dressed only in bikini panties and a lace bra. She moved into the hallway. "Dad," Tammy called, holding a hand to her crotch.

"Good morning," a Spanish female voice answered from the kitchen.

Tammy looked. The woman was plump, in her forties, dressed in a Silver Palace housekeeping uniform. Tammy could tell from the uniform the woman was a domestic. "Where's my dad?"

"Senior Larson. He had to work. Can I get you some coffee?"

"Holy shit," Tammy complained, dashing for the hall bath. When she came out, the woman was gone from the kitchen. Tammy found her in the bedroom. Dede was making the bed.

"NO, no, no," Tammy objected, moving to Dede to take her arm. She guided the woman to the door. "You don't come in here. I take care of this room."

Dede was annoyed, being pushed into the hallway. The bedroom door slammed behind her.

Door closed, Tammy went to her bag on the floor beside the bed. She set it on the unmade bed. She rummaged in the bag to find a pack of Newports. She opened the cigarettes and turned the pack upside down to shake out several cigarettes and a condom stuffed with a small tin foil packet. Her hands shook as she worked the small packet from the condom. Packet in hand, she opened it carefully and sank to her knees beside the bed. With the packet open, Tammy leaned toward it. She pinched the side of her nose and sniffed hard at the waiting smear of white crystals. It was meth.

The cloud of meth found its way from Tammy's nostril into her lungs, where it dissolved into her bloodstream to be pumped through her body. The meth slammed into Tammy's psyche like a truck. Her eyes looked at a distant fuzzy horizon as she collapsed to the floor beside the bed.

EIGHT

CHANCES ARE...

LUKE HEARD the announcement from surveillance on his radio. It was Gayle Turner's voice.

"Ace of Clubs is in the house," Gayle's filtered voice said.

Luke and everyone with a radio understood. The general manager, Greg Larson, had arrived on the property. Luke was pleased. He wouldn't have been surprised if Larson hadn't come in. The arrest of his eighteen-year-old daughter for prostitution had to be a shocker. Luke thought about going to go see Larson but decided against it after Gayle Turner called to tell him about the buzz on TikTok. Tammy Larson's booking photo and word of her arrest were there. Luke remembered a Chaplin in Afghanistan after they had a tough time with the death of six other Marines. Luke could still hear the Chaplin's voice, *This too, shall pass.* Luke hoped it would be true for Greg Larson.

Luke had presented the challenge of tracking Vegas Skin to his officers. The nick name *Vegas Skin* seemed more user-friendly than calling them whores. Working girls in Vegas weren't whores. They, like everything else in Vegas, had to be wrapped in some kind of provocative mistic. Mistic or not, he couldn't let whores tarnish the sign above the Silver Palaces' front door, WELCOME. He rode a guest elevator down to the casino level, sharing it with two Millennium couples. Their bags and suitcases told Luke they were on their way to check out. They were still smiling and talking about the fun they had in the Palaces' River where you could float, and drink and they had seen the Beatles at the Mirage. Luke decided they were the bright side of Vegas.

On the casino level, Luke walked through the maze of tables in the card room. This was midmorning in Sin City. The twenty-one tables were busy. Weren't they always? The chime and pulse of electronic sounds drifting from the swarm of slot machines mixed with laughter from the long line for the morning buffet. A crowd of seniors sat at the buzzing, flashing slot machines. It seemed seniors were less intimidated by a machine taking their money than they were with a smiling, smooth, quick-handed dealer. Machines or a practiced smile, odds were the house would be the winner. Luke glanced at his watch. Remembering there had been a problem with the currency counter, he headed for the cash cage. He walked to the thick, protective windows in front of the cashiers. He didn't see any that recognized him. He lifted his badge from beneath his jacket and held it up for the supervisor behind the six cashiers. The supervisor, looking like an escapee from a casino chorus line, studied the silver and gold badge through the thick glass. Luke almost gave in to irritation after what seemed to be her prolonged look at the badge. The supervisor finally raised her eyes to his and offered a nod. Luke stepped to the unmarked, nondescript outer door of the mantrap. A buzzer sounded, and Luke pushed the heavy metal door of the mantrap inward. He stepped inside to find windowless white walls, intense silence, and harsh, shadowless light. Luke allowed the door to thud shut and lock behind him. He glanced up at the camera in the corner of the trap. He knew a buzzer sounded in surveillance where an officer and Gayle Turner would be watching. He also knew he had looked at only one of four cameras in the trap. The buzzer sounded a second time. Luke pushed through.

In the cool, clean air of the cash cage, Luke knew he was near the heart of the Silver Palace, although this heart wasn't pumping blood, it was pumping cold, hard cash. Money had its own moldy smell, and in the nearby hidden count room, there would be a billion dollars in cash.

The cash cage served guests, some wanting change, others making a deposit into a casino account, or more importantly, making a cash withdrawal. The cage also provided records for dealers, signing in or out. They also exchanged casino chips for cash, as well as a myriad of other cash transactions. The cash cage was the visible money laundry the world could see. It was covered with an arsenal of surveillance cameras. Some visible, some not. A mix of PTZs, pan tilt and zoom cameras capable of turning on a three-sixty axes as well as zooming in close enough to read the serial numbers on bills. The staff of six women all wore the same uniforms and shoes. There were no pockets on their blouses or pants. Jewelry was prohibited, including wedding rings, necklaces, and earrings. The six cashiers, as well as their aging supervisor, all wore similar hairstyles, nothing below the collar of their logoed blouses, but all fit the Vegas mold. They were attractive.

"Is there something I can assist you with?" the supervisor said with a short-lived smile as she greeted Luke just inside the door of the mantrap.

"Yeah," Luke answered, ignoring the supervisor's interest in his unscheduled presence. "Your PM watch had a problem with the currency counter last night. I heard it ate a couple hundred-dollar bills last night."

"Yes, we have a new one. Loaner from the Hard Rock," the supervisor explained, gesturing to the machine setting on a countertop in the center of the room. "Seems ours may be down for the count."

Luke looked at the machine. He laid a hand on it as he walked around the table, pretending he really knew what he was looking at. Then he moved from the counter to the back of the cashiers. Three of the six were servicing guests. Luke chose the youngest of the three who weren't. There was a number five on the back of the chair the girl sat in. He stepped close to her shoulder. "Can you tell me the total in your drawer?"

The young cashier, intimidated by Luke, glanced at the supervisor who offered a reassuring nod. The girl's eyes returned to Luke. "Six thousand four hundred and twenty-two dollars and seventy-two cents," she answered in a near whisper without opening the drawer.

Luke nodded approval as he returned to the supervisor's side. "Can you give me a ballpark figure on what number five has in her drawer?"

"Certainly," the supervisor answered. "Six thousand four hundred and twenty-two dollars and seventy-two cents."

"Thank you." Luke wanted out of the cash cage. He was moving for the door of the mantrap when he saw something on the floor. He paused and looked, hardly believing what he saw. A purple five-hundred-dollar chip laid in plain sight on the polished floor of the cash cage. A smile teased at his face as Luke reached down for the token. Wait until the supervisor sees this. Luke's fingers grasped the edges of the token. He pulled. It wouldn't move.

"It's glued to the floor," the supervisor said over Luke's shoulder. "I thought you would know. Surveillance uses it for camera focusing."

Emerging from the mantrap, smarting with embarrassment, Luke found the morning atmosphere of the noisy casino floor comforting. Why the hell didn't he know about the token? He was the director of security. No, he was the dummy who went for the bait in the cash cage. He'd have Gayle Turner's ass when he saw her. As the head of surveillance, he relied on her to tell him everything. Was she part of the lets humble Luke Mitchel club? Luke refused to turn and look back at the windows of the cage. He knew they were all smiles in there. He took a deep breath and walked away.

As the director of security, Luke lived and worked in a world of numbers. The number of guest rooms occupied, the number of employees on duty, the number of vehicles in guest parking. Even the proverbial bottom line was a number. Luke didn't like numbers. Maybe because numbers were pure, and his business wasn't. His business was to find what was unpure, untrue, false, lies, and then one of the lies walked by. A shapely server with a tray full of iced drinks dressed in skimpy snug black shorts, a red top barely covering her boobs, black lace nylons and high heels marched by. The girl offered Luke a smile from painted red lips as she swept by. She didn't know him, and he didn't know her, but they both knew Vegas. Luke knew he'd just seen the real face of both. Money and skin. Lots of it. It was bizarre, but real. The irony was the Silver Palace, like all of Las Vegas, promoted sex. An army of scantily clad servers, a mix of attractive female dealers, and an evening floor show with topless dancers. Attractive females were more than suggestive, they were a Vegas commodity, and the Silver Palace was a gold mine for beauty. All of which seemed in conflict with Luke's mission to ban those selling sex, and there were many. Luke knew he couldn't stop guests from bringing in whores. *Vegas Skin* was simply a mask to avoid the harsh reality. Sex for sale was a crime, but Las Vegas turned the other cheek. What happened in Vegas, *stayed* in Vegas. Guest privacy was the gateway. What went on behind the closed doors of guest rooms was protected and guaranteed. Working girls knew this and hid behind it. Many of them were known, often identified by facial recognition on entry, but when on the arm of a guest, they were never challenged. Luke knew he couldn't stop them, especially when the Silver Palace, like every casino in Vegas, promoted sex, but it was his job as director of security to stop the rain. The Nevada State Gaming Commission, always looking over his shoulder, watched his every move. It was much like the five-hundred-dollar token glued to the floor in the cash cage. He could see it, touch it, but he couldn't have it. He could see the working girls. He knew who they were, but he couldn't touch them.

———

JACKIE FALLON, the dark-haired, thirty-year-old, attractive executive assistant to the general manager, sat at her desk just inside the GM's office, telephone in hand. "Yes, Francis, I know," she said. "I've seen what's on TikTok. Thanks for the heads-up."

As Jackie hung up the telephone, Greg Larson came through the door from the hallway. He was troubled. It showed on his face. Jackie had been Larson's assistant for three years. She knew this man and given his composure as he marched into his office, he knew his daughter's mug shot had appeared on TikTok. The banner below Tammy's picture read, *GM's daughter arrested for prostitution. Tammy Larson, the eighteen-year-old daughter of Greg Larson, GM of the prestigious Silver Palace on the Vegas Strip, has run out of luck! She's been arrested for prostitution.* Jackie had gone on the internet after the third call. She found the picture and the story. No wonder Larson was troubled. Her telephone was ringing again. She ignored it and pushed from her chair to follow her boss into his palatial office.

Larson sat down at his desk to find a cup of coffee waiting. "Would you like that heated? It been sitting there a while."

"No, it's fine." Larson tasted it, set the cup aside and glanced at his watch. "I missed the staff meeting. Sonofabitch" He slapped his desktop with an open hand.

"I went to the boardroom," Jackie explained. "I told them the meeting was postponed. Unexpected arrival of one of our Chinese investors. They understood."

"Thanks, but you know words out. Hell, I could feel it walking in." Larson took another sip of coffee. "Did I teach you to lie like that?"

"It was one of my qualifications," Jackie said, trying to lighten the tension, but she knew she had to tell him about the calls. The telephone on her desk was ringing again. "There's been a lot of calls. What would you like me to tell them?"

Larson looked to Jackie. He didn't understand. "Calls. Tell them all to go to hell."

"They're calling because of what's on TikTok."

Larson was annoyed. "What about TikTok?"

Jackie could tell he didn't know about Tammy's picture on the internet. Her heart raced. She wasn't sure what to say. She decided truth was not only best, it was her only choice. "I'm sorry. I thought you knew."

"Knew what?" Larson's tone was harsh. He was on edge. His hands gripped the edges of the desk. Charlotte had abandoned him when he needed her, and his daughter had been arrested for prostitution. He was in the midst of a bitter divorce and now Jackie was telling him there was more. He knew it wasn't good. The constant ringing of the telephone in the outer office warned of that. Jackie's ability to read Larson's mood wasn't a one-way street. He could read her too," Jackie, Tell me."

"I'm sorry," Jackie said, lacing her fingers together. She looked much like a teen in the principal's office. "I thought with all the calls, you must know."

"Quit pissing around. What is it?"

Jackie looked at the floor. She talked to the rug surrounding Larson's desk. "Tammy's picture is on TikTok. The one from jail. They said she was arrested."

"The internet, fuck!" Larson slammed a fist on his desk. Pens and loose items danced in the air. He pushed out of his chair and turned to the floor-to-ceiling windows overlooking the Strip. The sun was bright, and the street below was crowded with traffic. The familiar towers of glass reaching into the sky on both sides of the Strip stood tall and silent. Larson studied them but found it hard to believe this was the city where the world came to play. He was desperate, alone. His office was the center of the universe for ten thousand-plus employees. Already, they knew of his daughter's arrest. It was true,

Larson reasoned, it really was *Sin City*. He didn't want to turn back to Jackie because tears welled in his eyes. Larson sniffed and stared. He wondered what would come next. What should he do? The man who usually had all the answers was finding he had none.

"Would you like to see what's on TikTok?" Jackie questioned carefully.

It was quiet for a moment before Larson answered. "No," he said without turning to her, "If I don't see it, maybe I can't answer the questions."

Jackie nodded and turned for the door.

"Close the door on your way out," Larson said without turning from the window. He heard the door close as he watched a flock of black crows wing their way over the top of the distant Flamingo. For a moment, he wished he were a crow.

———

CHARLOTTE JOHNSON TRIED to make her morning coffee at her office in the Cosmopolitan normal. She failed. Closing her office door was unusual for Charlotte, but it was closed. She ignored at least twelve calls from Greg Larson, but she was now waiting for the next one. Hours had passed. His call hadn't come.

"Damn it," she whispered, gritting her teeth while checking her phone once more.

It was silent. As the director of rooms, she did a daily count. Occupancy was at seventy-six percent. Based on the daily reservation report she was projecting they would sell out by the weekend, but she didn't care. Screw them. Didn't they know? But how could they? She had told no one. No one other than the man she loved. The man she trusted. The man who left her alone after the call from his estranged wife. The bitch. She was to blame. Don't go, she pleaded with Greg, but he went. He made the choice. His daughter was in trouble, and he put her first. Did that make him more of a man, more of a father? She warned him. You go, I go. He was torn. She saw it. Had she made the right choice, had she said the right things? Why didn't she answer his calls? Why wasn't he calling again? Was she right in leaving Greg after forcing him to decide what path he would take? A path that could lead back to his wife. A path any father would choose. Was she right in leaving? If she was right, why was it so painful? Love was like walking on ice. Charlotte was afraid she had fallen through the ice. The telephone on her desk rang. The caller ID told her it was the general manager.

She drew in a deep breath and picked up the receiver. "Good morning, Mr. GM."

"Charlotte, David Griffin, the president of Bankers United is coming in for coffee at eleven this morning. I'd like you to join us. Who knows our resources better than my director of rooms."

"It would be my pleasure."

"Good, give us a couple minutes. Say eleven thirty or so. You just happen to be passing by. We'll be in the main dining room. My resources tell me he is divorced. You understand, don't you?"

"I'll do my best," Charlotte assured.

The GM hung up. Charlotte did the same. The problem with being an attractive woman in Las Vegas, no matter your title, was the fact you became bait. Live bait. Charlotte knew her success in Vegas was linked to her beauty. Others claimed they saw it. She saw herself as average. She was pleased Greg Larson thought she was attractive. That was important to her. He had put it all on the line for her. His marriage, his career. He had kissed her, a Black woman, in front of the world at a casino managers meeting at the Bellagio. Why wasn't he calling? Was moving out a mistake? Were her words wrong? The reality was that deep inside she saw herself as a Black woman in a White world. Greg Larson had taken those thoughts away. At least until last night. Her telephone rang again. To her surprise the GM was calling a second time.

Charlotte gathered the receiver. "Yes, sir."

"Charlotte, I just had a call from Ken Hall in Food and Beverage. He tells me there is something online, TikTok, about Greg Larson's daughter being arrested for prostitution. You and Greg still a thing?"

Charlotte hesitated. If she admitted she hadn't seen what was on TikTok, it would be a confession she and Greg had parted. Charlotte found the answer, it was almost true. "Yes, I know his daughter is having problems. Doesn't every eighteen-year-old?"

"How true. Well, give Greg my regards and if we can help in anyway."

"I'm sure he'll appreciate that, sir."

"See you at coffee."

Charlotte hung up. She dammed herself. The GM of the Cosmopolitan was showing more sympathy than she, a woman allegedly in love with Greg Larson, had. She should call him. She considered it, even reached for the cell laying on her desktop. Then stopped. No, the choice, no matter how painful, belonged to Greg, not her.

PAIN WAS NO LONGER an issue for Tammy Larson, and she knew why. She was floating, smiling, humming. The packet of meth, her last, wasn't enough to put her down, but it was enough to put a smile on her eighteen-year-old face. Feeling euphoric, she dug in her bag of clothes for something sexy. She was happy, carefree, but conscious enough to know she needed to go out in the world. A world she knew, not a world crowded with a worried, disapproving father. Her world was filled with color, music, and approval. Approval from some connection she would be handing a wad of bills for another taste of life. The Snowman. She'd go see the Snowman. He'd have what she needed. Tammy was buttoning her blouse when she felt something in a pocket. She dug out the paper and unfolded it. It was a notice to appear in the Superior Court of Clark County for arraignment on a charge of prostitution. It sobered Tammy but only for a fleeting moment, then her smile returned.

"Fuck you too," she spat at the paper, crumpled it and tossed it onto the unmade bed.

Tammy did have one obstacle in her path—money. She didn't have any. She dug in her purse after pulling on knee-high boots. She found three dollars and seventeen cents. Hardly enough to excite the Snowman, but then she remembered she was still in her dad's condominium. He had money. Lots of it. He never gave her a dime, but he gave tons of money to her mother, not because he wanted to, but because he had to.

Dede Garcias was told to keep her boss informed. Being pushed out of Tammy's room was something Senora would want to know. Overtime pay or not, being the babysitter for the GM's eighteen-year-old had her on edge. Dede had seen her share of users up-close and personal. This kid was a doper. Dede went into the kitchen and dialed Senora's private cell number.

Boots on and still high, Tammy Larson checked her image in the floor-to-ceiling mirror on the closet door of the bedroom. She was pleased with what she saw. After seeing the Snowman, she might stop at Walgreens and get some hair color. Blue, maybe green. Her high-heeled boots were giving balance a problem. She promised herself to be careful, although she knew the real problem wasn't her heels. She tucked the front of her blouse into her skirt. She'd seen that on MTV. Now, she was ready. She took a deep breath, smiled at her image in the mirror and moved for the door.

Tammy found the plump housekeeper in the kitchen. She was looking out the kitchen window while speaking Spanish on a cell phone. She was making an obvious attempt to talk quietly. Tammy was pleased she went unnoticed. She moved away quietly. She had no problem finding her father's bedroom. Stepping into the room, she closed the door behind her. She noticed the bed in this room had been made neatly. Bitch. Two pictures atop a dresser brought a smile to her face. One was a profile of the Black woman her father was screwing, she couldn't remember her name, and another was a high school picture of the then-sixteen-year-old Tammy in a cheerleader outfit. She couldn't remember when the picture was taken.

Privacy an issue, Tammy began her search. She started with the bedside nightstands. In the first, she found a man's wristwatch. She looked for the brand. Van Cleef. She pushed the watch into the pocket of her leather skirt. She searched again. This time, she found a man's gold wedding band. He didn't need that anymore. It got pushed into the pocket with the watch. A third search of the drawer behind an open packet of Trojans and a folded white handkerchief revealed a man's gold bracelet. It was quickly added to her pocket.

On the other side of the bed, in a similar nightstand drawer, Tammy found a tube of lipstick, several soiled tissues, a handwritten shopping list and a single diamond earring. She searched hard for the earring's mate but found nothing. Dammit.

The housekeeper was in Tammy's room when she found her. She was making the bed. "I thought maybe you wouldn't mind now," Dede asked, carefully pausing from the task. Tammy noticed the woman had already gathered her clothes from the floor and hung them in the closet.

Gathering her purse from atop a dresser, Tammy forced a smile. "Hey, listen. I have to go meet a friend. I already called an Uber, but I don't have a dime. I was gonna stop at an ATM. Could I borrow a couple bucks until I get back? I'll only be an hour or so."

Dede balked at the idea. "Loan you money. I don't know if your father would…"

Tammy cut her short with an extended open hand and a smile. "You know who my dad is. We're good for it."

The reluctant Dede dug in a pocket of her uniform. She came out with folded currency. She unfolded a twenty-dollar bill and offered it to Tammy's open hand. Tammy widened her smile. "Remember it's an Uber. They're not cheap."

Dede's worries deepened. Her hand trembled as she pulled another twenty-dollar bill and placed it in Tammy's open palm.

"Thanks," Tammy offered, turning to disappear into the hallway. Dede pushed her money back into a pocket.

She wiped a hand on her uniform before pulling out her
cell phone.

————

WHAT HAD BECOME A MORNING ROUTINE, although Luke
deliberately varied the times, was a visit to the
surveillance unit. In the surveillance, two thousand
seven hundred and thirty-three cameras recorded
images from every corner and every floor of the Silver
Palace. Coupled with its facial recognition features and
an AI artificial intelligence algorithm, surveillance was
an invaluable tool not only for the Silver Palace but for
all of Las Vegas. The moment a visitor neared the fabled,
Welcome to *Fabulous* **Las Vegas,** sign, or tried an
approach to the Strip on a side street, a subtle sea of
discrete video cameras would find them, record their
movement, and assess their threat level.

In the surveillance unit at the Silver Palace, an array
of wide, tall video screens lined the wall, floor to ceiling,
behind a partition of glass where plain-clothed officers
watched a variety of images. Some of the images
switched through an automated program, while others
focused close on card tables, slots, and a variety of cash
points. The three women and four men watching the
screens were collectively and individually highly skilled
in casino gaming as well as behind-the-scene operations.
Facial recognition altered them to known cheats, which
was reinforced by the AI assessment of suspicious
activity or individuals. Underscoring surveillance's tech-
nological capabilities was the individual skill sets of the
assigned officers. They knew the games, traditional and
electronic, and they read cards, spotted markings, short
decks, counterfeits, corrupt dealers, dishonest employ-

ees, slots, payouts, cheaters, all linked to their instinctive ability to read character.

In addition to the collective skill sets of the surveillance team, Gayle Turner, the surveillance director, a thirty-four-year-old dark-haired brunette, could dance. She was a refugee from a chorus line at the MGM who knew age was a wall she couldn't dance over. She loved cards and gaming. Both paved a way for her to become a dealer at the Rio, then a card room assistant at the Flamingo, and finally into surveillance when the Silver Place opened its doors. She worked for three years before becoming the director. She was in the position when Luke Mitchel was hired as the director of security. Luke liked Gayle, trusted both her skills and character. He appointed her as his assistant. She knew the Silver Palace, and she knew Luke Mitchel was the right man for the job. Gayle was at her desk in the dimmed blue light from the video screens. There were three smaller video screens on her desk. Gayle was watching activity in the employee dining hall when Luke entered. He chose a chair beside Gale and sat down. She offered a smile. "We saw you in the cash cage. Welcome to the club. We've all dived for the five-hundred-dollar token."

"Good lesson in humility," Luke agreed. He was a refugee from eight years with the LAPD followed by four years at the Wild River Resort run by the Mojaves in Del Rio, Arizona. The GM handpicked him after he had saved the life of a would-be jumper while he was a guest at the Silver Palace. Gayle, like everyone in security, held her breath until she saw what Luke Mitchel was, and it seemed Luke knew the nuance of the game. He not only knew it, he lived it. Long days and nights proved he led by example, not mandate. Security got over its anxiety about the guy in a sports jacket and black tee shirt while Luke wormed his way into their lives with proven hands-on work and trust.

"Seen anything this morning?" Luke questioned, moving his chair closer to Gayles to join in looking at the center screen on her desk.

"Yeah." Gayle nodded as she now watched employees march in and out a rear door employee exit where a uniformed officer checked handbags and backpacks. "Your guy at the back door picks his nose."

"Got an email from HR earlier," Luke announced, slumping in his chair. "Three more dirty and out the door yesterday."

"Drugs?" Gayle questioned with a glance at Luke.

"Yeah." Luke nodded. "That makes twelve this week. According to HR, that's an increase that can't be ignored. Director has already given a heads-up to the GM."

"Like the GM doesn't have enough on his plate," Gayle offered, pushing back in her chair. "You see what's on TikTok?"

"Yeah," Luke answered, deciding his role in picking up Tammy at the county jail was *need to know*. "It's been a week since we've been searching for this in-house doper. We won't be able to keep a lid on it much longer. Especially with HR trying to dodge the bullet."

"He's gotta know we're watching," Gayle suggested. "And he knows what we can't see. Candice says she's dangling a carrot in front of an informant in housekeeping. She's trying to get the girl to make a buy."

"Candice in tonight?" Luke questioned, pushing up out of his chair. Candice Harmon was the attractive blonde supervisor of the surveillance unit's PM watch. She was also a licensed real estate agent who had helper Luke find the condo he recently bought in nearby Henderson. In appreciation of her help, Luke bought

Candice dinner. He found she was more than helpful, she was gorgeous. The attraction Luke had for Candice seemed mutual, but both were savvy enough to know an on-duty relationship turned into a romance was against policy. Although the GM and Charlotte Johnson proved the wall could be climbed, the path was not for the faint of heart. Thus, Luke and Candice were being cautious. Complicating things for Luke was the fact he had left a lover, Barbara Nichols, behind in Del Rio. She had recently been promoted from senior barmaid to director of F&B (Food and Beverage) at the Wild River Resort. Whether or not she would move to Vegas was now in doubt.

"Candice will be in at four," Gayle said, answering Luke's question.

"I'll come by," Luke said, turning for the door. "Until then, keep the whores out."

———

TAMMY LARSON GOT her Uber ride to the fringe of Freemont Street. It cost her thirty-eight dollars from the forty she *borrowed* from Senora Perez. She didn't care. The wristwatch and jewelry stolen from her father's bedroom were waiting in her pocket. She hoped it would buy her enough meth to get her through the next couple of days. Plenty of time to ask Daddy to provide an attorney. The Uber dropped Tammy on Bridger Avenue, just off Fremont Street. The pawn shop was on the corner. Tammy had been there before. She had hocked earrings she stole from her mother. The woman had so many she hadn't even missed them. Tammy, feeling high and confident, noticed two working girls on the corner. They were young and Asian, wearing too much makeup and not enough clothes. She considered telling them about Vice cops working Fremont but then decided talking to them would put her at risk with their pimp. Maybe a pimp was what she needed. She decided to give it consideration after she got some money.

The pawn's illuminated sign flashed, EZ Pawn. The windows on either side of the glass door entry were filled with a mix of cell phones, digital cameras, watches, and jewelry. Tammy knew she chose the right place. A chime sounded as she entered the store. There were three people ahead of her. A gray-haired man in a suit and tie, and a middle-aged couple. She browsed as she waited. Finally, the couple walked away and a balding clerk wearing glasses signaled Tammy to the counter. "How can I help you?"

Tammy dug into a pocket and proudly emptied her hand onto the countertop. Her father's wristwatch, wedding band and gold bracelet, along with one diamond earring, rattled on the glass surface. She smiled confidently. The clerk picked up the watch to study it carefully. He turned it over and looked at its back. Then, laying the watch down, he pushed at the gold ring and the bracelet with a long fingernail. He looked at the earring but didn't pick it up, "The risk for me is do I get to keep these items, or will Metro come in and impound them?"

Tammy's high was still filling her with confidence. She smiled, spreading both hands on the glass counter, leaning deliberately toward the clerk, pushing her breasts toward him. "The risk for me is do I get a fair price for these...or not?"

The clerk smiled, looked at the swell of Tammy's breasts and then picked up the watch again. He looked at the back of the watch a second time and then Tammy,

"Seven fifty, Mixed bills. No receipts, no questions and you're out the door."

"Deal." Tammy smiled.

The clerk reached into a pocket. His hand returned with crisp folded bills.

Tammy stuffed the folded currency into a pocket on her leather skirt as she left the pawn shop and the sound of its chime. She made no effort to hide her smile or the click of her boots on the sidewalk as she marched toward Fremont Street. She was passing an alley near Bridger Avenue when a hand grabbed her by the back of the neck, forcing her in a quick, staggered gait into the ally.

"Wait, wait, what are you doing?" she cried, but the grip and the man's strength gave her little choice.

"Shut up, bitch," a gruff voice warned as a dark metal automatic pistol was pushed in front of Tammy's face. "You make a sound and I'll blow your motherfucking face off."

"Please, please, listen," Tammy sobbed as the hand on her neck moved to the pocket of her skirt.

"Shut the fuck up," the voice growled as he pulled the money from her skirt. "Ha, ha, I watched your ass in the fucking pawn shop."

"Please, I..." Then the heavy metal pistol slammed against Tammy's jaw and ear. The sound stung. Light flashed behind her closed eyes. She staggered and fell to her knees. Tammy braced herself with open hands. The pavement was wet and cold. She felt the heavy hand again pulling, jerking away her cell phone. Her ears rang with a deafening tone. She coughed and spit blood. The man and her money were both gone.

NINE
AFTER SHOCKS AND...

LEADING THE SURVEILLANCE UNIT, Luke walked to the
employee entrance at the rear of the Silver Palace. It was
almost time for the cash transfer. The older uniformed
officer Gayle pointed out as the one picking his nose was
busy checking IDs and bags of those coming and going.
Luke gave thought to telling the man about his on-
camera habit but decided it was just surveillance bullshit.
He wondered how many times they watched him adjust
his dick. He offered the gray-haired officer a nod. Luke
couldn't remember his name, but he did remember he
was a retired firefighter. Outside the glass doors stood
two uniformed officers. They both carried long guns
held at the ready, and their bulky appearance told Luke
they were wearing body armor. He glanced at his watch.
An armored car was due to arrive for the cash transfer.
Luke had seen the DDR (Daily Drop Report) earlier on
his computer. They would be picking up eight million
seven hundred thousand and fifty-eight hundred dollars.
Not bad for a weekday. Mario Lopez, his day watch
supervisor, always gave Luke an estimated count he got

from the team of officers stationed in the count room. Their estimate was always close. The guesstimate was necessary because it ensured the count's ballpark accuracy without a dependence on the manager supervising the count team. Luke knew surveillance would have their drone in the air and more officers, along with Mario, would be stopping traffic on the approaching driveway while three more armed officers stood by in the heavily fortified count room where the money, stacked on wooden pallets, concealed beneath plain heavy wrapping paper, awaited. The pick-up time, always varied and known by few, would take only minutes. The armored contract vans were usually a different make, model, and color. The weapons their guards carried were impressive, and the team of three, getting out to pick up the palettes of cash, with their black-hooded faces, looked like no non-nonsense armed Navy SEALs. Luke knew his presence could be a distraction. He turned and walked away. He was the director, not a participant.

With eight million plus going out the back door, Luke decided on a cheaper look at the front door. In the midst of the giants on the Strip, the Silver Palace with its ten thousand-plus employees and near seven thousand rooms, was like a bright light attracting bugs, even in the morning sunshine. What happened on the street in front of the Silver Palace reflected what was going on inside, and Luke knew that.

The escort services in Vegas, as well as freelancing pimps and whores, wanted the same thing from the Silver Palace that its average ten thousand guests wanted —money. In addition to a significant service fee, to get laid, pimps and whores alike were skilled at stealing cash, rings, watches, and credit cards and anything else they could get their hands on, and many of their victims, not wanting to be identified to wives, friends, and family, many times never reported their loss. Dawn Wilder, caught the night before, proved that.

Starbucks had an open sidewalk café just outside the front doors of the Silver Palace. The morning sun was bright, and the forecast was calling for a high of one-o-eight, but it was still cool enough to enjoy fresh air. Luke ordered a latte and looked for a chair among the shaded scattered tables. They were crowded. He finally spotted a thirty-something brunette sitting alone at a table by herself. She was dressed businesslike, not over the top Vegas. Her handbag suggested she was more business than guest, and more importantly, was the fact three chairs at her table were empty. Luke decided to be bold and friendly. Cup in hand he walked through the maze of crowded tables to the brunette, "Miss, it's crowded. May I share your table?"

The brunette offered a smile and moved her bag from the tabletop to a chair. "Of course, please." She gestured with a smile and painted nails.

Luke sat down. He had surveyed the sidewalk which was his real reason for being out front. He spotted two working girls. How did he know what they were? They were dressed over the top, not to be ignored, Vegas style. Their practiced strolls up and down the sidewalk, near the curb, offering subtle glances at slow traffic and male *peds*, assured him they weren't waiting on a bus.

"Thanks," Luke said, granting the brunette a smile. "Busy place this morning."

"It's busy every morning," the brunette suggested with a glance at the surrounding tables, "But who can get through a day without a Starbucks."

"You on your way to or from work?" Luke questioned after another look at the woman's attire.

"I'm already at work," the brunette answered, "and how about you?"

Luke deliberately avoided answering her question. "You're already at work?" Luke countered.

"Ellen Griffin," the woman answered. "I freelance for KTNV, better known as Channel Thirteen here in Vegas."

"Impressive," Luke suggested. "And you're already at work."

"Key word I used." Ellen Griffin smiled. "Was freelance. I find worthwhile stories and take them to the team at KTNV."

"Fascinating," Luke suggested. "So Vegas is home?"

"It is," Ellen answered. "I'm from LA. I found Las Vegas was the land of opportunity. I'm in my fourth year. And how about you…mister?"

"Sorry." Luke extended a hand across the table. Ellen accepted his invitation and reached for Luke's open hand. It was more squeeze than shake, but Luke found her hand warm. "Luke Mitchel. I'm from LA too. This is the beginning of my third year," he added after a glance at the street. An SUV pulled to the curb. One of the streetwalkers climbed in. "Vegas really is the land of opportunity."

"And what did you do in Los Angeles?" Ellen asked.

"Your skill set as a reporter is showing," Luke answered.

"Sorry." Ellen smiled, sampling her coffee. "Professional habit?"

"I understand," Luke agreed. "Fair is fair. I was a police officer, LAPD. Last couple of years on the job, I worked narcotics."

"Fascinating," Ellen suggested, leaning into the table. "Now that you mention it, it fits your persona."

Luke decided he had said enough. Ellen pressed for more, "So if I connect the dots I'm sitting at a table outside the Silver Palace with a former LAPD police officer who now works in Vegas. Wanna tell me how long you've worked here?"

"I don't want my story on Channel Thirteen," Luke cautioned with a smile, but he was serious.

"Your story isn't what brought me here," Ellen assured. "But what I saw on the internet did."

Luke's posture stiffened. He knew what she was talking about, and he felt as if he had just walked into quicksand. The phone on his belt chirped and vibrated. Luke reached for his cell. He looked at caller ID. The number had an area code he didn't recognize. He thought it was a spam call but its timing was perfect. He punched the answer button. "Luke Mitchel."

"Luke," Tammy Larson's panicky voice cried in his ear. "I need help. You said to call you. Some fuck robbed me. He hit me in the face with a gun."

Luke pushed out of his chair, motioning to Ellen Griffin that the call was important. She nodded understanding as he turned away. "Where are you?" Luke insisted.

"The Gold Spike. Right in front," Tammy sobbed. "I had to kiss a tourist's ass to use his cell. The prick took my phone, too."

Luke headed for the front door. Ellen Griffin saw the urgency. She hoped she wasn't seeing the last of Luke Mitchel.

The Gold Palace had a fleet of eight new highly polished four-door Mercedes parked on the employee level of the Silver Palace's multi-level parking structure.

Luke had a key. He and the GM had a single key that fit all the cars.

Luke got off the elevator on the employee level. He punched a number on his cell phone. He held it to his ear as he hurried to the line of parked Mercedes.

"Surveillance, this is Turner," Gayle's voice answered.

"Gayle," Luke said as he hurried to the first car. "I'm going off property in one of the company cars. Cover for me."

"You need help?" Gayle questioned. She could hear the urgency in his voice. She was already dialing up his image on one of the three screens on her desk.

"No, I'll explain later."

He pushed the cell phone back on his belt and scrambled in behind the wheel of the first Mercedes. Luke knew he had to avoid the slow traffic on the Strip. He drove to the Mayland Parkway. He knew it paralleled the Strip to Stewart Street, where he could turn toward the Gold Spike Casino at the end of Las Vegas Boulevard. Luke ran two red lights and one stop sign, speeding, and he ignored protesting horns from angry motorists. It seemed to take him forever, but Luke finally arrived. He parked in a Red Zone in front of the Gold Spike and scrambled out of the car. He didn't have to look for Tammy. She found him. She ran into his arms, crying. He held her by the shoulder and guided her toward the car just as a Metro Cop on horseback approached.

"We're outta here," Luke called to the uniformed officer on the horse. "Medical emergency." He pushed Tammy into the front seat and hurried around the car to get behind the wheel. He glanced in the rearview mirror at the police officer as they sped away.

Tammy wiped at her face slumping in the seat with

her head back on the cushion, "The prick took all my money."

"Try to relax," Luke said, worming the car through traffic. "Look at me. Let me see your face." He thought Tammy still looked like a whore, a young, weary one, but she managed a look at him. Luke studied her. Eye makeup from tears ran down her face leaving dark streaks. The left side of her face was bruised and swollen.

A trace of blood showed in an eyebrow. "Relax." Luke pulled out his cell. He keyed a number as he sped by two slower cars.

The weary Tammy didn't argue. Her head went back against the seat cushion with her eyes closed.

"Surveillance, this is Turner," Gayle's familiar voice answered. Luke had dialed a direct number.

"Gayle, it's Luke. I want this done quietly. You understand."

"I understand," Gayle assured.

"I need the GM's address, his condo. But before you do that, call him, tell him it's urgent he come home immediately. Right now, understood?"

"I'm on it," Gayle assured.

GREG LARSON WAS TRYING to put the pieces of his broken day back together. He was meeting in his office with Dave Thorton, Chief of Engineering, Dennis Torres, Head of Landscaping, and George Morrison, Chief of Building Design. Spread before the men, on the GM's conference table were large blueprints illustrating a glass-walled pool planned for the rooftop of the Silver Palace. Thorton, the engineer, was pointing out the plan for water sources and mandated drains when Jackie Fallon, Larson's executive assistant, knocked on the GM's closed office door. Opening the door partially, Jackie looked to the group.

"Sorry, gentlemen, I need to speak with the GM."

Larson read Jackie's expression. He crossed to her while the others waited. She leaned toward the GM and spoke in a near whisper, "Gayle Turner, from surveillance called. She said Luke Mitchel and your daughter need you at home, urgently."

Alarm showed on Larson's face. "What! What's happened?" He made no effort to be quiet.

Jackie was worried. She went on quietly, "I don't know. Gayle asked for your address and said they would meet you there. That's all I know."

"Sonofabitch," Larson said, bolting for a suit jacket on the back of a chair behind his desk.

The three men at the conference table exchanged worried looks. They all knew his daughter's arrest was on TikTok. It was not only the buzz in the Silver Palace it was the talk of the town.

"Meeting's over," Larson growled, pushing arms into his jacket. "I have to go."

"Yes, sir…sure, this can wait…anything we can do?" the three men offered their collective concern.

Larson didn't answer, bolting by Jackie and out the door. He literally ran to an employee elevator in the hallway, rushing by the director of human resources, who walked with a candidate for the vacated position of senior chef. The director was shocked. He looked at Larson as he hurried.

"Mr. GM, this is Harlen Rossi. He's here for our…"

Larson ignored the director as he rushed to the elevators, where he stabbed the down button repeatedly.

Finally, a car arrived. The doors parted to reveal three housekeepers, an engineer in coveralls with a vacuum and several women in dealer attire. They recognized the GM and backed away to allow him room. Larson stepped in and pushed the button to close the door.

———

LUKE MITCHEL CARRIED Tammy by the shoulder to the elevator and up to her father's second-floor condominium. Her pain and fright from being robbed and pistol-whipped had yielded to smiles, incoherent words, and an insistence she needed to sleep. Luke knew the symptoms. His days working narcotics in LA weren't that far behind him. A relieved Dede Perez opened the door and helped Luke get Tammy into the bedroom she abandoned earlier in the day. Luke helped get Tammy's boots off and then retreated to the living room. Dede went to work cleaning Tammy's bruised and swollen jaw, trying to make her comfortable.

Luke wasn't finding any comfort in the GM's condo. The idea of being comfortable there wasn't given much consideration. He paced, wondering how long it would be before Charlotte Johnson or the GM arrived. He decided to call Gayle Turner. She answered his call as soon as it rang.

"This is Gayle."

"Gayle, it's Luke. Did you call the GM? Is he on his way?" Luke was on edge.

"I spoke with his assistant. Jackie what's her name? I'm sure she told him."

"Well, where the hell is he? I've been here ten minutes."

"I'm sure he's on his way," Gayle answered.

"Yeah, okay. I'll call when I get back." Luke pushed the cell phone back on his belt and glanced at his watch. What the hell was taking the GM so long?

———

THE ANSWER WAS eight blocks away. Greg Marshal paced behind the Mercedes he pulled to the curb after the red lights on a police motorcycle lit up his rearview mirror. The helmeted officer, eyes masked behind sunglasses, stood writing in his ticket book as Larson continued his protests, "Listen, you know who the hell I am. Don't you people mail citations? This is bullshit."

"So is speeding past cars on the right," the gloved Metropolitan police officer answered soberly, lowering his citation book, "Now, either you stay at the rear of your car and stop yelling, or I stop writing, and this becomes something else."

"Yeah, okay, just hurry the fuck up," Larson urged.

Luke was standing at the kitchen sink staring out the window at the rows of towering condominiums and apartments wondering when he would get to see his place again in Henderson when Greg Larson opened the front door. "What the hell is going on?"

Dede Perez appeared in the hallway. She raised a finger to her mouth, giving both men a harsh look. "Please, she is sleeping."

Larson looked to Luke and he spoke softer, but his anger was obvious. "You called me because she's asleep?"

It had been a long day for Luke. They weren't in the Silver Palace, and he considered the playing field level. Luke matched Larson's tone. "You were called because Tammy went back to Fremont Street. This time she got her ass kicked and robbed."

"Robbed!" Larson was shocked. He looked to Dede. "Is she all right?"

Dede nodded. "She's got bruises," she answered in her Hispanic accent. "It don't look so bad."

Larson headed for the bedroom. Dede had left the bedroom door partially open. Larson opened it quietly. Tammy lay asleep on the bed. He grimaced, looking at the bruises on his daughter's face. He reached and laid a hand carefully on her shoulder. "I'm sorry, baby," he said in a near whisper.

When Larson returned to the living room, Luke and Dede were waiting. "She's got something worse than a bruise," Luke warned. "She's a got a habit. Drugs."

"Drugs." Larson tossed his jacket to a couch. "Jesus, why didn't her mother see this?"

"Same reason you didn't see it last night," Luke suggested.

"Mr. GM, sir." Dede clasped her hands together. "Do you want me to stay longer? Usually, I go home and..."

Larson cut her short, walking to collapse on the coach. He leaned his elbows on his knees to take his face in his hands, "Yeah, yes, go ahead," he answered without looking to Dede, "Thanks."

Dede looked to Jake. Jake nodded in agreement. Dede gathered her handbag from a table near the living room door. "Mr. GM, you should know. Your daughter, she was in your room with the door closed before she went away."

Luke opened the door for Dede. She gave him a quick look, crossed herself with gathered fingers and stepped out. Luke closed the door behind her. When he looked back to the living room, Larson was gone. Luke was uncertain what to do. Larson reappeared from the hallway to the bedrooms.

He cleared his throat and looked to Luke. "She took a Van Cleef watch Charlotte bought me, my wedding ring, and a bracelet. Who the hell knows what else? I don't know what to do."

"What time does Charlotte get home?" Luke questioned, knowing Tammy wasn't the only one needing help.

Larson crossed the living room to an ornate cabinet. He opened the cabinet to reveal a row of liquor bottles. He selected a bottle and a glass before looking to Luke. Luke shook his head. Larson poured his glass full. He gulped the liquor in three heavy swallows, before answering Luke. "Charlotte, left last night. She's not coming back."

"Shit," Luke mumbled as Larson poured another drink.

Luke knew he couldn't walk out. This man had saved his life. Larson shot and killed a man that was about to shoot Luke when he laid unconscious on floor in the GM's office. Greg Larson was more than a GM. He was the man who laid it all on the line for Luke Mitchel. Luke knew it was his turn. Payback. He had to help Larson. He crossed the room to take the liquor from Larson when Charlotte Johson opened the door and stepped in. She looked at Larson and then Luke.

"Luke, You can go," Charlotte said, "We'll work things out."

Larson bolted by Luke to pull Charlotte into his arms. He buried his face in her long hair. Charlotte's arms went around Larson's back. They kissed.

"Tammy's in the bedroom," Luke said, moving by the two and out the door. "Greg will tell you the rest."

————

IT HAD BEEN an exhausting night and a long day for Dawn Wilder. The prick from Texas, her arrest at the Silver Place, being called a thief, then a whore. She was neither, she hoped. She was an escort, but she left the Silver Palace carrying a guilt she had never felt before. She wanted to sleep, to forget, to run from it all, but the free-loading dick, Casy Lynch, stoned on weed, and who knew what else, was sleeping in her bed. She was not about to get in bed with another man. Dawn went to the guest room where she closed the blinds and the door, undressed, and got in bed. Sleep had always been her hiding place. She prayed it wouldn't fail her now.

Charlotte Johnson and Greg Larson were finding the best way out of their dispute, lovers quarrel, argument, disagreement, was to simply put it behind them. They found they didn't have to agree, which was not new, but they did find and agree a path forward in their relationship required put the issue behind them. There was no formal, *I'm sorry*, or the often-used, *we'll never do that again*. In its place was an acknowledgment and agreement not to look back, but to look forward. The love they shared was obvious to both, and what they needed and found was a solid common bond, as they climbed the rock-covered mountain facing them. The mountain was asleep in their guest room. Its name was Tammy.

The grasp on reality came from Charlotte as she and Larson sat on the couch in their living room. She took Larson's hand in hers before she spoke. "Greg, we need help. We can't fix Tammy. There are people and organizations that specialize in problems like Tammy has. The head of Guest Services at the Cosmo had a fifteen-year-old who had a drug problem. They put the boy in a home that provided security and monitoring as he went through recovery. In eight weeks, he came home convinced he wanted to live clean."

"Where did they send him?" Larson questioned, squeezing the warm hand he held.

"Red Rock Recovery up on the hill, toward East Mountain," Charlotte answered.

"I like the idea. We've gotta do something. Look what happened today. Let's give them a call."

———

LUKE MITCHEL WAS glad to return to the Silver Palace. He was giving sincere consideration to driving the Mercedes to his condo in nearby Henderson the next time he was fortunate enough to spend a night at home. He thought about the GM's policy dictating managers and director had to stay on property when room occupancy was above seventy-five percent. It was above that most days. The policy meant nearly thirty rooms would be occupied by employees when they could be rented by guests. It was a cost-effective argument he decided, and someday, someday when Greg Larson's life wasn't covered with storm clouds, he would do it. Luke waved to a uniformed officer on duty near the driveway entrance to employee parking. Pulling the security radio from his belt, he announced, "Gatekeeper-Ten is back in the house." He knew surveillance and security supervisors would be listening. Luke parked the Mercedes where he found it and walked to a nearby elevator.

His third-floor guest room was minor compared to those on the upper levels, but it was comfortable and quiet. Luke decided to go there, wash his face and hands, catch his breath, and maybe check in with his one-time lover, Barbara Nichols. They had met at the Mojaves

Wild River Resort and Casino in Rio Vista, Arizona. She was a bartender when he signed on as a security officer. She was an attractive blonde and a skilled bartender, which kept the Mojaves bar a busy place. Barbara had planned to follow Luke to Vegas, especially after he bought the condo and offered a serious invitation, but that had to be put on hold after the Mojaves wisely promoted her to head of food & beverage. Potatoes and meats won over love, at least for what Luke hoped would be short term. Wild River was nice, but it stood, eyes closed, in the bright lights from Las Vegas.

Reaching his room, Luke considered ordering from room service but decided sharing a table with those down in the employee cafeteria sounded better. There, he could pick from the buffet without deciding what he had to order. He unholstered his automatic pistol, and unclipped the radio and cell phone from his belt, dumping them on a tabletop beside a comfortable chair which he welcomed. He slumped into the chair and pushed off his shoes. Picking up the remote, he turned on the flat-screen TV. Anderson Cooper was talking to an on-scene reporter somewhere in the Middle East. Flashes from explosions and thunder roared in the background. Luke watched, realizing many were having a much more challenging day than his. Next, Anderson went to a reporter following a presidential candidate around North Dakota, and Luke, sinking a little deeper in the chair, fell asleep.

———

TAMMY LARSON, riding in the back seat of her father's Maserati, was cold and pissed. She was coming down from her meth high, and she had no hope ahead of her.

Her plan to visit the Snowman had turned into a nightmare. The sonofabitch that robbed her was probably somewhere getting high and calling everyone with her cell. The prick. Now, she watched traffic while her father and his Black lover drove her somewhere. What was it the bitch said? *Tammy, you need help. You're headed down a dead-end street. Dead end*, what did this good-looking Black woman know about *dead ends*. She smelled good, had pretty teeth, and nice hair. Why the fuck wouldn't they tell her where they were going. A pain-in-the-ass doctor was her guess. Once the car stopped, both of them, her dad and the Black bitch, could both wonder where she was going. Damn, it was cold.

She saw the illuminated sign as her father pulled the car into the lighted front entrance. Red Rock Recovery. What the hell was this? There were two people waiting under the canopy covered near the glass doors. A woman and a man. There was another man in some kind of uniform just inside the doors. When the car pulled to a stop, the waiting man and woman moved to the car and opened the back door. Tammy leaned away from them, "What the fuck?"

"Tammy, come with us," the man ordered, reaching for her. He looked buff, and his grip on her shoulder was firm.

"We've got a nice room waiting for you," the thirty-something woman added.

"Go to hell."

Greg Larson was out from the front seat. He opened the back door of the car and pushed Tammy toward the man who pulled on her.

Charlotte joined the waiting thirty-something. "Tammy, they're going to help."

"Fuck you too." Tammy's resistance, mixed with her

meth crash, didn't amount to much. She was pulled out of the car and hustled toward the glass doors, where the uniformed man inside pushed the door open.

"Mr. Larson," the muscle man said with one hand on Tammy's shoulder and another on her back pushing while the thirty-something held her other shoulder. "You don't have to come in this evening. We've got all we need."

"What the fuck?"

"Tammy," Larson called. "I love you."

"Good night, Tam," Charlotte added.

Charlotte put an arm around Larson's shoulder as he watched his daughter disappear behind the now-closing glass doors.

THE RING of a bedside telephone in Luke Mitchel's guest room woke him. He was surprised. Damn, how long had he slept? The math waited as Luke pushed out of his chair and moved to gather up the telephone as it continued its annoying ring.

"This is Luke."

"Chief, it's Anakoni Stone. PM watch."

"Anakoni, what's up," Luke said to his Hawaiian security supervisor. They had shared much. Luke liked his island import.

"Chief, we have a problem on sixty-two."

"Tell me about it."

"Lucy Mendoza, housekeeping. She was twenty-seven."

"Was." Luke picked up on his supervisor's tone.

"Tom Langley from engineering found her about ten minutes ago. He tried CPR. Then we tried. Paramedics are on the way, but it's not looking good. We're guessing drugs."

"Shit," Luke complained, knowing the loss was serious, serious in a multitude of dimensions. "You at the scene?" he questioned.

"Yeah, we're in the stairway between sixty-two and nine."

"I'll be up." Luke hung up, grabbed his gun, radio, and cell. Shoes were next. He grabbed his jacket, moving for the door. He found a back-of-the-house employee elevator and punched the button for sixty-two. The business of the Silver Place hadn't died. The elevator stopped first on twenty-six for room service with a dinner cart, then again on forty-three for two housekeepers. Luke was frustrated with the delays.

He looked to those sharing the elevator. "This car is going up, you know."

The two Hispanic housekeepers chose not to answer. The younger twenty-two-year-old White kid from room service didn't know who Luke was. "I'm betting they tried," he said with a glance at the housekeepers. "It's faster to go up and then back down. Beats waiting for a downer for ten minutes."

Luke nodded understanding. He felt like he just found another token glued to the floor. The elevator bumper to a stop on sixty-two. Luke got off and headed for the stairway. It was crowded inside. There was an emotional housekeeping supervisor who was being comforted by a younger male housekeeper, Tom Langley from engineering, who was also being emotional. Anakoni Stone, the uniformed PM security watch commander, two uniformed officers, one a young Black woman, the other, an older Hispanic male, and three uniformed paramedics from the LVFD, who with heavy equipment bags, were crowded around the body of the young housekeeper laying hidden by them, on the flat floor of the landing.

Anakoni Stone offered Luke a nod as one of the helmeted uniformed paramedics stood and turned to them. He recognized Stone's sergeant stripes as the one in charge. "She's gone, Sarg. No pulse, no heartbeat, no breath. Choice is yours. We can't establish a cause of death, so we transport her to Morning Side, or you call Metro. Given her youth, there's going to be an investigation. She's got the remains of what appears to be crystals in her left nostril. Coupled with her collapse in here you know what that indicates. Phenol."

Stone looked to Luke. Luke knew the choice was his. "We'll call Metro."

The paramedic nodded acceptance and turned to the two men kneeling over the body. "Okay, guys, we're out of here. Metro's gonna own this."

The paramedics gathered their heavy equipment bags and headed for the door. Luke looked to Stone. "Okay, tactfully get everyone out of here. Have someone take Langly down to engineering. Brief them on what happened. I want a man up on the sixty-ninth. No one comes down. Put another one on sixty-seven. No one comes up. Then get me two more in here. Make sure they understand no one touches anything. No railing, no walls, nothing. What was this girl's name?"

"Lucy Mendoza."

"Okay, go down to housekeeping, find the supervisor that was in here and connect her with the MOD, the manager on duty. Tonight, that's Tom Roberts from the card room. He and the supervisor will have to go out to the girl's home and find her husband or family."

"She's single. Lived with mom and dad," Stone offered. "She's been here a couple years."

"Mom and Dad need to be informed. Tell Tom to call me if he wants. They need to know the Silver Palace will help with whatever they need. Anything."

"Jesus," Stone said as it sank in.

"Tell them to take Jesus along. He'll help," Luke suggested. "Get me two more troops up here for whatever. I'll take care of things here. Okay?"

"Got it." Stone was on his radio as he moved away.

Luke looked at the young housekeeper's body after the crowd thinned. She lay exposed on the floor with both her arms and legs in awkward positions. Her hands were open, fingers extended, eyes closed. Her head was surrounded by discarded blue paper towels and a pair of wrinkled latex gloves left behind by the paramedics. Some of the towels were folded, others wrinkled. Urine began to soak through the crotch of the girl's uniform pants. It collected and ran down in a crooked wet stream onto the tile floor. Luke hadn't seen a dead body in a long time. The last was his boss and mentor at the Wild River Casino in Arizona. Luke found the man in his car in the parking lot with a bottle of Jack in his dead hands. Before that was his police partner in Los Angeles who was shot in a liquor store by a Black teenage would-be robber. Luke pushed the memories aside. There was much to do. He pulled the phone from beneath his jacket and punched a predial.

Candice in surveillance answered. "We've been watching and listening," she said. "What do you need?"

"We've got a dead housekeeper in the stairwell on sixty-two. I need to know what time she came in here and from what floor, and who she met, if anyone. We need to know where that individual went after they met.

Tom Langley from engineering claims he found her. Doesn't mean he isn't a suspect. Got it."

"We're on it," Candice assured. "Back to you in a couple."

Luke pushed the phone onto his belt as two uniformed officers arrived. "Watch Commander said to meet you here," the older of the two advised after he looked at the body and grimaced. Both officers looked young.

"Yeah," Luke answered. "Just hang with me. You're my gophers, and don't touch anything."

"She really dead?" the second officer asked, staring at the lifeless body and the stream of urine.

Luke chose not to answer. He stepped around the urine tracing away from the housekeeper's body and looked up the stairs for a camera. There was none. He turned and looked above the entry door where they all stood. He found a camera. It was a small gray one, fixed with a wide-angle lens focused on the stairs. Luke moved to the stairs leading down to the sixty-seventh floor, again eyes searching. The landing below made a forty-five-degree turn to the right to connect with steps leading downward. The walls were naked. The fixed cameras were mounted on floor entrances. There were none on the landings. Luke knew it meant there were blind spots. If it was a dope deal that killed the girl, the transaction may never have been seen. It all depended on how smart the doper was.

His cell phone chattered. Luke pulled it from his belt. Candice was calling.

"What have you found?" Luke questioned.

"Maybes," Candice answered. "We see this guy go into the stairway on seventy-four. He's young, twenty-five maybe, Hispanic, wearing a room service uniform.

Connie Quinton recognized him. She says his name is Jose Alonso."

"Tell Connie thanks."

"There's more."

"I'm listening."

"So, Alonso goes down the stairs. We see him on every landing until he gets to sixty-seven. There, he must have stopped on the landing, off camera, just above sixty-two. Then we see Lucy coming out of the house-keeping closet on sixty-two. She walks to the entrance of the stairway, goes in, still on the camera inside, until she goes up the steps to the platform, where we conclude Alonso is waiting."

"But you can't see either of them?" Luke pressed.

"No, but there is nowhere else they could be."

"Okay, okay, go on," Luke urged.

"Forty seconds pass and then Lucy reappears. She wipes her nose as she comes down the stairs to sixty-two. She pauses when she reaches the platform, puts a hand on the wall, and then falls."

"Jesus," Luke said. "Phenol. Okay, where did this Alonso kid go?"

"We watched. He comes up the stairs, all the way to seventy, went out into the hallway and took an elevator down."

"The little prick."

"But we didn't see anything."

"Yes, you did. We'll go get him. Where is he?"

"Connie stayed on him. He's in the kitchen. Looks like he's loading a room service cart for delivery."

"Okay, stay on him. I'll have Stone go introduce himself. Cover him, too."

"We're on it."

Luke pushed the cell beneath his jacket and unclicked

his small handheld. "Gatekeeper-ten, to thirty," he said, keying the radio.

Stone's filtered radio voice answered immediately. "Thirty here. Go, ten."

"Surveillance has a room service employee on camera. His name's Perez."

"I know him."

"He's in the main kitchen. I'll send the two guys with me down to meet you. Go get him. Put him in cuffs. Take him up to detention in surveillance."

"Will do," Stone answered. "Have the two meet me in the card room. I was talking with Charlie."

Luke looked to the two young uniforms. They had been listening. Their faces showed their excitement. "You heard. Get out of here."

The two uniforms disappeared out the door in a rush. Alone, with the young dead housekeeper, Luke switched from the radio to his cell. He aimed it at the body and took pictures. He moved to the left, took more. Then the right, taking picture after picture. Close-ups, wide shots, the stairs, the door to the hallway, the face of his wristwatch to capture the time and then to the body where he knelt to shoot close-ups of the girl's face and nostrils. When done taking pictures, Luke punched in a cell number he wished he didn't have to make. His call was to the GM.

"This is Larson," the familiar voice answered quickly. Luke could tell from background noise that the GM was in his car.

"Luke Mitchel, here, Boss. I'm sorry I've got some unwelcome news."

"Damn," Larson answered. "You're going to take that spot over at Mandalay Bay, aren't you?"

Luke could tell from Larson's humor that Charlotte's

return was having a positive impact. "No such luck for you," Luke answered. "On a serious note, I'm calling to inform you of a young housekeeper's death. Lucy Mendoza was found in a stairway. It looks like a drug overdose. There's reason to believe a room service employee may have supplied the drug. He's being detained. We'll have to call in Metro PD. This is criminal."

"I'm sorry to hear that," Larson responded. "Is there anything I can do to help?"

"No, I've got the on-duty housekeeping supervisor and Tom Roberts, the MOD, on their way out to notify the girl's parents. They will be offering any support they may need. I'll have a detailed report waiting on your computer."

"Yes, we'll provide anything the girl's family may need," Larson assured. "I'll call them when I get in tomorrow. If you can, Luke, try to keep this quiet. The death of an employee on property could be challenging."

"This is Vegas. Unfortunately, death by drugs isn't big news anymore."

"I hope you're right, Luke. You need anything else, call me."

"Bet on it. Is that spot over at Mandalay really open?"

Larson didn't answer. He had hung up. Luke took a breath, glanced at the body, and dialed 911.

TEN

A GARDEN PARTY

AT THE SILVER PALACE, Anakoni Stone, the armed PM security watch sergeant, paced in the card room. Finally, the uniformed officers arrived. The order from the director of security, based on the images found by surveillance was, *Find the sonofabitch and show him your handcuffs.*

"Let's go," Stone said, leading the officers to a door into the kitchen.

Twenty-five-year-old Jose Alonso, a room service employee, was at the main grill in the expansive busy kitchen watching a secondary chef lift flaming steaks from a sizzling smoky grill onto an array of plates atop his service cart. Alonso would take the order to a suite on the eighty-third floor. The expansive suite was a guarantee of a big tip. The big tip, coupled with his drug sales, would put him close to having enough to buy the Camero he'd seen on Russel Road. In the Camero, he could do some serious cruising. The car had three woofers. It would not go unnoticed. Lucy Mendez would go along. She was hot. Alonso had no idea she was dead in a stairway awaiting the arrival of the Metro police.

Alonso may have been just twenty-five, but he was savvy enough to know the three uniformed security officers entering the kitchen, especially with the fucking muscle-bound Hawaiian guy, Anakoni Stone, not only leading them, but mad-dogging him with threatening look. Alonso studied them for a moment as they worked their way through the maze of hot grills and salad stations. Sergeant Stone's eyes never left his. It was a warning he could not ignore. Some piece of shit had for certain snitched him off, and security was closing fast. Alonso bolted toward an open overhead door where a kitchen team was unloading a truck full of potatoes.

"Jose, stop," Sergeant Stone yelled over the noise in the expansive kitchen. The array of chefs, food service employees, and the army of grunts all turned to look as Alonso ran toward the open overhead door with the three security officers in pursuit. "Stop, you little bastard," Stone shouted as he and the two officers chased the fleeing Alonso in an attempt to arrest him as the suspect in the drug death of Lucy Mendoza.

"Get 'im," one of the pursuing uniformed officers screamed as Alonso bolted by the tractor and trailer where kitchen grunts labored at wheeling a palette of potato sacks down a ramp from the trailer.

Anakoni Stone was running, but his two younger subordinates were far ahead of him. The labor team unloading the trailer simply stared as Jose Alonso ran by them and into the oncoming night. Alonso had good reason to run like a frightened antelope. He knew his capture meant not only the loss of a job he wasn't all that fond of, but a high probability he would go to jail. He dared a glance back. He had a lead on his pursuers, he could hear their commands to stop, but they proved to be little more than an incentive for him to run faster. He had a car parked in employee parking. It was an old black Hyundai Sonata, but Jose knew if he could get there, and get in his car, he'd wave goodbye to these dicks in his rearview mirror. There were two more tractor and trailers waiting to unload outside the overhead doors. Alonso disappeared between two of them. His choice divided the trio chasing him. He ran faster. A three-foot-high wrought-iron fence divided the kitchen docks from a driveway for employees and guests leading up into the multi-level parking structure. Signs with directional arrows, near the entrance of the structure, cautioned guests, **Employees Only**, while a second, with another arrow, pointed arriving guests, up to another level, with the sign reading, **Guests Only**.

"Catch the sonofabitch," Luke yelled at his phone where he watched the live images of the foot pursuit provided by an array of surveillance's fixed and PTZ cameras under Candice Harmon's direction. Luke had dialed into the link providing him exclusive live, twenty-four seven, images of the Silver Palace's seldom-seen inner sanctum. His teeth were clamped tight as he watched with Lucy Mendoza's lifeless twenty-seven-year-old body, and its trail of urine, lying just a few feet away.

In surveillance, Candice had three monitors on the desk in front of her. Each carried different images of Jose Alonso running like a gazelle. Beyond the towering glass wall separating Candice and her PM shift of two men and four women, a large floor-to-ceiling video screen carried more live images of the pursuit. Jose Alonso appeared, jumping over a four-foot-high cement wall to land on the driveway entrance of the parking structures. He chose the side with the sign announcing **Employees Only**. He knew two uniformed security officers were posted for guests driving up into the multi-level structure where they would be stopped and asked for evidence they were guests, while the second officer would look under the front, sides, and rear of every vehicle, with a light and mirror positioned on a three-foot arm. Only after this would the car, SUV, limo, or pickup be allowed to continue. Employees were given far less attention.

Candice watched the image of Alonso running up the driveway toward the level reserved for employees. A three-foot-high cement barrier in the shape of a large triangle separated the two driveways. It was at the rear entrance of the Silver Palace, so it had to be more than practical, it had to be attractive. Thus, the head of landscaping had filled it with a thieving array of native cactus. Not only were they low maintenance, they were attractive.

Alonso, out of breath, was shocked as he neared the top of the long driveway. Three uniformed security officers were running toward him. He turned and began running back down the ramp. "Stop, halt, get on the ground," a combination of loud voices filled the air behind him. An asset not seen by many, and those who did notice it, gave it little thought, was a wide overhead iron gate that could be lowered to lock out, or in, vehicles or those on foot. There were matching overhead gates on both the guest and employee sides of the driveway.

The gates were designed for security, but this was Las Vegas. Again, the iron gate's practical implementation had to be masked behind beauty. The attractive design resulted in an iron lace design allowing light and vision through, but once lowered, mounted sharp iron spikes on the bottom of the gates would sink into preset reinforced holes, making them impenetrable. They were controlled by the on-duty surveillance supervisor, or at the direction of the director of security. The Red Button controlling the gates was on Candice Harmon's desk. Watching and providing live images of the chase, Candice saw Alonso turn to run back down the driveway after seeing the arrival of yet another trio of security officers intent on his capture. Candice pushed the Red Button. The overhead wide iron gate shook when the electrical jolt awoke it. Electric motors hummed, and the heavy gate's metal wheels screeched as they followed the track downward. Jose Alonso, approaching on the run, saw the wide, heavy iron gate coming down in his path. He knew he would be trapped.

"Holy Mother, save me," he pleaded.

The big gate was even lower and would soon send its spikes deep into the precut reinforced holes. Alonso ran full speed, heels clicking on the cement. He fell and rolled under the metal gate as one of its sharp metal spikes ripped through the back of his shirt. The gate thudded into the driveway, locking his trio of pursuers on the other side. Pushing to his feet, Alonso glanced at the officers on the other side of the gate and ran on.

Officer John Mattingly of the Metropolitan Police Department was behind the wheel of the patrol car as it approached on the long driveway. Officer Ron Hanson sat on the passenger's side. They were responding to a 911 call reporting the death of a housekeeper at the Silver Palace. The man running down the driveway toward their patrol car made Hanson stiffen in his seat.

"What, look out!" he shouted.

Mattingly slammed a foot on the brakes. The patrol

car's tires screeched as they slid on the concrete. Jose Alonso screamed, too, arms wide, as momentum carried him into the front of the police car. A deadly thump sounded. Jose hit the front of the sliding car and rolled onto its hood, slamming into the windshield. The glass windshield shattered into a myriad of spidery cracks. Alonso slid off the dented hood as the car braked to a stop. He fell, rolling over the low cement wall into the cactus garden. His screams filled the air as a multitude of sharp needles pushed into his clothing and flesh.

Anakoni Stone, gasping for breath, and the men with him were the first to arrive at the walled cactus garden. Joze Alonso lay sprawled and screaming on his back atop an array of bent, broken and crushed cactus plants. Blood seeped from long, sharp needles sticking into his neck, arms, hands, legs, and ankles. He was helpless and unable to move without causing more pain, but unable to tolerate the pain he was in. His cries chilled the faces of those watching.

In surveillance, Candice Harmon raised the iron gate. As it rose, the three officers behind it scrambled under and rushed to join Stone. The two Metro officers climbed from their black and white patrol car with its shattered windshield to join the security officers rimming the cactus garden. Looks of disbelief filled their faces as they stared at the fallen, trapped Alonso.

"We got no choice," Stone said, stepping over the low cement garden wall, being careful where he set his foot.

Another officer, gritting his teeth, followed Stone's lead. Together, they reached the sobbing, helpless Alonso. Stone grabbed him by his belt, and the officer grabbed a pant leg and a shoe, which came off and fell away. Together, they pulled. Alonso filled the air with more chilling, high-pitched screams. Stone and the officer dragged him to the wall where an army of hands joined to lift him up and over the wall. Alonso was out of the cactus trap, but he was covered with needles sticking in his flesh and riddling his clothes. Alonso mumbled Spanish prayers as he was laid on the cement.

Cars lined up behind the patrol car setting in the traffic lane with its broken windshield and flashing red lights. Many were out staring, looking, inching close to look, taking pictures with their cell phones. The chase, with its dramatic climax, resulted in every security officer on duty wanting to join in, or at least come to take a curious look at the fallen Porky-Pine-looking Alonso lying face down on the cement with his wrists handcuffed behind his back. His screams reached a new high when Officer Mattingly searched his pockets. A sandwich baggie with small tin foil packets inside was discovered in one of Alonso's pant pockets.

In the stairway on the sixty-eighth floor, Luke Mitchel continued to watch the images from the driveway on his phone, but he had been alone, waiting with the body of the young housekeeper for what seemed to be a long time. Damage to the Metro police car and Alonso's injuries told him his time in the staircase was getting longer.

An ambulance was called to carry away Alonso. One of the Metro police officers went with him. A second Metro unit arrived to provide support for the first, followed by a sergeant who would assess the damages to the patrol car.

Stone got a team together to clear the driveway and get the growing line of guests' cars moving. It all took time. Candice Harmon, watching from her perch in surveillance, knowing the clock was running, called KC King, and asked him to come in, bringing as many of his

AM watch troops as he could find. King did not hesitate. He told her he'd be in.

Two metro police officers, with Anakoni Stone escorting them, finally reached the stairway on the sixty-eighth. Luke, tired of standing, had surrendered and sat down on the steps. He got up when Stone arrived with the police officers. The dead body told the story. They looked and said what Luke expected, a detective team would have to be called.

———

TAMMY LARSON WAS FINDING the aftershocks from her last hit of meth were worse than the room she was in. She had no appetite, and pain was creating spasms in the muscles in her arms and legs. She wanted to sleep, but she knew without a hit, she never would. She looked to the placard on the inside of the door that had no lock.

Caution—Excessive Noise Prohibited. Visit the Social Room at any time. TV is provided 24/7. Channel section is decided by Majority. Telephone 9AM/5PM by request. Calls are monitored. Breakfast 8AM, Lunch 12 PM, Dinner 6PM. No in-room food or drinks. Snacks prohibited.

All room lights out 11PM. Talking to or soliciting security personnel is prohibited. Keeping Appointments with Staff Physicians & Councilors is mandatory. For your protection, all exterior doors are secured. Your cooperation is appreciated.

"Fuck you too," Tammy told the placard.

She checked her tinted, barred window. It was locked. The bathroom was shared by whoever the fuck was in the next room. She was finding the naked walled room with its chair, nightstand, and single bed was much like her. It was lonely, cold, and in need. No TV, no phone, and a door with no lock. This was just fucking great.

Surrendering to meth aftershocks, Tammy zipped open the suitcase on her bed. Her dad and Charlotte had packed the suitcase. Like the fuck they knew what she needed. She flipped the bag open. A white envelope lay on top of folded jeans. Tammy picked up the envelope and opened it. A wad of folded bills, held together with a paper clip, fell to the top of the jeans. Tammy tossed the envelope aside and picked up the money. She pulled the paper clip away and counted. There were ten twenty-dollar bills, four fifties and three-hundred-dollar bills.

"Wow," Tammy mouthed.

She thumbed through the bills, trying to count. The meth aftershocks got in the way. She gave up and pushed the wad into a pocket of her jeans. She rubbed at her face with both hands. What did the Snowman call this, Mitch, you know, M, for meth, and then, itch, making Mitch. *Your little white ass was going to itch.* She giggled. The Snowman was cool. She wished she hadn't sold her car. She would drive down and see him now that she had money. Get some good shit. How the fuck was she going to get through the night. She picked up the envelope. There was a note inside. She tossed the envelope and unfolded the note. It was her father's handwriting.

Tammy,
I love you. You need help. I'll see you get the best. I'll take care of the court thing. Forget it. The little girl I left behind. I'm sorry I wasn't there for you, but I am now. I want you back.

Try to do what they ask. It will help. Then you can come home. I put money in for anything you might need. They said I can come see you on the weekend.

  Love, Dad

Tammy's eyes filled with tears. She crumpled the note, drew it tight to her chest and sank to her knees beside the bed, weeping.

———

TWO METRO DETECTIVES ARRIVED. Luke briefed them in the stairway where the dead housekeeper still lay. They did their thing, which wasn't much different than his, although there was one major difference. In the world of Law Enforcement, Luke, no matter what his title was at the Silver Place, was still a Rent-A-Cop while they were real cops. It helped bridge the *don't get in our way* when Luke tactfully explained he was a refugee from nearly a decade with the LAPD. The real cops relaxed and went to work taking pictures of the body, from every angle, wide, close, the stairway, the guest hallway. Then came their drawings and measurements. Luke gave them the story of the suspected drug deal. He promised to reinforce it with video recordings of the encounter on the stairs, the chase, the arrest, and the arrival of the Metro patrol unit. The detectives came to the same conclusion Luke had. Jose Alonso was a drug dealer who supplied the dead girl a deadly dose, probably, as the paramedics suggested, Phenetole. Jose would be charged with possession, dealing and murder. When they finished, they called the Clark County Coroner. Then, again they waited.

While they waited, Luke called room service and ordered sandwiches and cold drinks. The kitchen knew what was going on. They did their best to make it their best, and it was impressive. The order was delivered by elevator to where an unfortunate security officer stood watch with the body in the stairway while everyone else including Luke, the two detectives, Sergeant Anakoni Stone, KC King, and two security officers from the chase, gathered in the carpeted quiet hallway to enjoy the feast set up on an unfolded tray by and two attentive servers, who stood by pouring drinks. They ate, talked, and laughed about the latest win by the Raiders. A highly dressed middle-aged couple appeared from a nearby suite and walked toward the elevators, passing the group dining in the hallway. They gave the men suspicious looks. Luke noticed.

"Did you hear," he said, raising his glass. "The Raiders beat the Broncos."

The couple offered smiles of understanding and moved on.

The coroner finally arrived, forty-eight minutes later. It was a busy night for the dead in Vegas. A suicide from atop Mandalay, a deadly crash on the 15, an OD in front of the Bellagio, and a hit and run on the Maryland Parkway. Luke was glad they finished eating before the talkative coroner and his aide arrived. As soon as the body was loaded into a bag and onto a cart, Luke had them escorted to a back-of-the-house elevator. He promised delivery of the surveillance images to the detectives in the a.m. He shook hands with both, and they left. Luke looked to KC King, "Cleanups waiting. Find whoever you have to find and get the stairway cleaned. I want it spotless, sanitized. Careful who you pick. Everyone knows what happened, and it's not pretty."

KC King nodded. He understood.

————

WHEN DAWN WILDER woke up in her second-story apartment three miles west of the Strip, it was dark. She ignored the darkness. Peeing was more important.

She was surprised finding her way to the hall bath that Casey hadn't turned any lights on. When she came out of the bathroom she called to him, "Casey."

Silence answered her. Dawn went to the master bedroom, where she had seen him sleeping earlier. The room was dark. She switched on a light. The bed was unmade, empty.

"Casey," Dawn called again as she moved the living room and turned on more lights.

The only sign of Casey was an empty can of Coors Light on a coffee table and a dirty ashtray. Clad only in brief panties, Dawn turned to the kitchen. Casey must have gone to Burger King. There was one on the corner just a block away. He liked it. She would call his cell. An order of fries sounded good. Switching on the lights in the kitchen ended any thought of french fries. Dawn's purse lay open on the kitchen counter. Its contents were scattered. Lipstick, a compact mirror. Dawn's heart raced. Her wallet lay nearby. She grabbed it. Nevada State driver's license, social security, a faded picture of her late mother, and Baxter, the family dog when they lived in Ohio.

"God, no," Dawn mouthed. It wasn't what was in the wallet. It was what was gone. Gone was a Visa card, a Citibank, and her ATM card. Casey Lynch wasn't at Burger King. He was gone. Dawn felt weak, destitute, frightened. The cell phone she had left on the counter was gone.

Leaving the open purse and wallet, Dawn hurried to the master bedroom. There, she went to a nightstand beside the unmade bed. She opened a drawer and searched. Pushed aside a soiled Kleenex, a room service menu from the Bonaventure, a packet of matches from the Luxor and a bottle of nail polish. It didn't take long. The jewelry kept bedside in a velvet-lined box was gone. Gold chain necklaces, bracelets, an assortment of rings, earrings, and a variety of pins and broaches. Some she had from her years as a teen. She looked to the mirrored closet. Standing, she slid the door open. Her clothes hung neat, intact. Casey's side of the closet was empty. Two coat hangers hung on the closet's chrome bar. They looked lonely. Dawn sank onto the side of the unmade bed. Dressed in only pantyhose, she felt cold. It was as if she had been raped. Casey Lynch was gone, but he had taken Dawn Wilder's heart and money with him.

Casy crossed her arms beneath her breasts. Dressed only in her lace panties, she felt cold and alone. She knew what she had to do, and her thoughts were taking her beyond the thief she had invited into her home only to feel the pain of his betrayal. She was thinking of what she had left. Something more valuable than what Casey Lynch had taken. Dawn stood and studied herself in the closet doors full-length mirror. She had to find a way to call Pam.

———

LUKE WAS HUNGRY. A psychological conflict haunted him after spending so much time with the young dead housekeeper, and then coming away hungry, but rational logic prevailed. He had to eat. A visit to the employee's dining room put the thought to rest. The sight of two security officers sitting at a distant table with others made Luke feel better about it. He walked the buffet line, selecting scrambled eggs, bacon, lots of it, french fries, chicken wings, toast, and a piece of pineapple upside-down cake. Luke shared a table with a blackjack dealer, an attractive one, a young valet attendant with steak and potatoes and a front desk agent. They talked about the Sphere, the price of gasoline, the weather, and David Copperfield's show at the Grand—the valet attendant had just seen it. None mentioned what happened on the sixty-two or who Luke was. They all knew.

Luke felt better about the day, which somehow, when he wasn't watching, had become night. Dinner proved there was life after. Luke was glad he'd done it. Sharing the table with others, others who knew what happened but had a life ahead of them with demands not to be ignored. Leaving the employee dining room, Luke headed for the casino level.

The Strip was proving itself right. You couldn't tell time by looking at a clock or at a window. Vegas didn't have many, and the Silver Palace had fewer than most. Occupancy at the Silver Palace was above seventy-five percent, which meant it had about ten thousand-plus guests. GM, Greg Larson's policy dictated when occupancy was above seventy-five percent department heads were to stay on property. Seldom did a department head get a room above the third floor. Luke Mitchel was headed for his. A pass through the card room seemed a promising idea, or a stall to get to his less than palatial room. Based on the crowd and the noise, Luke thought most of those guests were in slots. The Silver Palace housed over two thousand slot machines. The slots were set in floor design by marketing, and they worked. Slot machines were kinda the secret in Vegas. And the secret was they were the casino's *big dog*. Luke knew as he walked through the maze of machines that the slots paid out whatever management wanted. Slot payouts were adjustable. They usually brought in seventy percent of the Silver Palace's daily take. Luke wasn't a numbers guy, but as he walked among the slots, he marveled at their level of sophistication. The slots were a blend of ever-changing digital video images mixed with movement, flashes, sounds and numbers, all fueled by folded currency and hopeful players. Reinforcing the allure of the machines was an army of scantily clad beauties in brief tops who supplied iced drinks to the players or anyone else. Along with the exposed flesh were roaming technicians who were quick to any player who needed attention. A plain-clothed security officer also mingled, watching for pickpockets and cheats. A multitude of surveillance cameras and several uniformed security officers also added to a secure feeling. Clark County had recently passed a law that made it a crime to carry a flashlight in any casino. Cheats knew a high-intensity light aimed deep into the face of the slots could result in malfunctions favoring them.

Luke drew little attention as he walked and studied the players. There were as many women as men. He found most middle-aged or sometimes seriously old. Dressed comfortably, eager, hopeful, and vocal. Most players had support standing at their shoulders, offering encouragement. Luke could see they were having fun. He was pleased. This was what Vegas was all about. With so many machines and players, there were near-constant shouts from those winning. At least they considered themselves winners, although odds were, the fifty-dollar jackpot they had just won was a result of the one hundred and fifty dollars they put in, but they were winners, and so was Vegas. Luke was walking away from slots when he saw the girl. He looked at her for the same reason other men were looking—-she was beautiful. The young brunette, bag over her shoulder, appeared from the restroom along the wall of the card room. She marched confidently on heels across the card room. Her long legs were wrapped in dark mesh nylons that accented their shape. A short, dark skirt wrapped her torso, yielding to a flowing, unbuttoned blouse, gaping wide over her breasts. Many of her admirers thought they were looking at a Vegas icon, and they were. Director of Security Luke Mitchel knew he was looking at Vegas Skin, an escort, a working girl. All the titles, the names, made the reality less stinging. She was a whore.

Luke spoke discretely into the mike concealed on his lapel. "Surveillance, Gate Keepers, got a probable Vegas Skin. Twenty is the card room. Crossing diagonally toward twenty-one."

"Ten, we've got one of our soft clothes following. Watch where she goes." The voice in Luke's earpiece was KC King.

Luke watched silently as the brunette waltzed through the maze of tables until she reached a twenty-one table where a high roller sat alone in the center seat. He was surrounded by a circle of admirers and the curious. Drink in hand, he encouraged the female dealer to put down a card on the seventeen she had showing. The brunette pushed through the crush to put an arm around the shoulder of the high roller. Her odds just got better. So did the high roller's. The dealer put down her card. It was a five of spades. A roar of approval came from the crowd around the table. The high roller reached out to claim a stack of tokens.

Luke knew the attractive young brunette was no longer a security target. She was the companion of a high roller. Given how he was playing the odds, he was a guest, and that made the girl his companion. The Vegas irony, the unwritten law of the Strip, the shadow of cash, don't fuck with those with money. Luke knew the girl was a pass. Surveillance would track her. Photos would be emailed to the others on the Strip. Her world would get a little smaller.

Luke spotted Charlie Johnson, the card room manager, at his desk on the raised podium in the middle of the sprawling, busy card room. Charlie had been watching the twenty-one table, too. Luke headed for him. As MOD (Manager On Duty) at the time of the girl's death, Luke sent Charlie and Dede Garcia from housekeeping out to notify Lucy Mendoza's parents of her death as a result of a drug overdose. Charlie, at thirty-four, in his tailored suit and expertly knotted tie, looked like a male model. Luke, in his black tee shirt, sports jacket, and jeans, was intimidated. Charlie not only looked iconic, he was the captain of the ship. Under his supervision, the army of dealers spread across the expansive, busy card room obeyed his every command. Poker, Twenty-One, Roulette, Craps, Baccarat, Pai Gow and more. Charlie knew them all. In addition to the games and staff was the money. Millions. Charlie's skill set, known by most, was the envy on the Strip.

Luke looked around as he reached Charlie's podium pretending he knew the strategies of how and where the tables were placed. "Charlie, haven't had a chance to get by. How did it go with notification to the Mendoza's?"

Charlie stood and straightened his jacket. "It was

difficult. Ms. Garcia did most of the talking. They was saddened, but oddly, they seemed to have sensed it was going to happen."

"High side of twenty. Still living at home with mom and dad. They may have seen the truck coming," Luke suggested.

"Perhaps. Nevertheless, they were shocked. Dede assured the Silver Palace would cover all their expenses. They wept and asked us to join hands. They prayed in Spanish. It was difficult."

Luke nodded in agreement. He'd heard enough. He wanted out of the card room. "Thanks for going out there." He stepped down off the platform.

Charlie reached and laid a hand on Luke's arm. Luke paused.

"Until today, I always thought what you did in security was of little consequence. Today changed that."

"Death will do that," Luke suggested.

Charlie extended an open hand. Luke took Charlie's hand. They shook firmly. Luke walked away.

ELEVEN

THE REARVIEW MIRROR

LUKE FINALLY REACHED his guest room. He turned on the flat-screen. A reporter for CNN was talking about the war in the Middle East. Luke turned the volume low and pushed off his shoes. His socks followed. Neither brought relief. He was glad to hear KC King's voice on the radio which he pulled off and tossed to the bed. He appreciated King and his men coming in early. There was little doubt there were tired troops on the PM watch. He knew who put this together—Candice Harmon. If the girl was trying to impress him, it was working. Sergeant Anakoni Stone and his men ran their asses off to capture Jose Alonso. Candice kept them in the loop with Alonso's every move. Little doubt they appreciated her. Luke got up, tossed his jacket, opened a Diet Coke he found in the fridge, turned down the TV, returned to his chair, sank into it, and punched a number on his cell phone.

Candice answered, "I saw the party in the hallway. Looked like fun."

"You wear a badge and carry a gun, and you appreciate a good sandwich."

"Along with those sandwiches were a lot of guns."

"I get the picture." Luke smiled. "You want me to buy you a sandwich."

"If I don't have to bring a gun and it's a night we're both off. Then we could have our sandwich and…"

"Got it," Luke answered. She was baiting him. Luke welcomed it. "Listen, before we break bread, I called to say thanks for what you did today, and tell your crew thanks. We couldn't have done it without them."

"Will do. Good night, Luke."

Luke was glad to set his phone aside. The flat-screen was still on but muted. The images were from a war half a world away, or was it? War had once been something he woke up to. The conflict he faced in the day ahead would be different, but nonetheless, still a conflict and still scared by death. Early in the day, he would brief the GM on Lucy Mendoza's death and the arrest of Jose Alonso. The realization he would be talking to a man whose daughter had a drug problem unnerved him, but it had to be done. The GM would have to have answers ready when the questions came. Luke wondered how much press the drug death of a young housekeeper at the Silver Palace would get. Vegas was a town where more often than not, the Strip would be pulled up, and the dirt would be swept under the rug. He was finishing the remains of his Diet Coke when his phone chirped. Luke gave it an annoyed look, but he had to answer.

"This is Luke."

"Luke, it's Barb."

The familiar feminine voice of a lover from a life left behind comforted him. A rush of memories filled his mind. The scent of Barb's hair, her smile, her naked beauty. She was exotic yet warm and sincere.

"Barb! Barbara who?" Luke teased.

"You know, the woman who traded you for a sack of potatoes and a keg of beer?"

"Oh, the one who turned down my invitation to move to Vegas."

"Yeah, okay, that one. Director of Food and Beverage for the Mojaves at the Wild River Resort."

"I miss you, Barb," Luke said, giving the call a more serious tone as memories of their laughter, teasing, and lovemaking flooded in.

"Need I remind you who called who," Barb answered.

"Okay, we've confessed to missing each other. So, what else is new?"

"I'd like to try and put Humpty Dumpty back together. If the invitation still stands."

Luke was surprised. "You mean come to Vegas. Give up F&B?"

"That's exactly what I mean. I like the Mojaves, they're a lot like real people, but with you gone, the place is empty. I'm betting I can find something in Emerald City. Especially if I get to share that condo you've been bragging about."

Luke's surprise was turning to excitement. Barb had been an integral part of his life. He never said it, but they both knew it. They were in love. "It's blue and green inside. I need to paint, but the furniture's nice."

"So, I'll help you paint. Do you want me to come up there or not?"

"Yes, I want you to come up. What's your timeline?"

"The Tribe can replace me in about three minutes. I've got a suitable number two. He can step in. I can be out of here in two, three days."

"We won't need your furniture. I bought the condo furnished. My stuff is still in storage down there."

"So, I'll add mine to it."

"This is great. I'll overnight a key to you. I'll make room in the master for your clothes, but you always looked better without them."

"You're such a romantic, Luke."

"I shouldn't like you naked."

"Might be a way to celebrate our reunion," Barb suggested. "Okay, I'm calling from the casino. We've got breakfast for one hundred and six realtors, so I have to go. See you soon, Luke Mitchel."

"Bet on it," Luke answered, laying the cell phone aside. He hoped he'd be able to sleep. Barbara Nichols surprised him. Not only had she surprised him, but she excited him. He could see them painting, getting rid of the blue and green, shopping for groceries, taking in a headliner. The day filled with death and drugs just got brighter with hope, and okay, he had admitted to himself, love.

———

THERE WAS an ATM in the 7-Eleven a block from Dawn Wilder's apartment. Walking to it, she realized she had no ATM card. Not only didn't she have an ATM card, she didn't have a dime. Casey Lynch had taken her ATM, a Visa card and what little hope she had after being jammed by security at the Silver Palace. Dawn was desperate. She went into the store with the hope the thirty-year-old Asian usually behind the counter would be there. Fate was kind. The girl was there. Dawn waited until a customer walked away. "I don't know your name, but you remember me. I shop here. Snacks, beer."

The Asian gave Dawn a suspicious look. "Yes, I remember you."

"I've been robbed. I don't have a dime. He even took my cell phone. I need to call the lady I work for. It's a local call. Could you let me use your cell?"

A young Black man in a hoodie stepped to the counter with a can of Red Bull. He pushed a ten-dollar bill at the Asian. Dawn waited. The Hoodie took the change and walked away.

Dawn resumed her plea. "Please, you know me. I'm not lying. Just one call." She dug in a pocket to find a crumpled note. "Here, look. See, it's a local call."

"All right, one call." The Asian reached beneath the counter, gathering a cell phone. "You make quick call, and you tell no one." She offered the cell to Dawn.

Dawn took the cell and walked down an aisle lined with potato chips on one side and snack cakes on the other. She punched the number into the cell. She walked on, holding the cell to an ear. It rang and rang. Finally, the voice she hoped for answered, "Who is this?" It was Pam's voice.

"Pam, it's Dawn, don't hang up."

"Dawn, I called your cell. A guy answered. What's going on?"

"I've been robbed. He took my ATM card, my credit cards, even my cell."

"Are you all right?"

"Yes, he did it while I was sleeping."

"Don't call the police. They won't help. Call your bank in the morning. Tell them what happened. Then call Verizon. Tell them your phone has been stolen."

"I need help tonight. I don't have a dime. I borrowed this phone. I was hoping you could make me a loan?"

"Listen, you're all right. Can you work? I've got a request from a guest at the Luxor."

"Work." Dawn was shocked at the suggestion.

"Escorting could get you a tip tonight," Pam suggested. "Then five hundred in tomorrow morning, but you've got to talk to your bank."

"Pam, I don't have anything. What should I do? Hitch hike to the Luxor."

"I'm sorry this happened, Dawn, but you called me. Either you work, or your life's going to get even more difficult. You don't have to be at the Luxor until ten. I'll have an Uber pick you up at nine thirty. No charge. When you get to the Luxor, ask for Ken in valet. Tell him your name. He'll tell you how to find your date."

Dawn's eyes filled with tears. She'd been jammed by security at the Silver Palace, Casey stole everything from her, and Pam was urging her to work. She felt trapped, hopeless, alone.

"Dawn, you're either in or out," Pam pressed after Dawn hesitated.

"Doing this will get you through the night. Tomorrow will be a new day."

Dawn had no choice. "Okay, okay," she blurted.

"The Uber will be at your apartment at nine thirty. Look beautiful, Dawn. You know you can. Are we agreeing?"

"Yes, we're agreeing." Dawn ended the call, wiping her tears from the cell phone.

———

TAMMY LARSON WAS JOLTED awake by a heavy knock on the door of her room at the Red Rock Recovery Center.

"Breakfast buffet in fifteen minutes," a firm, mature feminine voice declared from the other side of the door.

Tammy sat up but chose not to answer. A moment later, a knock sounded on another door with the same announcement. Tammy wiped at her face. Her eyes itched, her fingers ached. She pushed a cover aside to swing her feet to the floor. It was cold. God, how could her father do this? How could she find relief? The idea of food made her nauseous. She stood and staggered into the shared bathroom. At least no one was in it.

She was pulling on a pair of jeans when a knock sounded again. This time, the door opened. The woman was in a nurse's uniform, a thirty-something, no makeup, hair pinned up in some kind of roll and dark eyes that disapproved of what she saw. Tammy, struggling with withdrawals, was pushed closer to her emotional edge.

"Have you had anything to eat?" the nurse questioned.

"I'm not hungry," Tammy answered.

"It's called no appetite," the nurse corrected. "Come with me."

Tammy pushed on a pair of flip-flops and followed. She was surprised seeing the others. Male, female, mostly young. She tried to keep up with the nurse crossing the wide reception area. All of them looked displaced, annoyed. Some gathered in the media center, joining others, sitting, whispering, sleeping. A large flat-screen TV played Beavis and Butthead with no audio. Another room with a wide doorway revealed the buffet where more stood in a slow-moving line. No one seemed to notice Tammy, but then she thought, it wasn't that they didn't see her, it was more like they just didn't care.

The nurse led Tammy into a treatment room and closed the door.

"Sit down and give me your full name and date of birth."

Tammy did as she was told. The idea of not cooperating unnerved her. The nurse weighed her, took her temperature by ear, checked her blood pressure, and then examined both of her arms, looking for needle puncture wounds.

"When's the last time you used and what was it?" The questions, probing, and pushing turned from minutes to hours, but Tammy was hiding somewhere, somewhere where the nurse couldn't find her.

Finally, the nurse said, "Put your shirt on and follow me."

Tammy was escorted to the buffet, where she was ordered to a table while the nurse, pushing others aside, went through, preparing a tray. She returned to Tammy, setting the tray in front of her. It was jammed with scrambled eggs, toast, several kinds of sausage, and bacon. In the corner of the tray, a collection of seven pills and capsules lay waiting. A server, dressed in uniform, but looking like most of the others, approached to set a glass of juice on the table in front of Tammy. She moved away quickly.

"You will sit here and eat until this tray is empty. How long that takes is entirely up to you. After you eat, take the drugs. They are for your withdrawals. Do you understand?"

Tammy chose not to answer. She was against a wall the nurse couldn't see.

"Don't answer." The nurse added, "The cameras will be watching."

The nurse marched away. Tammy looked at the tray.

She thought she was going to vomit. She closed her eyes and tried to calm herself. The movement of a chair brought her back to the moment. She opened her eyes to find a young man with a bad complexion in need of a haircut had sat down at the table. He was followed shortly by an attractive blonde woman close to Tammy's age.

"You going to eat all that?" the blonde asked, picking up Tammy's glass of juice to drink from it.

"Count me in," the long hair added as taking several pieces of bacon from Tammy's plate.

"You two don't look like buzzards," Tammy suggested sarcastically.

"You're a newbie," the blonde answered. "They want newbies bragging about how much food they give you. Wait until you go through the line yourself." She used her fork to take a part of scrambled eggs from Tammy's tray.

"So, you like weed, right?" Tammy suggested sarcastically.

"Weeds for pussies," the long hair defended, taking a piece of toast. "Coke brings it home quicker."

"So, got any?" Tammy questioned.

"Yeah, right, I just like hanging out here. Spend some time finding my true soul."

Tammy tried a different tactic. "Okay, I'm Tammy. Can't you see the big M on my forehead?"

"You're hurting, aren't you," the blonde pressed.

Tammy nodded in agreement. She had no reason to lie.

"We're all fucking hurting." The long hair added, "My old man sells more cars than any dick west of the Mississippi. He's worth the better part of a billion. Look where the fuck he puts his firstborn." He took more of Tammy's eggs.

"So, maybe you can get me a deal on a Rolls. I'm tired of walking the fucking streets," the blonde said with sausage in her mouth.

"Prostitution?" Tammy questioned with a look at the blonde.

"Do you really think they've got a cure for being a whore in here?" She smiled sarcastically, picking up another piece of toast.

"Unfortunately, I'm a whore who likes codeine. Little something for aftershocks. You know, no pain, no gain. So, how about you and this no appetite shit."

Tammy took a breath before answering. "Meth. I just like the shit. I never hurt anyone. It just makes me feel good, you know like, everything's cool."

"Until somebody dumped you here," the long hair said, chewing on bacon.

"Okay, you don't look poor. What happened?" the blonde asked.

"I had a shit job at Jack in the Box. You know, just so my mother would shut up. Guy there got me started. It was cool until Jack no longer paid enough, you know. So, I tried hooking. First time out, fucking Metro busts me."

"You need a pimp, girl."

"And how did that work out for you?"

"My dad's a surgeon. He knows drugs and shit. I stole some stuff from his office. He dumped me here."

"So, what fast track you on, girl?" the long hair asked with a look at Tammy's remaining eggs.

"Take them," Tammy suggested. "Parents are divorcing. It's all about fucking money. It was like they didn't even see me anymore. Didn't give me shit, not a dime.

Until I got popped. That got their attention. My dad did this."

"Attention, please." The amplified female voice came from an overhead speaker. "The buffet is now closed. Dump your trays and exit immediately. Attendance in the media center is mandatory. Patient rooms and restrooms will be checked. Attendance is mandatory."

The long hair took Tammy's last piece of toast while the blonde gulped down the remaining juice.

The media room was crowded. Bevis and Butthead had been turned off. Tammy didn't count but she guessed thirty-plus. Most were about her age. None looked pleased. Wardrobes ranged from impressive to poverty level. Tammy fit in the middle. She was surprised when the long hair sat down beside her.

"What's this all about?" Tammy said in a near whisper to him.

"They bring in speakers to tell us what fuck-ups we are and how they have all the answers. Listen, I know somebody if you're in need."

"In need. Here, this place?" Tammy was annoyed.

"Just saying. You got money, I got a source. He works in security. You order he gets it. Same day delivery."

Tammy's sarcasm changed to interest. She looked to the long hair. "I got money."

"Three hundred, and I can hook you up. Name it."

"Crystal meth."

"Show me the money."

Tammy dug in her bra.

———

THE DISTANCE from the Red Rock Recovery Center to the Las Vegas Strip had to be measured in more than eighteen miles separating them. They were worlds apart. On the Strip, the management team of the Silver Palace had been summoned to an unscheduled but mandatory meeting in the Sky Light Conference Room by General Manager Greg Larson. The room was filling, and it was abuzz with rumors and speculation. "He's so resigning," was among the whispers. "I heard his replacement is from Singapore," another suggested, while others were saying. "He'll blame all his problems on us, and he's got a lot."

Director of Security Luke Mitchel, was among the waiting. He heard the speculation, and like others, he was worried. The whispers and small talk ended when the GM and his executive assistant entered the room. Jackie Fallon sat at one of the tables with others. Greg Larson, looking fit, and filling the Vegas persona for a GM in his forty-seven-hundred-dollar suit, walked to the podium in front of waiting faces.

"Good morning," Larson began, with both hands gripping the sides of the podium. "I want to talk to you this morning about transparency. Mine. Over the past few months, and especially the last few days, I've given you, and the world, much to talk about. Since I'm the source, I need to bare my soul. Most recently, my eighteen-year-old daughter was arrested for prostitution on Fremont Street. Her arrest revealed she has a drug problem."

The silence in the room was profound. Larson paused to take a drink from a bottle of water. He took a deep breath and continued. "How could I not see this truck coming? Last week, here at the Silver Palace, we suspended nine employees after they failed their random drug tests. It gets worse. Yesterday, Lucy Mendoza, a twenty-seven-year-old housekeeper who's been with us for almost three years, was found dead in a stairway. Her death was the result of a drug overdose. We believe a room service employee supplied the drug. He was turned over to Metro, but we must ask, how was this missed? A drug dealer in the Silver Palace. Lucy knew who was dealing. She isn't the only one that knew, but because we didn't see it, she's dead."

Larson paused for a moment. His eyes went to the ceiling, then the floor as he struggled with his emotions. "Lucy's death is a tragedy that belongs to all of us. We need to watch for the signs. I'm talking signs. Signs that point at me. I didn't know my daughter was a user. Was it because my twenty-two years of marriage is ending in a divorce? Maybe it's because I know the room projection for next month, or the daily drop, or how about the cost of uniforms for housekeeping. I know all that, but I can't tell you the last time I spent an hour with my daughter."

Larson paused, lowered his head, cleared his throat, and looked to the waiting eyes. "TikTok, the rumors, the gossip, all of it hurt, but none of it hurt as much as knowing that I, Tammy Larson's dad, wasn't there. I failed." Larson wiped away a tear. "Tammy's in rehab now. I didn't know what else to do. I love her. I'm going to make sure she learns that, and I'm going to make sure she gets the best care."

He paused to lace his fingers together. "Divorce? I won't ask for a show of hands, but the woman I married years ago is no longer the woman I love. There's a high probability I caused the divorce. You don't become general manager, or manager, or director of anything, without spending most of your life here. I do it, you do it. I created a policy dictating when occupancy is above seventy-five percent, you must be on property. As of today, that's over. Either we have subordinates who are capable and trustworthy, or we don't. Let's find out."

A hardy round of applause came from the crowded room.

"There's been talk about me creating a double standard," Larson said, losing his tie. "I'm talking about the policy prohibiting on-the-job relationships that develop into romantic relationships. Most of you know what I did. You need to know why. I won't mention Charlotte's name, but at the time, she was our director of human resources."

A ripple of laughter rippled across the room.

"We fell in love. When we were discovered, Charlotte resigned. I felt guilty. She did what was right while I did nothing. Feeling guilty, I decided to declare my love in front of the world by kissing her at a *Big Ten Meeting* at the Bellagio. It worked. A few million watched us on the net and it got mentioned around town. I held my breath afterward, while the investors decided if I was good, bad, or ugly. They granted me a pass," Larson explained. "Why? Because it was the right thing to do. So, here's our new standard. No more blanket guilt. We judge each case on its individual merit."

Larson reached into a pocket to pull out a handkerchief. He wiped his face, studied those who sat waiting in silence, then continued. "I've heard the rumors. I'm not leaving. TikTok's not going to kick my ass. Neither is gossip or rumors. They want truth, I'll provide it. I'm proud of what I've done here at the Silver Palace. We're a Vegas landmark. You don't visit the Strip and not see us. You don't stay here and forget us. You don't see a picture of Vegas without us in it. Why is that? Why are we one of the billion-dollar big dogs? I'll tell you why, because we deserve it, we earned it. I'm not going to let any of this personal bullshit tarnish my *Vegas gold*. We're in this together. I need you, and you need me. I called you in here this morning because you needed to know the truth. There are shadows in this town, but I'm not hiding behind any of them, why, because I've got nothing to hide."

Larson turned and marched from the room. Most pushed to their feet. Applause followed.

TWELVE
SKIN COVERED BADGE

LUKE WAS PLEASED with what the GM said. Truth was important and although he knew more than Greg Larson confessed, like the others, he was leaving the room feeling good. In the Corps, it was called *team spirit*. The applause the GM got at the end of his confessional was an assurance that they had *team spirit*. A glance at his watch told Luke he missed the briefing for day watch. He wanted to see who the day watch commander, Mario Lopez, had assigned to Vegas Skin, the special ops to keep whores out of the Silver Palace. The duo was the first, and they were to dress like guests. Maybe a look at them from surveillance Luke decided, leaving the conference room.

The radio beneath his jacket told Luke a guest in slots had just punched a man playing a machine beside him. A serious fight followed. Mario Lopez was on the scene. So was guest relations and the slots floor manager. Good response, Luke concluded, as he reached the door to surveillance. He was surprised at what he found inside. Candice Harmon was at the supervisor's desk. Gayle

Turner, the surveillance supervisor, was nowhere in sight. Candice read Luke's surprise.

"Is that pleasure or surprise I'm seeing." Candice smiled.

"Would you allow both," Luke answered, choosing a chair beside Candice's desk.

"Okay, but just this once. Gayle called me early this morning. She said she's got miseries. Bad enough to make her want to stay home. You're looking at putting a Band-Aid on the schedule. What was going on up in the conference room? There was enough of you in there to start a bunch of new rumors."

"Sorry, it was confidential about the new wing the Palace is adding."

"A new wing, you're kidding."

"Yes, I'm kidding."

"*Gate Keeper-Six to surveillance,*" the filtered voice of a female security officer said on a speaker on Candice's desk. Candice keyed a microphone sitting in front of her.

"Go ahead, Six."

"*Surveillance, I need a twenty on Gate Keeper-Ten. I'm at the front entrance. There's a Vegas Skin here insisting she talk to him.*"

Candice glanced at Luke and punched a keyboard in front of her. Three screens switched to three different angles of the uniformed officer at the front door. The shapely blonde, Dawn Wilder, wearing knee-high boots, a short leather skirt and a blouse open to the shadow between her ample breasts, stood beside the officers.

"Should I ask?" Candice said.

Luke moved for the door. "It's business."

"Yeah, she's dressed for business."

Dawn's impatience was showing when Luke reached

the front entrance. She was not going unnoticed by those passing. Luke looked to the young Black female officer. "Thanks, Clark. I'll take it from here."

The officer nodded, gave Dawn a final look and walked away.

"Can I buy you a coffee?" Luke suggested, gesturing to the Starbucks sidewalk café.

"I don't do coffee," Dawn answered soberly, adjusting her shoulder bag. "Make mine an apple smoothie…"

Luke looked at Dawn as he led the way through the tables. "I don't think they do smoothies."

"I do," Dawn answered as Luke selected a vacant sidewalk table. He pulled a chair out for her. She sat down.

"I'll be back," Luke said, moving for the service counter.

Two men at a nearby table offered admiring glances. Dawn pushed her chair back and crossed her legs to allow a better view.

Luke returned with a coffee and an apple smoothie. He set Dawn's drink in front of her, gave the two men an annoyed look and sat down across from her. "I was beginning to think you weren't coming."

"Think of me like a smoothie. You were wrong, and you paid for it."

Luke smiled at Dawn's pun. He was impressed with her beauty and her intellect. He sampled his coffee, knowing surveillance was watching. "Our agreement was hinged on you providing me a number."

"I've got your number," Dawn answered, tasting her smoothie.

"You could have called."

"No, I couldn't, not until I get a phone."

"You lost your phone?"

"No, I was robbed. He took my cell, ATM, credit cards, and my cash."

"Sorry. Was it a client?"

Dawn leaned her elbows on the table. She gave Luke a sober look. "You know I do have a life. Not everything is linked to what happened here," she said with a glance at the wall of the Silver Palace.

———

LUKE ACCEPTED HER CHALLENGE. "You were with a uniformed officer when I came out here." He looked into Dawn's eyes. "You knew what she was by what she was wearing. Same goes for you. Everyone can tell what you are."

"And you?" Dawn questioned, leaning into the table. "I don't even know your name. What's with the black tee shirt and jacket? You one of these guys that gets paid to break fingers in a back room."

Luke sipped his coffee. Dawn had pushed back hard, and he was giving her words careful thought. Finally, he set his cup down. "Breaking fingers is Hollywood, not Vegas. I'm director of security here at the Silver Palace. My name's Luke Mitchel."

"And I'm Dawn Wilder. I'm an escort. That's why I dress the way I do. Look around, Luke Mitchel, this is Vegas. The servers in your casino wear less than I do. Your chorus line is topless. The Silver Palace is like every casino on the Strip—you promote sex, you suggest sex, sex brings in money. Guests are welcome with escorts, if we're pretty enough, but when asked, when you're pushed for answers, sex for sale is a crime. Vegas without sex would be like ice skating in Death Valley." Dawn paused and sampled her smoothie. Her irritation was obvious. She pushed her cup aside. "We both get paid for what we do. Where did you get the idea you're better than me? You're not better, you're just different."

Dawn's words stung. Luke decided to turn the conservation in a different direction. "Who robbed you?"

"Guy I rented a room to. Although he never paid any rent. Just ate all my food. When I got up, he was gone. So was all my stuff. The dick. When I leave here, I'll get a new cell, go by my bank and give them my sob story."

"Did you report it?"

"Report it? To who. Kinda hard to find someone who cares, and then they have a handout."

"I'm sorry, Dawn. Do you want help?"

She studied Luke, saw he was sincere. "No thanks. I'll handle it. You like working here?"

"Most days," Luke answered. "It pays the rent. And being an escort?"

"It pays the rent." Dawn smiled, pushing blonde hair from her face.

Luke knew Dawn was flirting. He had to remind himself she was an escort. She was employed by an escort service—*sex for sale*. A crime in Las Vegas and a crime the Silver Palace wanted stopped at their front door, or did they? Where was the line?

"We were going to talk about a number," Luke said, wanting to avoid more talk about sex.

Dawn dug in a pocket and pushed a note across the table. "You promised you wouldn't give me up."

"And I won't. I just need to know who she is."

"You won't get that by calling Cloud Nine Escorts?"

"Agreed, it's a little more challenging than that, but this will help."

"So, our date is over and all it cost you was an apple smoothie?"

"What's the cliché?" Luke smiled and pushed out of his chair. "Live and learn. You be careful out there in the world, Dawn Wilder."

"You too, Mr. Director."

———————

WALKING into the cooler air of the casino, Luke saw what Dawn Wilder meant. He watched a card room server cross the card room with a tray of drinks in hand. She was dressed in a low-cut top which barely covered her breasts, a short skirt over shorts just covering her buttocks and high heels. She was paid by the Silver Palace, but her real money came from tips. The line was blurred, Luke decided, as he headed for the elevators, but he had learned as a cop the line was often blurred. Luke knew the difference was intent and the law. The law said paying to get laid was a crime for both the individual paying, and the individual providing. His job was enforcing the law in the Silver Palace. As both he and the escort had just agreed, "It paid the rent."

Candice Harmon was at the supervisor's desk in surveillance, hanging up from a call when Luke entered.

"Your sidewalk conference over?"

"For now," Luke answered, sitting down in the chair beside the supervisor's desk. "The dynamic duo in today?" He was asking about the team of electronic wizards, two young refugees from Taiwan, housed in a surveillance backroom that seemingly did what others could not do in electronics, and the Palace often called on them.

"You mean AC and DC," Candice answered. "They're at a one-day thing over at the Grand learning how to protect us from hackers."

"Better late than never," Luke suggested, sliding the note from Dawn in front of Candice. She looked at the paper. Luke continued. "Allegedly, it's the number for Cloud Nine Escorts. They don't advertise. Their number isn't listed. Reputation for quality keeps them busy. The number is for a woman, what are they called, a *madame*. Her name is Pam. I need to know who she is and where she is. Put the duo on it when they get back."

Candice nodded. "Will do," she answered, pushing the note into a drawer. "Listen, I talked with Gayle again just before you came back"—Candice pushed back in her chair to look directly at Luke—"something just doesn't fit. I'm not sure what it is, but you know it just isn't her."

"That's a little vague," Luke suggested.

"I asked how she was feeling," Candice continued. "She answers by saying she may need a couple more days. I told her I didn't want to continue this sixteen-hour-a-day thing and that Carter had raised his hand, he's in there." She pointed to the glass wall separating the supervisor from the team of four on the other side, watching an array of images on large flat-screens. "And Gayle says, stay away from him. I told her I'd stop by, and we could work out a schedule. She tells me, put it together, just don't put Carter in charge."

"What's with Carter?" Luke questioned, glancing at the four inside. He knew the man by sight but little about him.

"He was part of our opening act. Came up here from Laughland. Riverside, I think. That's about all I know. He's not one of mine."

"But Gayle knows him. Maybe I'll call her."

"Don't. You do, she'll know I gave her up. Give me a little time. When I get away, I'll go see her."

"You'll keep in the loop?"

"As long as you don't put the loop around my neck."

Luke's cell phone buzzed beneath his jacket. He reached for it, glanced at the caller ID. "Jackie Harmond," he said, keying the call. "Luke here. What's up Jackie?"

"The General Manager would like to see you. Is it convenient?"

"I'll make it work. Ten minutes. Thanks, Jackie."

Luke looked to Candice as he pushed out of his chair. "Duty calls."

"Listen, if it's about me and the note I put on his windshield asking for a raise, tell him I'm tired waiting,"

JACKIE FALLON WAS at her desk on the telephone when Luke arrived. She finished her call and offered Luke a smile. "That was much less than five minutes."

"Call me the early bird," Luke suggested.

"Don't sit down," Jackie advised. "I'll tell him you're here." She picked up her phone and punched a number. "Sir, Luke Michell is here." Cradling the telephone, she looked to Luke. "His majesty awaits."

"It's not about…" Luke hesitated.

Jackie understood Luke's question was about the GM's daughter. She shook her head, *no*.

Greg Larson, jacket off, was sitting behind his desk, leafing through a cluster of papers. When Luke entered, he glanced up, gestured to one of the chairs in front of his desk, and returned to attention to the notes in front of him.

"Holy shit!" Larson said, pushing the papers aside. "You know what a Red Bull costs downstairs?"

"Been a while since I've had a drink here?"

"Thiry-eight bucks! It's nuts. A White Russian, thirty-six dollars. Who the hell drinks here? One of our beers goes for eighteen dollars."

"I think we're probably competitive," Luke suggested.

"I gotta stop shopping at Walmart and pay attention to what's going on here," Larson said, studying Luke. "Ironically price is what I wanted to talk to you about."

"I'm listening," Luke assured, but he was tense. Being summoned to the GM's office wasn't unusual, but the day had been.

"I'm like you, Luke," Larson began. "Our paygrades are a little different, but we both know you can learn a lot by just listening."

"As I'm doing now," Luke agreed.

"So, I'm talking to somebody who knows what's going on in the Silver Palace, and I'm told you have a security program called Vegas Skin. Fill in the blanks for me."

"Vegas Skin is just what its name implies. No whores in the house."

Larson raised a hand. "Unless we're talking an escort with a guest. A guest who wants to play a little Sports Book or Twenty-One, who knows, but we do know, if he can afford a little, what did you call it?"

"Vegas Skin."

"Vegas Skin, right, but in the company of a guest, we don't get in the way. I think you understand why, it's called money. And once that guest room door closes, it's none of our business. Right?"

"Right, but recently an escort stole a guest's money, a lot of it, along with his watch and ring. Lucky for him, he got it back. I hope we can agree these so-called escorts aren't in the business because they like sex. It's like you said, it's about money."

"We agree on that, but I want balance. When

someone complains about what an escort has done, you and your people own it, but I'm talking about what might be perceived as too much effort put into what you think might happen. *Might happen* is a gamble. Gambling belongs to our guests, not you. Nevada State Gaming Commission prohibits you from gambling. We agree on that?"

"So, get rid of Vegas Skin?"

"No, just make damn sure your people know where the line is."

The GM's remark about the line took Luke back to an Apple Smoothie and Dawn Wilder. The line between Greg Larson and Dawn Wilder was a narrow one. "I'll make sure our efforts regarding Vegas Skin are understood by all and in complete agreement with management."

Larson rocked forward in his chair to rest his elbows on his desk. "Two weeks from today, Tex Mitchell will be premiering his opening act for a two-week stay with us. Reservations for his show and rooms are already on the edge of a sell-out. You know what that means to you?"

"Means I'll be talking to the head of security at the SoFi. Mitchell did a sell-out there last week."

"Big difference between SoFi and us is Tex Mitchell didn't sleep there. He's booked our penthouse tower two days before his opening until the day after he turns out the lights."

"I'll get our ducks in a row."

"You may be ducking a lot. Tex is a player. In addition to the penthouse, he's got another eleven rooms booked for his entourage. All said to warn you, your Vegas Skin is about to get stretched. Every resort in this town has been chasing Tex for the past couple years. We got him.

When he leaves, I want him to be as happy as he was when he arrived. You're gonna have women crawling through the cracks to get in here. Don't stop them all. You understand what I'm saying?"

"I understand," Luke assured.

"I wanna know everything that goes on. Well, most of it. All right, get out of here. I gotta kick some engineers in the ass."

Luke pushed out of his chair, he paused to look at Larson. "Chief, can I ask…"

"Tammy, yeah, she's a work in progress. She's in rehab. Thanks for your help, Luke."

"Yes, sir."

———

AT THE RED Rock Recovery Center overlooking the sunlit panorama of Las Vegas, Eighteen-year-old Tammy Larson was lying in her bed feeling no pain. She was floating in the backyard of her home. It was the house she'd grown up in. Her father won it in the divorce from her pain-in-the-ass mother and gave the house to her. Now, she was hosting a party and a barbeque. Most of the crowd were young, and most were high and loving it. Fuck the police. Some she knew. One was a jailer at the Clark County Detention Center. She had been kind, offering help when Tammy threw up in the cell's toilet. Then came the birds, thousands of them swirling around her singing, and then it all disappeared as she fell. Help, she cried. The pit was dark and black.

The double hit of crystal meth had cost her three hundred dollars. Thanks to her father, she had the money. Long Hair, who she met in the buffet, made the deal with the security officer, but when delivered, he insisted on a forty-dollar tip.

"Fuck, I could have been busted," Long Hair argued, but settled for thirty dollars and a quick sniff.

Tammy's hit was not so subtle. After the evening meal, which she couldn't remember, she went to the semi-privacy of her room and snorted the double hit. Logic assured her since the fuck, Long Hair, had sucked some of it, the reduced double was okay. She was wrong. Methamphetamine, a powerful, highly addictive drug, slammed Tammy's central nervous system. It increased the activity of her neurotransmitters, including dopamine, a brain chemical for motivation and behaviors. Tammy felt a euphoric *rush*, an intense and pleasurable feeling, but it lasted only minutes before fading. Her heavy dose with the false hope of maintaining a high now pushed her toward death.

An evening nurse, making her final rounds, saw the open condom, the foil wrappers and Tammy convulsing on the bed. She filled the night with her screams.

Tammy, unconscious and strapped on a stretcher, was transported by ambulance to the University Medical Center on West Charleston, where efforts to save her life began. She was unresponsive, had an irregular heartbeat, seizures, and difficulty breathing. Her costs so far were only nine hundred and thirty dollars. A gift from her father. She was in the hospital ER for two hours before a low-paid management trainee at the Red Rock Rehab Center made the call to her father's private cell.

He was having dinner in one of the Silver Palaces private, but palatial dining rooms with Tex Mitchill's attractive blonde agent when the call came. "Sir, we don't want to alarm you, but your daughter has suffered a drug overdose. She is in the ER at the University Medical Center on West Charleston."

Larson bolted from the table spilling a bottle of wine Tex Mitchell had sent as a gift.

Larson called Charlotte Johnson as he tried snaking his way through the Strip's evening traffic. "Charlotte, don't ask. Just meet me at the University Med ER." Larson was not informed a similar call had been made to his estranged wife.

Larson's arrival at University Med didn't go well. He wanted to see his daughter. When refused, he insisted on seeing the doctors treating her. "Maybe you don't know who the hell I am." Again, his request was denied. A patient advocate arrived and briefed him on what was going on to save his daughter's life. She was escorting him to a private waiting room when Charlotte arrived. She was followed shortly by Larson's estranged wife which added to the already high tensions.

Greg Larson was sitting with his face buried in his hands, sobbing and praying when the woman entered the room.

"Who are you?" Charlotte questioned.

"I'm Tammy's mother."

THIRTEEN
ALL THINGS OLD AND NEW

LUKE MITCHEL WAS MAKING his evening rounds. He started on the roof of the Golden Tower. The Silver Palace had two. The Silver Tower stood two floors higher than the Gold. Work had begun on the glass-walled pool that would allow swimmers a panoramic view of the Vegas Strip from atop the Tower's sixty-two floors. Luke had to visualize the pool because a forklift, a crane, stacks of thick heavy glass, palettes loaded with bags of cement and several mixers, cluttered the roof, making it difficult to know what was planned. An early evening breeze, although still warm, made it inviting. Luke walked to the front rim of the tower to look down at the Strip. Darkness had found the street below. Head-lamps lit the street, people filled the sidewalks. Night-time Vegas was beginning to show its face. Luke's eyes swept over the array of lights and colors. He realized he was looking at visitors. He was no longer one of them. For Luke, Vegas was home. As he watched the glow of the fading distant sunlight and the sprawl of the city, he wondered where Greg Larson was. The Silver Palace's rumor mill was alive and well and word that the GM had spilled a bottle of wine and abandoned a VIP guest in his rush to get away told everyone there was trouble. Luke thought he knew what that trouble was, Greg Larson's daughter, Tammy.

From the top of the tower Luke wished them well. He raised his face to look into the dark sky, hoping God was listening, and spoke, "God, have mercy on them." He took a breath of the fresh air and turned away.

An elevator had brought Luke up, so he decided it would be the stairs going down. He was on the fifty-fifth floor, descending when he realized what was ahead. He paused for a moment. The towering stairwell was quiet. Luke moved on, slowing his descent as he reached the forty-second floor. The lighting in the stairwell was bright. The floor was clean and polished. There was no evidence a young housekeeper had died there. Luke had only seen the girl in death, or had he, like most, never saw the woman she was. He spent hours in the stairwell with her. He wondered how many times he had passed her in a hallway, on an elevator, and never spoke. He moved on.

Luke's footfalls on the stairs were far from quiet, and as he approached the thirty-ninth floor, he heard a door slam below. As he neared the landing, he could smell the odder. It was marijuana. Someone had been smoking a joint. On the floor of the thirty-ninth landing, he found what he suspected. A joint was crushed on the floor. Luke reached for his radio. "Surveillance, this is Gate-keeper-Ten, have a look at the video for the thirty-ninth. ID who exited the stairwell into the main corridor less than a minute ago. Possible employee smoking a joint. Give the info to Gatekeeper-Twenty for follow-up."

"Roger, Ten, will do," a filtered male voice answered him.

He expected Candice to answer. When she didn't, he wondered why. Meal break, nature calling, there were a lot of reasons for her to be away from the supervisor's desk. Twelve-hour shifts in Gayle Turner's absence was among them. Surveillance was among his planned stops. Luke switched to the back-of-the-house elevator when he reached the thirtieth floor. He shared his ride to the third with a server and a cart full of dirty dishes. They still smelled good. Getting off on the third, Luke chose a shortcut through the men's locker room to surveillance. He was surprised to find Anakoni Stone, the PM security watch commander standing with a shirtless KC King, his AM watch commander, in front of an open locker. Both men saw Luke approaching.

"Got a taste of cannabis." Stone smiled. "Maybe that's why they call it upstairs."

"I'm betting on an employee," Luke suggested.

"You're right," Stone agreed. "Surveillance already ID'd him. Engineer by the name of Stillman. I was on my way down there when I found KC in here."

Luke looked at KC King who was pushing his arms into a uniform shirt from the locker. "My wife's sister is in town," King explained. "They dropped me off and went to the Mirage, Cirque du Soleil. I'm going down and see what's cooking in employee dining."

"Sounds good," Luke agreed. "I'm glad I ran into both of you. GM called me in earlier. He heard of our Vegas Skin operation and wanted to know precisely what it meant."

"And that would be?" Stone questioned as he leaned against the lockers.

"No whores allowed," Luke answered.

"And that means what?" KC King asked as he tucked in his shirt.

"That's where it gets vague." Luke explained, "We see escorts, call girls, whores, as a crime, a threat to guest safety, and we made a proactive effort to identify them and keep them out."

"And the GM disagrees?" Stone questioned.

"We see these women for what they are," Luke continued, "the GM sees them as an asset, no pun intended, because those inviting them in aren't the young couple here to see some headliner, or the seniors that crowd around the slots. He knows who enjoys these women, those inviting them in, after paying fifteen hundred to get laid. They've got money, and they gamble. The numbers are on his side."

"So, our position is?" KC King asked.

"We focus on guests. We do what we can to keep them safe. We want them to come back, so unless a guest is getting *head* in an open hallway or the escort is in dire need of a bath, we observe and report. We only get in the way when and if a crime is overt."

"Not much in Vegas that shocks me," KC King suggested as he pinned a gold and silver badge on his shirt. "I get the GM's message. If a customer can't shop in our store, guess what? He's gonna shop somewhere else."

"But no shoplifting's allowed," Stone added. The three men laughed.

"What do we do with the *Skin Teams*?" KC King questioned.

Luke had an answer ready. "Keep them. Make sure they understand the GM's policy. In addition to identifying *Ladies of the Evening*, have them watch for pickpockets, electronic cheaters in slots, car thieves in guest parking, or employees stealing silverware from guest dining. I'm sure the two of you can find significant roles for them."

"I like that," Stone agreed.

"I'm going down for dinner. I promise not to *fork around*," KC King offered.

They laughed again, then Luke looked at Stone. "Anakoni, when you find this engineer that likes pot, remind him smoking weed in Nevada may no longer be a crime, but it could get his ass fired when he smokes in the Palace."

"Will be my pleasure," Stone assured.

"And tell him he's the one who cleans up the mess he left upstairs."

Luke did a fist bump with both men and moved on. Reaching surveillance, he opened the door to the subdued light of the expansive complex. As his radio alerted him earlier, there was a man at the supervisor's desk. It was Carter, the man Candice had mentioned earlier. A man Gayle Turner cautioned her about. Luke wondered if Carter had been part of the original hiring, what was going on? Obviously, Carter had the skill set they needed.

"Evening, Chief. Welcome to the heartbeat of Vegas."

Luke's eyes panned the multitude of video images on the large flat-screens on the other side of the glass partition, separating the supervisor from those watching and maneuvering the inventory of cameras.

"Candice gone for the day?" Luke questioned, watching an image inside focusing on a Twenty-One player with a stack of tokens stacked at his elbow.

"Yeah, she said she was going to do a pop in on Gayle. Ask me to sit in," Carter explained. "Guy you're looking at is a counter. Card room manager reached out, but we were already on him. Either he's counting or he's just one lucky sonofabitch."

"Who makes the call?" Luke asked.

"Card Room, unless we catch a move first."

"Okay, I'm out of here. Send me an email. I'd like to see how this turns out."

"Will do," Carter answered. "Listen, the schedule for Candice, with Gayle out, has made for some long days. I'd be glad to fill in, but nothing to push, and upset the ladies. Nevertheless, you need help, I'm your man."

"I'll keep that in mind," Luke answered with a final look at the suspected card counter before he turned to the door. His thoughts were on Carter's ambition. Was it wrong to want more? Was this the issue Gayle had warned of?

———

CANDICE PUSHED the doorbell of Gayle Turner's second-story condo on Valley Boulevard just a few blocks off the Strip. The view told Candice that Gayle's rent wasn't cheap. When the chime sounded inside, a dog began barking. A moment later, Gayle Turner opened the door. Candice wasn't sure what to expect but what she saw surprised her. Gayle was dressed in a white robe and flip-flops. Her Vegas look was on. Eye makeup, which Candice always envied, hair curled and pinned up on the back of her head and a sincere smile baring her white even teeth. If she was ill, it was hidden.

"This is a surprise," Gayle said, opening the door wider. A Yorkie jumped at Candice's legs, "Smokey, stop. Go lay down." The dog disappeared inside.

"You had me worried, girl. Phone only counts some-times." Candice smiled. Her surprise was showing.

Gayle gestured Candice in. "I was just going to pour a glass of wine. Shall I count you in?"

"Only if it's a big glass," Candice answered, choosing a chair she had sat in before. The Yorkie was back, but he lay down under a glass cocktail table. Gayle went to a kitchen counter and poured white wine into two tall glasses. Finishing, she carried them to Candice. "I was down in the spa. That's why the robe."

Both sampled their wine and then Candice spoke. "Gayle, we've been friends for almost three years. You're my big sister. My closet friend. What's with this *I'm sick* crap? You look like a model."

"Models get sick," Gayle answered, taking a drink of wine.

"Okay, I'll play the game. You've been offered a job somewhere else and you're thinking about it?"

The Yorkie climbed into Gayle's lap. The robe fell from one leg. Gayle smiled at Candice's question but answered bluntly, "No job offer. I like the Silver Palace."

"Then why aren't you at work? You're not sick."

"It's complicated." Gayle set her glass on the cocktail table as she adjusted the dog in her lap. "We all live three lives. A public life, like when we're at the mall in a crowd. Then there's our private life, the life we share with friends. And then there's the big one, our secret life. The life we never share, a life we never talk about. Thank Shakespeare for all that."

"Shakespeare was a man, screw him." Candice took a heavy drink as if to mimic Gayle. "I can't help you if you won't tell me what's going on."

"Sorry, this one's all mine." Gayle put the dog down.

Candice emptied her wineglass. "Let me take you back a couple years. You took me into the closet in surveillance and closed the door. I'll quote what you said,

'I'm your best friend, Candice. What the hell's going on?'"

"I remember." Gayle picked up her glass from the table. She stared into it as if wishing she could hide there.

"I told you what I have never told another human being. I was pregnant. Pretty personal, huh? You told me the choices, helped me pick the right one. That's what friends do, Gayle. You gotta let me in."

Gayle massaged her wineglass, continuing to stare into it. Then, with a nod, she raised her eyes to Candice. "Okay, I lied about an arrest when I applied at the Silver Place." Her tone was emotional. The confession scared her.

"BFD," Candice answered without hesitation. She set her wineglass on the table and leaned to rest her elbows on her knees. "Who gives a shit. You're talking about a file buried in human resources that's at least three years old."

"This one's big," Gayle argued. "That dick Carter is pulling the strings. He wants me out. Either I resign, or he blows the whistle and moves up."

"What's in Carter's whistle, Gayle?"

Gayle tipped her glass for the remaining drops before setting it down. There were tears in her eyes. "I was arrested for prostitution."

Candice was shocked. She tried to hide it, but her face was of little help. "Fill in the blanks for me."

Gayle pulled the robe over her naked leg and took a breath before she began. "I hitched a ride with a trucker from Tuson to Laughlin. I was eighteen, running from a mother I was glad to get away from. The only job I had in Tuson was passing out shoes at the Tuson Wonder Bowl. Minimum wage, and I got fired. I hitched a ride with a trucker who dumped me in Laughlin. I looked for work, couldn't find shit. Slept in unlocked cars at Riverside. I didn't have any ID, no skills. I saw this streetwalker. She was no older than me. We talked. She bragged about the money she was making from bikers. They like Laughlin. So, I put on shorts, but instead of getting laid for a couple bucks, I got arrested. Prostitution. I served forty-seven days. Girls in my cell block told me to try Vegas."

"I got a job at the Hyatt, in the laundry. Next, I got a driver's license, a new name, and eventually a new life. Vegas was user-friendly."

"That was decades ago," Candice suggested as Gayle wiped tears from her cheek. "Nobody's going to give a shit now."

"Human resources isn't in the business of forgiving lies, and neither is the Nevada State Gaming Commission."

"How does Carter know of this?"

"His brother-in-law has some kind of county job in Laughlin. He was looking for ways to help Carter when he found it."

"How! You got a new name in Vegas?"

"He matched pictures. My booking photo in Laughlin, license photo for Nevada. They were only seven months apart. Carter showed me the pictures. Said I might want to move on before the roof fell in."

"The little prick," Candice blurted.

FOURTEEN
THE DARK SIDE OF LOVE

GREG LARSON, the GM of the Silver Palace, was learning it was easier to manage a property with six thousand, nine hundred and eight rooms, with over ten thousand employees than it was to get a divorce. Tammy Larson, his eighteen-year-old daughter, was in a coma in the ICU at the University Medical Center on West Charleston Avenue in the heart of Las Vegas. She had suffered a near-fatal overdose of a yet-to-be-identified drug while a patient at the Red Rock Recovery Center.

Larson arrived at UMC after a call to the Silver Palace. He called Charlotte Johnson. She left her office at the Cosmo and joined him. Tammy was stable, she would live, but the aftershocks, they were told, could be life changing, brain damage, a weakened heart, loss of balance, an inability to walk and more. The news was devastating. Greg Larson, still struggling with shock, waited in a patient room UMC provided. His shock worsened when his estranged wife, Naomi, arrived. She wasn't alone. She brought an attorney with her. Charlotte Johson excused herself thinking there would be talk of the Larson's pending divorce. She was right, but there was more.

"I'm attorney Jason Cross. I represent your wife in the divorce action you filed several months ago. As a result of your daughter's hospitalization, Naomi called and asked assistance this evening." He pushed several documents into Larson's lap. Larson tossed the papers aside and bolted to his feet.

The move surprised the attorney. He backed away several steps. Naomi did not. She stood, burning Larson with a look of contempt.

"You can play badass all you want, Greg," Naomi warned, waving one of the documents she held in Larson's face. She read from it.

"This is a court order signed by Judge Henry A. Reynolds of the Superior Court of Clark County, Nevada. Effective immediately, the care, and all subsequent care, as well as all related executive actions, of and for, Ms. Tam Marie Larson, also known as Tammy Larson, shall be made by Naomi Larson, Tammy Larson's natural birth mother, who herewith, is granted sole and exclusive custody."

A blue vein pulsed on Larson's forehead. He grabbed the document from Naomi's hand. Crumpled it in a fist, spit on it and held it up close to her face. "Go to hell," he growled. "You, and this *Bumper Sticker* you call an attorney. You both better get the fuck out of here."

"Or what?" Naomi matched Larson's tone. "You'll call the police? Go ahead. We already provided the hospital a copy of the judge's order. If anyone needs to get out of here, it's you. The man who gave his daughter money to buy drugs."

———

LUKE HAD FINALLY FOUND his way out a back door of the Silver Palace and into the employee parking structure when Anakoni Stone, reached out to him on the radio. *"Gatekeeper-Ten, can you call my cell."*

Luke kicked the tire of a nearby car in frustration as he pulled his cell phone from his belt. He punched the number for Stone.

"Hey, Chief," Stone's Hawaiian dialect answered.

"Anakoni," Luke warned. "You better be standing over a bloody body in the front lobby or I'm coming back in there to spill yours."

"Sorry, boss, I thought when we were over seventy-five percent, you spent the night in-house."

"GM put that away. Key word is away. Which is what I'm doing."

"Got it. You read about this in the morning. It'll be in my log."

"Right, and I won't give it another thought. Come on, fill in the blanks."

"Okay," Stone explained. "Housekeeper comes in to thirty-six seventeen for turn down and finds a pistol under a pillow. She calls security. Rollins comes up and finds it's a loaded Glock Seven. Under the other pillow on the bed, he finds a condom filled with white packets. Looks like the big H. Rollins calls me. I didn't want to call Metro until you were in the loop."

"Appreciate that."

"There's more. I run the serial on the gun, it comes back stolen from New Orleans."

"Who's the guest?" Luke questioned.

"Janet, from guest relations, looks at his record for me. He's from New Orleans. Ken Fredricks. He's in every month or so. Likes Twenty-One. Big spender."

"Maybe a mule, maybe a dealer."

"Wait a minute." Luke heard voices in the background, then Stone returned, his voice was cheerful. "Rollins just found a boot stuffed with dope in the closet."

"Great," Luke agreed. "Any idea where Fredricks is?

"Yeap, surveillance is on him. He's playing Twenty-One. Got an escort at his side."

"Okay, he's no longer a guest," Luke suggested. "He's a felon. Call Metro, tell them you've got a gift for them. Take lots of pictures before they arrive. And tell surveillance to stay on him. Advise you if he moves."

"Will do, now go home, Chief. We'll put it together."

"Thanks, Stone. Kona will be proud of you."

Luke resumed his walk to his car. His troops had done a good job. He was proud of them. Relaxation returned. He unlocked his car and climbed in. Starting the car relaxed Luke even more. He was going home. He waved at a uniformed officer at the entrance of the parking structure. Luke's decision was now a choice between a drive on fast Interstate 15 to Henderson or a drive north on Las Vegas Boulevard, better known as the Strip. Luke chose the Strip. It would be slower, but he was in the mood for slow, bright lights, crowded sidewalks and bridges, the feel of Vegas.

The fountains at the Bellagio danced high into the night, New York New York was awash with color, and the Cosmo stood tall and massive. Luke's drive was slow, bumper to bumper. He put down windows on both sides of the car to let in the sounds of the night. The Luxor was coming into sight with its bright column of intense light reaching skyward from atop the Pyramid. Luke was drinking it in like a tourist when he saw the girl on the corner. Her thick blonde hair, her attire, knee-high boots, a leather miniskirt, a tight sleeveless blouse, and a purse hung high on a shoulder told him what she was, but what shocked him, what made him stare was the fact he recognized her. It was Dawn Wilder. A horn blew behind Luke. He turned right at the next corner. He sped up, turned right again and then another right until he was back to the Strip. He waited for a break in the traffic and then pulled onto the Strip, staring ahead, looking for her, hoping he was wrong, but knew he wasn't, and then he saw her. Walking close to the curb, smiling at passing cars. Luke slowed, pulled to the curb and stopped. Dawn leaned, looked into the car.

Luke didn't wait for her to speak. "Get in," he ordered.

"What!" Dawn answered in shock as she recognized Luke.

"Dawn, get in the car." Luke reached across and opened the passenger's door.

"I know you. You're not a cop."

A horn sounded behind them.

"Get in. Let's talk." The car horn beeped again. Dawn looked, hesitated and then climbed in.

"This is creepy," Dawn said as Luke pulled into the traffic.

"This isn't a date," Luke cautioned.

"Then pull over," Dawn said, "I want out."

"We need to talk. What the hell are you doing?"

"Working," Dawn blurted. "You got me fired, you dick."

"Fired?" Now it was Luke's surprise.

"The calls to Pam after I gave you the number. She connected the knots, and one of them went around my neck."

Luke spotted a sign ahead. *The Pepper Mill*. He slowed and pulled into the parking lot to find a space near the front entrance. He pulled in, turned the car off and looked to Dawn. "I understand you're frightened. All I want is to talk. Nothing will happen to you inside."

"Sure," Dawn agreed sarcastically. "What else could you do? Make me pay for my own drink?"

"Only if you order an apple smoothie," Luke answered, trying for a lighter tone.

Dawn opened the car door, climbed out and slammed it. Luke followed her.

"TWO FOR THE LOUNGE," Luke announced to a greeter inside the Pepper Mill. The greeter motioned to a shadowed lounge. Inside, Luke guided Dawn to a padded booth. They sat down. Luke sat down almost across from Dawn, allowing as much room as he could between them.

"This is the first time I've been picked up for a drink," Dawn said soberly.

"Let's hope it's your last," Luke suggested as a waiter arrived. "I'll have a Jack and Diet Coke," Luke said to the man. He nodded and looked at Dawn.

"Margarita with salt, lots of ice," Dawn said.

The waiter smiled and moved away.

Luke laced his fingers together on the table. "I'm sorry if I did cost you your position."

"That makes two of us. Why did you stop?" Dawn demanded.

"After seeing you, I couldn't believe it. I drove around the block."

"So, we are talking date?"

"No," Luke answered. "It's not a date. I was shocked to see you on the street."

"I was robbed, remember? Money is an issue. The street is all I had."

The waiter returned with their drinks. "Enjoy," he said and moved away.

Luke dug in a pocket and pulled out his wallet. He dug money from it and counted the bills. "Three hundred and forty-six dollars." He pushed the money across the table to Dawn.

The waiter returned. "Sir, monetary transactions are not permitted in our lounge."

Luke looked at the man. "Get away from us or I'll throw this fucking drink in your face."

The waiter nodded and moved away.

Luke looked at Dawn. "I picked you up. I owe you. Take the money."

Dawn hesitated for a moment and then gathered the bills.

"I don't know what went wrong, Dawn, but I'm going to find out. The two men who handle matters like this are very competent."

"Not as competent as Pam," Dawn suggested.

"Did you get a new cell?"

"Yes."

"You have my cell number. Call it, so I have yours."

"And why would I call you?" Dawn questioned.

"Because I screwed up. I'll find a way to help."

"Could you start by dropping me at my apartment?" Dawn asked.

———

GREG LARSON LEFT the University Medical Center with Charlotte Johnson after being humiliated by his estranged wife and her attorney. Larson was quiet most of the drive deliberately avoiding the Strip. Charlotte respected his emotions and stayed quiet.

"All I wanted to do was help," Larson said as he wheeled the car down into the condo's underground garage, where he stopped for a security gate. He pushed a coded control near the rearview mirror. The metal gate began a slow rise. "I gave Tammy money because I love her. Isn't that why we put her in that place? Because we love her."

"Yes," Charlotte agreed.

The gate was open. Larson drove through, guiding the car to an assigned parking space. There he turned the car off and leaned his head forward against the top of the steering wheel and wept. Charlotte reached across and massaged Larson's back. She ignored the tear tracing down her own cheek.

———————

LUKE DROPPED Dawn Wilder at her apartment complex. There wasn't much talk between the two after they left the Pepper Mill. Luke couldn't help but smell the scent Dawn was wearing. It filled the car. It was heavy but pleasant. Much like Dawn, Luke decided. She was the three-hundred-pound gorilla in the car. She was a prostitute, but she was more. Her beauty could not be ignored but it was more than her being attractive. Beneath the blonde hair, behind the glossy lips and hidden under the tinted cheeks, was a complex woman. A woman whose life he turned upside down. A woman twenty years younger than he, but a woman who had pointed out they had much more in common than the distance between a director of security and a whore.

When Luke pulled to a stop in front of the apartment

building Dawn directed him to, he was at a loss for words. Dawn wasn't. She looked at Luke. "Maybe next time you should carry more cash. On second thought, the next time you see me anywhere, turn the fuck around." Dawn climbed out and slammed the car door.

Luke's navigation system guided him toward his condominium in Henderson. "At the next light, stay in the left turn lane," the soft recorded female voice told him. Luke made the turns, listened to the directions, but the drive was long and laborious. Dawn's words stung, but it was more than her words, it was her attitude. She was a desperate young woman, and he knew he was the cause.

Reaching his condominium, Luke parked in back and headed for the stairs in the front courtyard. He wished he had chosen Interstate 15. Then he would have missed Dawn on the street near the Luxor. Then he would have been excited about reaching his condo, taking his shoes off, drinking a beer, watching *Rock the Block* on HGTV. Life was a bitch, but he knew life was more of a bitch for Dawn Wilder and he caused it. Tomorrow he would wake up and still be the director of security at the Silver Palace. Climbing the stairs to his second-floor condo he wondered what Dawn Wilder would wake up too.

Unlocking his door, Luke found the condo warm and dark. He turned on the AC and then the lights in every room. He didn't want it dark. Comfort came quickly. He left his shoes and socks near a recliner in the living room and collected a can of beer from the refrigerator. His thoughts kept going back to Dawn Wilder. They weren't sexual, he told himself, but had to admit she was attractive. She was a Vegas Beauty. She was also thin ice. Luke knew picking up a prostitute on the Strip for any reason was a danger for him. The answer to it all, Luke reminded himself, was Barbara Nichols. She was also a beauty. A beauty he knew inside and out and she'd soon be on her way. Not only on her way but coming to Vegas to live with him. She would love the condo. Who wouldn't? Luke went back to the fridge a second time. This time he collected a cold slice of pizza. He took it back to the living room. Barbara Nichols would erase any thoughts he had of Dawn Wilder. He reminded himself Dawn was a hooker, a streetwalker, an escort, a prostitute, a whore. The names didn't work. He was swimming in a sea of guilt. He tried the cold pizza. It did little to help. His cell phone chimed. Luke quickly picked it up from the table where he had dumped it. He hoped it wasn't Stone or KC King from the Silver Palace. He looked at the caller ID. He was surprised, it was Candice Harmon.

"This is Luke."

"Luke, you may recall we're almost neighbors," Candice said. "If you don't count the six miles between us. I know it's late, but we need to talk. It's about Gayle. We can flip a coin, you come see me, or I come see you. Okay, you win. I'll be there in ten." She hung up.

Luke quickly gathered his socks and shoes, the near-empty can of beer and got them out of the living room. He wondered if she would be offended by his bare feet. To hell with that. He hurried to the master bath, relieved himself, flushed and the doorbell rang.

"Hi, Candice." Luke smiled as he opened the door.

"Appreciate you allowing this," Candice answered, pushing by him. "You got any cold beer?"

"I do," Luke said, leading the way to the kitchen. The blonde busty Candice, dressed in jeans and a short-sleeved blouse, followed. Luke collected two beers from the fridge as he enjoyed her scent. They returned to the living room. Candice chose Luke's recliner. He sat on a couch. "So tell me what's going on with Gayle."

"You want the bad news first?" Candice questioned.

"Try me," Luke answered.

"Gayle was arrested for prostitution...and she lied about it."

"Holy shit," Luke blurted in disbelief.

"Now the good news," Candice continued. "It happened twenty-four years ago when she was eighteen...and you never got a word of this from me."

"I'm not the Nevada State Gaming Commission," Luke cautioned. "If Gayle lied when she was hired at the Silver Palace, it's a big deal."

"That's why I'm here. I know it's a big fucking deal and so does Gayle. That's why all her bullshit about being sick. She doesn't know what to do."

"Where did this come from? How do we know it's true?" Luke questioned.

"Gayle confirmed it and it's Ted Carter, that little weasel. He threatened to expose her. Why? Because he's a dick. A dick who wants her job."

"So, words already out, shit." Luke was worried. The room was quiet for a moment. Luke was thinking. Candice drank from her beer. "Okay, here's plan A," Luke shrouded. "There's no way we can solve this tonight,"

"Shock me," Candice added, "you know that means we're both going to get a good night's sleep."

"It's a big deal, and I don't want it getting any bigger."

"Count me in on that. Then it's good night?" Candice questioned.

"I think it has to be," Luke answered.

Candice pushed out her chair and turned to the door. Luke followed, brushing her, reaching for the doorknob.

Candice took Luke by the shoulder, surprising him. She looked into his eyes. Luke suddenly understood. He pulled Candice to him and kissed her, again, and again. Their arms searched each other's backs. Candice moaned as he tightened his body to hers. She gasped for breath as his kisses moved to her neck, first on one side and then the other. She pulled him back to her mouth. A hand pushed under the back of her blouse and moved slowly forward to grasp a breast. Candice moaned, pushing into him.

The cell phone on Luke's cocktail table chimed and vibrated in a circle. Candice pulled away from Luke's kiss. "It's not mine," she said breathlessly.

Luke released her and went for the cell which continued chiming. He grabbed it and looked at the caller ID. "Damn," he groaned, answering the call, "Hi, Barb, what's up?"

Candice, breathing hard, was tucking in her blouse.

"Good news," Barbara Nichol's voice said in Luke's ear. "The Tribe said they're done with me. I'm outta here. I'll be in Vegas by this time tomorrow."

Luke looked at Candice. She hadn't heard the words, but she did hear a female voice and Luke using the name Barb. She took a final breath, waved a hand at Luke, opened the door and stepped out into the night.

———

CHARLOTTE JOHNSON GOT the emotional Greg Larson into their second-floor condo. He tossed his jacket, pulled away his tie, pushed his shoes off and collapsed onto a couch. "I don't know what the hell to do. I never saw this coming."

Charlotte sat down on the edge of a matching couch

across from Larson. She folded her hands in her lap and studied him. Larson saw Charlotte's sober look and sat up to return her look. "Come on, say it."

"Greg, I never saw this coming either, but while I waited for you and Naomi to finish talking, I got five calls from the Cosmo. The last one was from the GM. He didn't say it, but I know he's not happy with all the drama, and my office being empty. I like being a director, but I have to be there to direct. I can't do anything about Tammy. I hope you can, but whatever is decided it involves you and Naomi. Her mother and her father. I just don't fit in. I think it's time we called a pause. No breakup, no goodbyes, just a time out. It allows you to concentrate on problems that can't be ignored, and me a chance to figure out how to get seventy-four surgeons into sixty-eight rooms."

Larson, now sitting with his elbows on his knees, nodded in agreement. "All I can think about is Tammy. My ex just muddied the waters. I have to fight what she's done. It's going to get ugly, naw, it's already ugly, and you, my love, you're no part of ugly. So, go to the Cosmo. They have a new feature on their flat-screens that allows guests to plug in their phones and watch videos."

Charlotte pushed to her feet. "I know, Greg. It was my idea."

"Should have known."

Charlotte walked around a cocktail table to where Greg sat. She leaned to him, and they kissed. Charlotte made it light. "Promise you'll stay in touch," she said, moving for the door.

"You know you're gonna miss me," Larson tried to be lighthearted, but his hands were gripping one another in a tight ball.

Charlotte did not look back as she stepped out and closed the door.

———

DAWN WILDER TRIED WATCHING TV after Luke Mitchel dropped her in front of her apartment, but even with three hundred and six channels, she was still searching with a remote. At least the asshole didn't take that. She was no longer an escort, fired from that, and even though Pam never learned of her problems at the Silver Palace with the Texan, she connected the dots on who gave up her private cell. And then Luke Mitchel finds her on the street. Is he a director or a game warden or some shit? Call me in the morning he orders. So, what if I don't? Wicked Tuna caught her attention on TV. Tyler, his hat on backward, at the helm of the Pin Wheel, was yelling at his sister, tying down equipment on the rear deck. Dawn wondered if Tyler was divorced. She guessed he was. Marissa, soaked from the choppy water, came into the cabin. Her appearance made Dawn think of her own sister—Jill. Jill was three years older, married, the mother of two, a cashier at Walgreens, and the care-taker of their widowed mother. Dawn sent money every month to her mother. It was never acknowledged, but she continued sending it anyway. Dawn envied Jill with her good-looking husband and her life in Anaheim, Cali-fornia. Jill had it all, while Dawn had nothing. She thought for a moment she was much like Tyler's sister. She was on a boat going nowhere with someone yelling at her. She hadn't called Jill in months. Dawn decided to call. Hearing Jill's voice on such a shit day would help. She turned off the TV, dug her new cell phone from her purse, looked at contacts, and there was Jill. She punched the number and waited. The telephone rang once, twice and a third time. Dawn was about to give up when Jill answered,

"Hello."

"Jill, it's Dawn. How are you? It's been a long time. Too long. How's Mom?"

"Are you still in Las Vegas?" Jill questioned.

"Yeah, still here. It was warm today," Dawn answered.

A dial tone sang in her ear. Jill had hung up.

Dawn bit her lip as she laid the cell phone down. She wiped a tear tracing down her cheek.

———

NAOMI LARSON HAD BEEN bedside for six hours in the Intensive Care Unit at UMC with her daughter. She was uncertain what to do. Life in Vegas had become a gamble in the truest sense. Nothing seemed certain, not even Tammy's life. Her oxygen mask had been removed. She was breathing on her own, but she had yet to open her eyes or move. A bedside monitor displayed Tammy's heart rate and blood pressure. Naomi thought of going home. Sparky would be barking at everything after being alone for so long. The thought made Naomi smile. She lived with a dog. She had once lived with a husband and a daughter in a hillside home overlooking the panorama of Las Vegas sprawled in distance sunshine. Now, it was a daughter in a coma, a husband wanting a divorce, and life with a dog, all wrapped in the dark of night. She closed her eyes and took a deep breath. Enough pity, Naomi promised. It was time to be a mother, and anyone or anything that got in her way, was in for a surprise.

"Mom," a raspy, dry voice called.

Naomi opened her eyes. Tammy had turned her head, eyes open. She looked at her mother with a hand gripping the rail of her hospital bed.

"Tammy," Naomi cried, bolting to her feet. She leaned over the bed railing and kissed Tammy's forehead. Her hand covered Tammy's on the railing.

"I thought it was you, sitting there. I…" Tammy paused, coughed. "I thought it was you. I wasn't sure."

"It's me," a tearful Naomi assured.

A nurse entered and moved bedside, across from Naomi. "Welcome back, young lady." She smiled at Tammy and then looked at the bedside monitors.

"She just called my name." Naomi was excited, relieved. "I was sitting there, and she said mom." She wiped away a tear.

"Heart and pressure look good," the nurse suggested. "I'm sure the doctor will be in for a look." She looked to Tammy. "Is there anything you want or need, dear?"

Tammy hesitated at answering. She pulled her hand from the railing and pushed it into Naomi's. She looked at her mother.

"We'll be fine," Naomi answered.

The nurse nodded and turned away.

Naomi gathered a bedside cup filled with water and a straw. She moved it to Tammy's mouth. Tammy sucked on the straw heavily. She gasped when she finished. Her head fell back into a pillow. "Mom, please, don't, please don't leave me."

"I won't leave you. I promise." Naomi raised Tammy's hand and kissed it.

"Is Dad here?" Tammy asked.

FIFTEEN

ALL THE KING'S MEN...

BARBARA NICHOLS'S call announcing her would be arrival the next afternoon, made for a troubled night's sleep for Luke Mitchel. The last time he glanced at the illuminated clock in his bedroom, it showed 1:24 a.m. He reminded himself Barb was coming because he invited her. They met in the Wild River Resort Casino in De Rio, Arizona, where they became friends, then lovers. They lived independent of one another, but Luke spent many nights in Barbara's bed. Their relationship was serious, until Vegas got in the way. When Luke joined the team at the Silver Palace, he invited Barb to move with him and find work among the lights. She decided to stay, until now, after he and Candice Harmon kissed passionately. They had flirted for months, and it finally happened, and it was great, but now more than great, it was a genuine problem. Candice was not only a subordinate, she was now an obstacle in his relationship with Barbara. He knew he couldn't have both. Damn, it was a choice he didn't want to make.

There was a third woman haunting Luke's night.

Dawn Wilder, a young prostitute, a beautiful one. Complicating this relationship was the fact he picked her up on the Strip. Why? He didn't have an answer. There probably wasn't one. Dawn claimed she was on the street because Pam, whoever the hell she was, had fired her as an escort because of him. Finding Dawn walking the street filled Luke with guilt.

He reasoned he picked up a whore on the Strip because he knew her. It sounded lame, and it was lame, but he knew he had to find a way to help her, although he had no idea how. It was much the same with Gayle Turner, his director of surveillance. He learned from Candice Gale was calling in sick because someone discovered she was once arrested for prostitution. A fact she omitted when she was hired by the Silver Palace. Luke's night was filled with troubled women. Women, he knew he had to help, but thoughts of how, were fleeting. Shit, Luke reasoned, combat in Afghanistan wasn't so bad after all.

———

GREG LARSON, the GM of the Silver Palace, was giving serious thought to going to work. At least at the Silver Palace, he would be recognized as someone in charge of something. His estranged wife, Naomi and Charlotte Johnson had both ran a truck over his ego. He was saddened by Charlotte's departure, but she was right. His life was in shambles. His eighteen-year-old daughter had been arrested for prostitution, and she now lay in a comma at UMC, where he had battled and lost with his soon-to-be ex and her attorney. If he had learned anything this night, and he hoped he had, it was that his threats, cursing and unreasonable demands, solved nothing, except for making most think he was an asshole.

Looking around his twenty-four hundred square foot condo furnished with whatever a couple million dollars could buy, showed Larson a cold reality. He was alone. He made a confessional speech to his management team at the Palace, and now, ironically, the words he spoke were coming back to haunt him. Transparency, truth and reason were claimed as his watchwords, the rudder for the great ship they sailed on. Yet, somehow, he was asleep in the cabin, not seeing the danger ahead. That had to change. He thought of the challenges he had. The most important one was Tammy, his daughter. Naomi, his estranged wife, was right—he created Tammy's crisis by giving her money, not once but twice. It was against everything in Vegas, but the reality was, money didn't equal love. What Tammy needed most from him was love. He had to find a way to give that to her. He headed for the master bathroom. He would shave and get dressed for work, but first, visit Tammy at UMC.

Larson hoped, prayed, if God still listened to him, Tammy would survive. He owed Naomi an apology. Her intent was good. Maybe if he was humble enough, she would allow him to help. Larson's cell buzzed. It was his private number. He hoped it was Charlotte. It wasn't. It was Naomi. His heart pushed up into his throat. God, please, don't let it be word that Tammy had died. "This is Greg."

"Greg, she's awake. One minute she was sleeping, the next she was awake. She asked about you. She wanted to know if you were here."

Larson leaned against the back of a couch as emotion gripped him. "I, I'll be right there."

"Be careful."

"Thank you, Naomi." Larson tossed his cell phone onto the couch and hurried toward the bathroom and then suddenly stopped and looked to the ceiling. "And thank you, God."

――――

"Loss my ass." Gordon Harris smiled as he stepped to the cashier's window near the card room at the Silver Palace. "I'm going up to my room, pack and get out of dodge." He pushed a handful of twenty-dollar bills to the cashier. "I'd like to trade these for two Franklins."

The young brunette cashier accepted the bills through the glass hand portal, straightened them, pressed out the wrinkles and leafed through the currency, laying them out on the countertop in a fan-like pattern. She studied the bills and then pushed the spread wider.

"Come on, I haven't got all night. Two Franklins. That's it." Harris was loud and demanding.

"One moment, sir." The brunette pushed out her chair and moved to an older, balding senior cashier. They spoke softly to one another with glances at Harris on the other side of the glass.

"Okay," Harris growled, reaching through the hand portal, trying to reach the spread of twenty-dollar bills. "Just give them back."

"Sir," the senior cashier barked. "Remove your hands. That's not allowed."

Harris withdrew his hands, closing one into a fist he thumped on the glass. "I want my money back."

Two uniformed security officers appeared, one a muscular middle-aged Black man and the other, an attractive young female. They took up positions on either side of Harris.

"Sir," the Black officer said in a firm tone. "Step away from the glass."

"This is bullshit. I want my twenties back."

The Black officer moved closer to Harris and spoke into his face. "I said, step away from the glass."

Harris looked angry but backed away from the window to watch the action inside. KC King, the security watch commander, was now inside the cash cage speaking with the cashier and her supervisor.

"We haven't tested the bills yet," the young brunette explained.

"The minute he reached inside to get them back, we knew it was time to call you," the senior cashier added.

"And he claims he's a guest here in the Palace."

"He said he's going upstairs and pack," the brunette answered.

"Okay," KC King suggested with a glance through the glass at the impatient Harris and the two officers. "Let's have a look at the bills."

"Only if the ink's dry," the brunette added sarcastically as she moved away to gather the collection of bills. Money in hand, she joined the senior cashier and KC King at the back of the cash cage behind a partition masking their moves. The two men watched as the brunette fed a twenty into an electronic counterfeit testing device. The machine flashed a green light as the bill was drawn into its printer-size shell. A yellow caution light followed and then a red light blinked as the bill was spewed from its opposite side. KC King and the senior cashier hid their reactions as the younger cashier continued the process. Finishing, she offered the bills to

KC. "Don't try to buy gas with this." She smiled. "Arco's got better detection than we do."

KC took the counterfeit bills, thanked them with a nod and headed for the mantrap. A moment later, he joined the two officers standing with Harris. He held the collection of bills up for Harris. "Where did you get these."

Harris pointed to the card room. "Right in there. An ATM at the back. Maybe twenty minutes ago."

"Show me your ATM," KC ordered.

Harris dug in a back pocket for his wallet. He opened it and pulled out a card. He waved it in their faces with a smile of contempt.

"Got a receipt," KC asked.

"I didn't want one," Harris answered, putting his wallet away. "Now can I have my money?"

"You told the cashier you had a room here. Do you?"

"She's lying. She probably switched my bills to make herself look good."

"Why would she do that?" KC questioned.

"You know, so you'd think I had the counterfeit ones."

"Who said anything about counterfeit? I didn't." KC looked to the Black officer and then his female partner. "You hear me say anything about counterfeit?"

The two officers shook their heads.

"You're trying to trap me," Harris argued, less than convincingly.

"No," KC answered. "I'll let surveillance do that. We've got a camera on that ATM, twenty-four-seven."

"I wanna talk to an attorney," Harris pleaded.

"First, you've gonna talk to the FBI," KC told him holding up the counterfeit bills. "That's who we're going to call. Possession of counterfeit currency is a felony. A federal crime. Now, you can go quietly with us, or we'll be glad to put cuffs on you out here in public."

"Yeah, okay, but I have a right to an attorney."

"Shut up," KC warned, leading him away.

———

GREG LARSON SKIPPED SHAVING and took all the back streets he could remember to get him to the University Medical Center. He parked in a space reserved for physicians and hurried inside to the elevators. He was surprised to find Naomi, coffee in hand, standing at the nurse's station outside ICU, talking with a doctor and a nurse. She saw Larson approaching and moved to him.

"She's sleeping," Naomi explained. "She ate a little oatmeal. They don't want her disturbed. The nurse promised she would find me when Tammy wakes up. I still have the room they provided. Let's talk there." Naomi led the way.

Larson followed Naomi into the patient room. There were two beds. A table near a wide window and a chair on either side. Naomi was the first to sit down. There was a pitcher of coffee on the table, along with paper cups, cream and sugar. Again, Larson followed Naomi's lead. He sat down across from her. He couldn't contain his excitement any longer.

"You talked to her. She was awake. She asked about me."

"Yes." Naomi smiled, sharing his excitement. "She asked if you were here. I told her you would be. Doctor came in and checked her vitals. She's stable. A bit confused, frightened."

"I can imagine," Larson agreed, wringing his hands

together. "Listen, Naomi," he said. "I'm sorry for all my crap earlier. I understand you wanting custody. You're her mother. I got it wrong. I'll do what I can to help you get it right."

"Is that really you talking, Greg Larson?" Naomi questioned. "That's a side I haven't seen in a while."

"Get used to it."

———

LUKE FINALLY FELL ASLEEP, running from passionate women, desperate women, and troubled women, but his cell phone ruined it. He was quickly awake, reaching for it, hoping it wasn't Barbara changing her mind. He found the phone in the darkness. "This is Luke."

"Luke, it's KC King. Sorry to wake you, but when there's an issue with an employee..."

"You're right. I'm listening," Luke assured, pushing the covers aside, sitting up in bed.

"You know a man makes a pass through employee parking every hour or so. Nolan is doing that when he sees what he thinks is two housekeepers at a car. They're under a light. He can't hear them, but he sees one of them hand something to the other. Nolan knows housekeepers love taking home food, leftover candy, and turn-down mints, so he walks from behind the van hiding him, and the two women react. One of them runs..."

"Runs!" Luke is surprised.

"Not very far. Surveillance helped. She's from room service, Linda Paulson, twenty-eight. Been with us about eighteen months."

"What's she running from?" Luke questioned.

"This is where it gets interesting," KC suggests. "Nolan

calls for help on the runner while he goes to the car. The housekeeper, at the driver's door, looks at Nolan, leans her head against the car, and begins sobbing."

"Sobbing! You're making this shit up, KC."

"You wish. Here's the short version. The housekeeper is Roberta Gonzales, age forty-six. Remember Lucy Mendoza? You sat with her body in the stairway for a couple hours. Turns out Roberta is Lucy's aunt. Why's she crying? Because Nolan walked in on her dope deal. Roberta is in possession of what we think is crystal meth and pentanol. Lots of it. She just got five hundred off the room service chic. She knows she'll be made as the mule that goes to Mexico every week or so. Want something, show me the money, but worst of all, Lucy Mendoza's mom, will know Roberta, her own sister, is the one that got her daughter her final dose."

"Damn," Luke responded, swinging his feet to the carpeted floor. "Another painful hit for Lucy's family. You'll have to reach out to the Narcs at Metro. They'll be glad to put these two in jail."

"Agreed," KC answered, cell in hand, as he paced in the watch commander's office, where several desktop computers displayed critical surveillance images. The walls were covered with memos, wanted posters, and a wide wipe board displaying schedules and deployment. "One other piece of business, then you can get back to sleep."

"You bet," Luke responded sarcastically as he headed for the on-suite bathroom. "I'll be right back to sleep."

"Cash cage had a walk-in with a handful of counterfeit twenties. He got him. Feds already picked him up. Details will be in my log."

"That's it? Luke questioned, turning on a bathroom

light and lifting the toilet seat, "just another quiet night at the Palace."

"You know what they say about Vegas," KC answered as he hung up."

TAMMY LARSON WOKE with daylight gathering outside the window in ICU. She studied the window wondering where she was. She knew it was a hospital. The blood pressure device on her upper arm and another clipped on a finger made that clear. She was filled with anxiety. She wanted to run, get away, hide, but she knew she couldn't, they would soon be there.

They, you know, the ones who would judge her, damn her, put her in jail again, and then one of them came into the room. A nurse turned on a brighter overhead light.

"You're awake. How are you feeling? Any pain, discomfort?"

"My mom still here?"

The Larsons were still sitting in the vacant patient's room UMC provided. They had talked for several hours. Greg Larson's candor surprised his estranged wife. Both admitted to ignoring Tammy's warning signs. Greg confessed to never stopping his role as a general manager. Especially when he came home to Tammy. "She didn't need a GM," he said. "She needed a father."

Naomi admitted to her faults too. "I was busy with my group at the club, my yoga class every morning, and then the afternoon walks with the girls, which was nothing but a bitch session for women who knew menopause was a path to aging. Which is prohibited in Vegas, you know," she teased.

They talked about many things—how the town was

growing, their dog Sparky, the price of gasoline, a herb garden Naomi had started, while Greg bragged about the new glass-windowed pool being built atop the Silver Palace. They talked about much, but they never talked about themselves, their looming divorce, or the days ahead. They both knew it, they could feel it, almost touch it, and it was their look at what had passed. Hindsight was proving much easier than finding a path out of the darkness haunting both.

Naomi dared to bring it all back to the daughter they shared. "Greg, we must find a way to help Tammy. I'm afraid if we don't, we may lose her."

Greg nodded in sober agreement. "Do you have any suggestions, ideas. Mine sort of went south."

"Most of what I know about drugs," Naomi confessed, "relates to aging or weight loss, but Joliot Alonso, remember her, she's been our housekeeper since we bought the place."

It was the first mention and suggestion for them to remember a life once shared, a time when the sky was blue, the house new, and Tammy was in the Seventh Grade Chores.

"Yes." Greg smiled. "I remember Joliot. She used to bring us fresh flowers she picked somewhere."

"I told Joliot about Tammy being in recovery at Red Rock," Naomi explained. "I had to talk to someone. She listened, and then she told me about her niece. A druggy. Cocaine, meth and then heroin. Parents had money. Dad's a veterinarian. They put their daughter in two different programs as an inhouse patient. Neither worked. The kid almost dies of an overdose. Then, mom, a devote Christian, learns of this group in Boulder called, Out of the Shadows. They put the kid in. She graduated five months later.

She's now married and has a child of her own. That was three years ago."

"Can we get Tammy in there?" Larson questioned, but the arrival of the Nurse put their talk on hold.

"Your daughter's awake." The nurse smiled. "She's asking for you."

Larson and Naomi were both quickly on their feet.

———

LUKE'S PLAN for the day was simple. Early in, early out. Barbara Nichols would soon be on her way. Her move-in, although invited, was going to be life changing. He knew that, but it worried him. Sharing a double wide in Del Rio, Arizona, was far different than sharing a life in Vegas. Although it was a life Luke wanted, and dreamed of, until he kissed Candice Harmon. Whoever said a kiss was just a kiss didn't know the emotional aftershocks they could carry. Aftershocks or not, plan A was to get in, get out, and get through the day. Luke parked in employee parking, wondering how close he was to the action Nolan had walked into hours earlier. He climbed out and headed for the employee entrance.

Luke chose his usual shortcut to surveillance by cutting through the men's locker room. There, he found KC King, dressed in jeans and a tee shirt, closing his locker, about to leave.

"Three people in jail and you're going home to watch GMA," Luke teased, pausing.

"My sister-in-law is still here," KC answered, hooking his keys on his belt. "I think she wants to move here. All some people see is the flashing lights, the big names, the money."

"That's what got me." Luke smiled.

"I heard what got you," KC said, offering a fist bump as they both moved for the door. "One naked woman. You know you don't have to jump off a building to find one of those in Vegas."

Luke and KC parted in a back hallway. Luke continued to surveillance. Reaching the unmarked door, Luke paused to take a breath. A lot had changed since the last time he had been inside. He now knew why Gayle Turner thought her career was over, Barbara Nichols would soon be getting into her car for a one-way drive to Vegas, and he had kissed the woman inside. He wondered if the kiss meant as much to her as it did to him. Luke decided he was acting like a fifteen-year-old. He reached for the door and stepped in.

Candice Harmon glanced up from the supervisor's desk as Luke entered the fainter light of the complex. "Welcome to the center of the universe." She smiled. Luke sat down in the chair beside her desk. Candice went on. "You remember the guy suspected of counting in Twenty-One yesterday."

"I do," Luke answered. He was both surprised and relieved Candice was being businesslike. Maybe that was the answer to his question. It meant more to him. He rejected the thought. What could she do? Greet him with a kiss. There was no privacy in the Silver Palace. Especially in the supervisor's office.

Candice adjusted an image of one of the three screens on her desk and then turned to Luke. "Turns out he wasn't counting. He was holding. Our PM watch saw it. We called security. They took him in the back, shook him down and found three cards in his right sleeve."

"Nice work. I'll put something on paper for them."

"What brings you in so early," Candice questioned, crossing her legs and looking at him.

"You were there when Barbara Nichols called last night."

"I remember you taking the call," Candice answered, soberly holding her look.

Luke leaned forward to place his elbows on his knees, deliberately avoiding eye contact. "She's driving to Vegas today. Should arrive sometime this afternoon."

"Does she need a place to stay?"

Luke knew he was being baited. He looked at Candice. "No, Barb and I were once a thing."

"You should have told me," Candice suggested.

"I didn't know," Luke answered. "I invited her when I got hired, but she decided to stay behind. Now she's changed her mind."

"And she'll be staying with you."

"Yeah." Luke nodded.

"That changes things a lot, doesn't it," Candice said, going back to adjusting the screens on her desk.

Luke knew there were no answers he could give to cover what had happened between them. He knew he was wrong in allowing it to happen. He had made advances on a subordinate. He was wrong, and he could feel the heat. He did know he had to continue before it all fell apart. "Frick and Fratt in this morning?" He was referring to the young oriental duo, both students at UNLV, who surveillanced, housed in a former closet the duo turned into a *don't ask room* full of electronics and digital gadgetry.

"Yes," Candice answered coolly. "They're both here."

"Here's what I have in mind."

"Been there, done that," Candice said without looking at Luke.

"I'm talking about Gayle's situation," Luke said, continuing. "Let's put the duo to work discretely and find out how the individual blackmailing her got his info."

Candice allowed herself to follow. "I can fill in some of the blanks. Gayle told me Ted Carter's brother-in-law works for the county down in Laughlin. I don't know what he does but he finds a picture of Gayle, you think maybe dickhead isn't part of that. Anyway, he matches the mug he has of Gayle with a picture of an eighteen-year-old arrested for prostitution in Laughlin twenty-four years ago by the name of Gayle Thompson. Carter gets the pictures and shows them to Gayle. She melts, so he knows he's onto something good. Either she resigns or this will find a way to HR, but like I said last night, none of this comes from me."

"We put the duo on this, and they succeed in pulling the curtain back, Gayle will never know anything."

"I'll get them in here."

Luke was pleased to see Candice excited.

————

DAWN WILDER, former escort for Cloud Nine, turned streetwalker, only to be picked up by a director of security, and then insulted with a hang-up by her sister because she was in Vegas, was up early getting ready for work. Only this time, after a night of soul searching, she was about to show the world they could all get screwed. Beauty was about to take on the beast. Dawn was going out to find a job. A job that had nothing to do with sex, if there was such a job in Vegas. She swept the long blonde hair back into a conservative fold she'd seen on a local Newscaster, tried her best for light makeup, chose a pair of wide-legged slacks she'd last worn at someone's graduation, a high-necked blouse and a pair of Sketchers. She liked her look. It was different, not likely anyone who knew her before would recognize her with this all-American girl look, but as she decided earlier, they could all get screwed.

She caught a southbound bus headed for the Strip. It was crowded. Young, old and in between. They were on their way to work, Dawn decided.

She noticed none of the men paid much attention to her. It made Dawn smile. Her disguise was working. She got off the bus at a stop near Mandalay Bay. The sun was out. She enjoyed the short walk. At the front desk, she asked a clerk how to find human resources.

"Do you have an appointment?"

Dawn smiled. "No, I'm looking for a position."

The front desk agent returned her smile. "You can go online and apply. Just go to our website, and you'll see the positions we have open. Click on the one that fits, and it will walk you through the application process. They'll probably ask you to attach your resume."

"Oh," Dawn said. "Just as I thought." She turned and walked away. The further she got from the front desk, the more she hurried. She wanted out. Once outside, Dawn thought about what she had been told. A resume, why hadn't she thought of that? She could surf the net with her phone, but she couldn't print shit. She didn't have a printer. Who came to Vegas with a printer? She came to Vegas from New Port Beach with a married neighbor who said he just wanted to have fun. Fun meant getting naked and dancing in front of him. He left Vegas without her.

A resume—Dawn couldn't imagine what to put on it. The truth wouldn't work. Graduate of Corona Del Mar High, french fry specialist at Jack in the Box, order clerk at Walmart, where she pushed around a four-wheeled cart with six shelves for minimum wage, or the Biggy she ran away from, server at Denny's, evening shift, where all tips were pooled and dived, to include the manager.

Dawn knew the casinos. She'd been to most, seen the best shows, had the best dinners, but it was all somebody else's money. Money, she knew, would go away. There were no career escorts, call girls, or streetwalkers. Sex for sale in Vegas was a crime. She had to find a way out of it. She had to get her sister to stop thinking what she was thinking. She sent them money every month, where was the thank you? The search continued. Dawn tried her walk-in approach at the Luxor, Paris, the Bellagio, the Wynne, and the Cosmo. All suggested she apply online.

Heat and reality were setting in. Dawn wasn't sure how far she had walked, but it was the most she had ever done in Vegas. Not only was the heat of the day becoming an issue so was the wall of reality she ran into. No one wanted to talk. No one cared she wasn't carrying a resume. The voices were different, but all were saying the same thing—apply online. She was not only searching for a new job, she was searching for a new life. She was walking with the crowd when she saw a familiar sign—Denny's. She stopped to stare. Denny's on the Strip. Why would she have noticed? Why would anyone? Dawn walked closer. A sign in the window read, Open— 24 HOURS. A smaller one read, *Help Wanted*. Dawn was desperate. Memories from her long years at Denny's in Hunting Beach poured in. It wasn't likely they would ask her to apply online. She adjusted the bag on her shoulder, and her pride and moved for the door.

"I saw a sign in the window saying help wanted," Dawn said to the man standing at a cash register at the end of a busy lunch counter. More sat at tables lining the windows with a Strip view. Dawn chose the man because he was wearing a tie. She knew he was likely the manager.

The man in the tie gave Dawn a look and smiled. "Sorry, miss, we only consider those living in Vegas." Dawn returned his smile. It was the first confidence she had felt all day. "I live here," she said with a glance around, "and your store looks familiar. I'd guess you've got at least five working the front, another six, seven in the back. I did four years at Denny's in Hunting Beach."

The *Tie's* smile faded. "How do I know you're not hustling me."

"Let's see," Dawn answered. "At the beach, my manager was Will Simpson. Then Jim Ferris. I started on evenings, then days. Like you, we ran with no less than five."

"When can you start?" The *Tie* questioned.

"I'm bringing you experience," Dawn suggested.

"And I'm offering you a job. I'll do twelve fifty and you keep the tips. No sharing. When can you start?"

A near-empty bus took Dawn north on the Strip until the crowds, the traffic, and the *Welcome to Fabulous Las Vegas* sign faded far behind. On the bus, Dawn did the math. Would Denny's wage pay her rent? Would tips be good? This was Vegas, tips would be more than the wage. Dawn got off the bus two blocks from her apartment. She had never walked so far without someone hitting on her. Her Fort Wayne costume was working. The reality of giving up sex and big money was grim when compared to what a return to Denny's meant. Maybe when she got home, she'd call her sister and hang up on the bitch. She climbed the stairs to her second-floor apartment and found an envelope taped on her door. She tore it open and read...

Due to rising costs of infrastructure maintenance for the complex, we are forced to announce a twenty percent increase in monthly rents. Please note the first and last monies deposited on occupancy must likewise be increased by twenty percent. These monies are due on or before your next scheduled rent payment.

Thank you—Horizon Palms Management.

LUKE MITCHEL and Candice Harmon met in the supervisor's office in surveillance with the Chinese duo, known as Frick & Fratt. Prior to the meeting, Luke went over the background of the two. He had met and worked with both before but hadn't looked at their resumes. He didn't need to. Gayle Turner, his OIC of surveillance, said they were good, and they were, but Gayle wasn't there, and this was all about her.

Their true names were Lee Kang, age twenty-four, and Jay Roberts, age twenty-three. Both were engineering students from UNLV. They met and became friends in college. Gayle Turner hired them as consultants after meeting them at the annual electronics show in Las Vegas. Kang, native Chinese, was from Beijing, and Roberts, a second-generation Chinese, was from Lompoc, California. Luke preferred the Frick and Fratt names they were tagged with better than their real names.

After the two were invited into the room, Candice asked a team member on the other side of the glass separating them from surveillance ops for cover while they met. Luke reminded the two what was going to be discussed was sensitive and had to be treated as confidential. Both nodded in agreement. Luke went further by advising that the tools and procedures they chose were their own and had nothing to do with the Silver Palace. Again, they nodded acceptance.

Candice began by announcing the subject of the inquiry was Gayle Turner, and her alleged arrest for prostitution when she was age eighteen, twenty-one years ago in the city of Laughlin. The two men exchanged looks. Gayle had hired both.

Luke added Gayle was being extorted by an individual who claimed to have learned of her arrest, as well as her concealment of it when the Silver Palace hired her. "We need the truth," Luke added. "We need to know who dug into these old records, when and why."

The two men made notes. Looking at their notes upside down, Luke saw they were writing in Chinese. He asked if they had any questions. Frick and Fratt exchanged a look and then Frick spoke. "You said Gayle is being extorted. Then you must know the identity of the blackmailer? Knowing who this individual is will be vital in understanding the motive."

"I'm not surprised by your question," Luke answered. "The blackmailer is among us. He's on the other side of the glass wall. You both know him. I thought I did, too. I'm talking about Ted Carter."

The two men exchanged a look. Neither looked to the six agents on the other side of the glass wall watching the montage of ever-changing video images.

"Time is critical," Luke suggested. "If you need help, reach out to Candice. She'll find me."

"Gayle has no knowledge of what we're asking you to

do," Candice added as the two men stood. "It has to stay that way."

"Have either of you spoken with her?" Luke questioned as the two men pushed to their feet. Both shook their heads. "Then the clock is ticking. Find us the answers."

Both men gave the customary Chinese bow and turned for the door.

"You don't suppose we'll see this on TikTok, do you?" Candice said with a look at Luke.

THE GENERAL MANAGER of the Silver Palace, Greg Larson, dressed in suit and tie was behind his desk as Jackie Fallon, his brunette thirty-year-old executive assistant, read through the proposed agenda for the day.

"At eleven, the card room manager will brief you on the proposal for the Poker Channel's coverage of our next tournament," Jackie read from her laptop.

Larson raised his hand. Jackie paused.

"Could you get us the numbers from the Poker Channel's last tournament? I'm not sure who hosted it."

Jackie made an entry and continued. "Lunch at the Shade of the Palm with Councilman Brenner. We need his vote on our plans for the Grand Prix, and he'll probably ask for a bump up with rooms when his adult son comes in next week."

"Can you handle that?"

"Of course. And then, at two thirty, two of our Chinese investors are arriving for their meet and greet. You may recall you made reservations for them at Hard Rock. Escorts, as per your suggestion, are being provided by Cloud Nine."

"All right, but after fifteen minutes max, you reach out and announce something important requires my presence, and we'll send them on the way. They'll be ready to go by then anyway."

Jackie made another note on her laptop before continuing. "Following the investors is your daily brief with the director of security and then at three the new chef would like—"

Larson raised his hand again. "Cancel Luke until tomorrow. He'll understand and tell the chef whatever you have to tell a chef. I'm out of here at three. Tammy's being moved from UMC to a recovery group in Boulder, called Out of the Shadows. Ever heard of them?"

"Sorry, I haven't."

"They're some Christian operation. I looked at them on Google. They look like a bunch of, *what do we do now* grads from ORU. Naomi set it up. She'll fill in the blanks for me," Larson added.

"Naomi, your ex?" Jackie questioned.

"Is that a problem?"

"No, but I thought you and Charlotte were deciding Tammy's care."

"True, but regardless of who decides what, Naomi and I are her parents. Charlotte and I talked, and she agreed this was best for all concerned."

Jackie nodded acceptance knowing there was more than what was being presented. "So, it's hello, goodbye to our Chinese friends on their way to the Hard Rock, and what's cooking for the new chef."

"Speaking of cooking, do you suppose you could order us a couple of those breakfast rolls with nuts on top."

———

TAMMY LARSON WAS SEDATED and strapped on a wheeled
stretcher in the ICU at UMC on West Charleton Boulevard. Her mother, Naomi, walked with her as two male
attendants pushed Tammy's stretcher to an elevator. On
the ground level, she was wheeled to a waiting medical
transport van. Naomi stayed with her daughter until she
was loaded in the van.

"You have the address," Naomi said to the attendants.
"I'll meet you there." Naomi waited until the transport
van pulled away before she turned to her SUV.

Boulder City founded with the construction of the
Hoover Dam in 1931, was twenty-six miles south of Las
Vegas. A population of just over fifteen thousand gave
Boulder a small-town persona. Eight miles from the
center of Boulder was the Out of The Shadows Ranch.
Its eighteen acres was surrounded by flat, barren desert.
The ranch house, a sprawling contemporary one-story
building, had fourteen bedrooms, a major kitchen, an
assembly hall, six counseling rooms and several offices.
A nearby barn and coral housed eight horses.

Add the chickens, a vegetable garden, three large
dogs and two cats along with two dusty pickup trucks,
and you have the makings of a ranch.

The transport van carrying Tammy Larson arrived
with Naomi's SUV not far behind. Several long-haired,
bearded thirty-year-olds in jeans came out as Tammy,
still quiet from the sedative, was offloaded and wheeled
inside. Others joined in unloading Naomi's SUV.

Naomi followed the attendants with her daughter. As
Tammy's stretcher was wheeled inside and down a hallway, a young man appeared. He signaled Naomi to wait.

"I'm Josh Logan." He offered Naomi a hand. He was
thirty-something, dressed casually. They shook hands as
Naomi watched her daughter disappear into a distant

room. "You must be Naomi. Welcome to Out of the Shadows. I appreciate you filling out all we need online. As I mentioned, we ask you to wait at least two hours before visiting. This assures your daughter will be drug-free when you come in. It also allows us to learn who Tammy Larson is, and how we might be able to help her."

"You might be able to help?" Naomi wanted assurance.

"You didn't create Tammy's problems. Nor did we. All we can do is offer our help in finding her a new path forward."

"You would call me." Naomi stared down the hallway where Tammy disappeared. "If there's anything."

"Of course, and you can call us as often as you like, but no private calls until later."

Naomi returned her attention to Josh. "This is difficult. Leaving her is painful. I didn't even tell her goodbye."

"Leaving your daughter here may be painful, but saying goodbye to her graveside would be far worse."

———

LUKE WAS in his office reviewing security logs. He was trying to concentrate but finding it difficult. His thoughts kept going to three women. Barbara Nichols, now only hours away from arriving, Gayle Turner, a frightened woman being blackmailed by a secret past, and Dawn Wilder, a former escort, streetwalker or whore. Whoever Dawn was, Luke felt he had turned her life upside down. He felt guilty about it, but other than picking her up off the street, he wasn't sure what to do, and then he thought of Charlotte Johnson. When he was once filled with doubt over what to do, or how to do it, Charlotte pushed him in the right direction. Maybe she could help again. Luke reached for the phone.

Charlotte was in her office at the Cosmopolitan several blocks away. She answered her cell after a quick glance at caller ID. "Well, this is a surprise," she said with the phone to an ear. "You finally ready to make your move over here, Luke?"

"Not right now," Luke answered. "But the day's not over."

"What has you calling, home boy?" Charlotte teased.

"Cutting to the chase," Luke explained awkwardly. "There's this twenty-eight-year-old, she turns a lot of heads. She knows the town, has a background in service. She'd make a great server in your card room, slots, somewhere?"

"You want help finding this girl a position," Charlotte countered. "What's her name?"

"Dawn, Dawn Wilder," Luke answered.

Charlotte noted, "Okay, Mr. Director, here's what I can do. I'll call HR and give them Dawn's name. We had a staff meeting this morning and HR talked about vacancies. Give me Dawn's number. If I have any juice, they'll call her. Tell her to be ready for it. Okay?"

Luke gave Charlotte Dawn's cell number.

"You realize you now owe me?" Charlotte reminded Luke.

"Big time," He was pleased.

"So, what's the latest on your GM and Tammy?" Charlotte questioned.

Luke was surprised. Charlotte and Greg Larson lived together, or did they? Her question suggested otherwise.

Luke avoided a direct answer. "Latest gossip today is

Tammy is being transferred from UMC to a recovery facility in Boulder."

"Let's hope they're not selling dope at this one," Charlotte answered sarcastically.

"Been uphill for them, hasn't it," Luke suggested, knowing he was on sensitive ground.

"Luke, I've got another call. It's the GM."

"Charlotte, you're gold. Thanks."

Luke's next call was to Dawn's cell. Charlotte had proven her worth, although her question about Greg Larson worried him. It was obvious something happened. The answer Luke got after dialing Dawn's cell surprised him. It was a recording. "The individual you are calling is not available. At the tone, please leave a message."

Luke was about to hang up when Dawn's voice answered, "This is Dawn."

"Dawn, it's Luke Mitchel."

"Oh, I'm so happy you called." Dawn's sacrarium was obvious. "I thought of you today as I walked by the Silver Palace and nine other casinos. Then I found Denny's. Did you know there's a Denny's on the Strip? I didn't, but I do now. I start there tomorrow night. Be sure to stop by."

"I understand this is a difficult time for you, Dawn," Luke said, ignoring her sarcasm. "But you need to listen and listen carefully. You need to go online, find the Cosmopolitan and apply for a position as a server. Human resources from the Cosmo will call you. They will offer you a position as a server. Their wage is better than Denny's, and tips at the Cosmo will likely exceed your wage. The choice is yours, but you have to act immediately. Now, just do it." Luke hung up.

Immediately his telephone rang. It had to be Dawn.

He'd had it with this kid. Didn't she understand help when it was offered. He was angry. He grabbed the receiver. "This is Luke."

"Luke, it's Jackie. Is everything okay?"

"Yeah, sorry, Jackie. It's been one of those days. You know."

"Oh, so, I'm not alone," Jackie answered.

"Hard to imagine you being alone," Luke answered.

"Let's save that for another day," Jackie suggested. "I'm calling because the general manager has a conflict. He would like to delay your daily until tomorrow."

"Tomorrow's fine," Luke answered. "Thanks for the heads-up."

"You're welcome," Jackie added and hung up.

Luke had one more call to make before he headed for his condo to make sure he was there for Barbara's arrival. He dialed surveillance.

"Surveillance, this is Candice."

"Candice, it's Luke. I'm out of here in a couple of minutes. Anything from the duo?"

"That's right, your friend Barbara arrives today. You must be excited."

Luke felt the sarcasm in Candice's every word. It angered him, but he wasn't about to show it. Showing it would reward Candice, and he'd had enough with sarcastic women for the day. "My question was about the duo," he repeated soberly.

"The duo, they're doing what duos do, I guess. No word yet."

"I'll be on my cell," Luke said and hung up. Luke's drive from the Strip to his condo in Henderson helped. He was speeding and he knew it, but he was glad to be getting away. The irony was he was running from Vegas to meet someone who was arriving. He pushed his speed even higher. Maybe he'd have time for a drink before she arrived. His plan worked. He arrived before Barbara's promised call. She was to call from when Route 515 brought her to the Henderson City Limits. The planned call would mean she was only minutes away. Luke's plan for a drink when he got home changed. He decided to straighten the place before Barb's arrival. He started in the bedroom. The Marine corps had taught him how to make a bunk. His king-size bed wasn't a bunk, but he made sure the sheets were tight, pillows straightened and positioned. The master closet was next. Everything was hung properly. He lined up several pairs of shoes on the closet floor.

Candice, as a licensed realtor, had not only sold him the condo, but she included a housekeeper from the Silver Palace who cleaned houses on her days off. Her schedule was a visit every two weeks. Knowing Barbara was coming, Luke paid her a bonus and had her clean earlier in the day. It showed. Luke didn't have to clean toilets, take out trash, or anything else. Isabella did an excellent job. The fresh flowers on his living room table proved it. Luke was pouring a Jack and Coke when his cell phone chattered. It was Barbara.

"Hey, lady, you're almost home."

"I haven't seen this much traffic since I left Pittsburg."

"Welcome to my world. Did you put my address in your nav system?"

"On my cell. I'm eleven minutes away."

"You'll see my car in back. I'll be the guy standing beside it."

"Been a while since I've seen you."

After Barbara's call Luke finished pouring his drink. He took a heavy swallow and headed downstairs. The afternoon heat was typical Vegas. Hot. Luke glanced at his watch. He still had five or six minutes. He wondered how much stuff Barb would have in her SUV. The heat drove Luke to the shade from a palm. First thing, he decided, would be the greeting, which excited him, and he knew from Barb's tone she was excited too. After the hugs, kisses, and the, *you look great* was exchanged, he'd take her upstairs for a look at the condo. She would love it, and he was going to love having her in it. Barb could relax, look around, while he unloaded the SUV. Two or three trips up and down the stairs should do it. It would be nice to have his closets full. Especially with Barbara's stuff. Luke looked at his watch. It was time.

He watched the driveway. Her SUV would have Arizona plates. A car appeared. Luke's heart raced. No, it was a tenant. Luke had seen the woman before. She parked several spaces away and hurried to the front courtyard.

Luke glanced at his watch. Barb's time was up, she had made a wrong turn. Missed the street. Come on, Barb, it's hot. His cell was clipped on his belt. He looked at it. It was silent. She would be weary from the drive. They could go to bed early. Imagining he'd be sleeping with a beautiful woman, in his condo, every night, brought memories of Barbara's naked beauty, her warmth. This woman belonged in Las Vegas. The heat was becoming an annoyance. Luke wiped sweat from his forehead. He moved closer to the palm, glanced again at his watch. Okay, she was lost. Come on, Barb. Where are you? Call me.

Luke gave in to his inpatients. He pulled the phone from his belt and punched Barb's contact number. Cell phone to his ear, he listened to it ring. She had to be nearby. Any moment she would turn into the driveway, but whatever the reason was, she didn't answer. Luke's excitement gave way to worry. He walked to the head of the driveway and looked in both directions. The street was quiet. He called her number a third time. Again, there was no answer. Where was she? Luke called again. It rang five times, unanswered. Luke gripped the cell in hand as he again looked both directions on the street in front of his complex. A kid went by on an electric skateboard followed by a truck loaded with bottled water. Luke wiped more sweat from his forehead. He looked at his watch as if that would solve the problem. "Damn it." He groaned, turning to the courtyard.

In the kitchen, Luke laid his cell on the butcher block where he hoped it would ring. He downed the rest of the drink poured earlier. He was worried. He wouldn't allow himself to accept it as fright, but where the hell was she? What could he do to find her? He tried calling her twice more. Both calls went unanswered. Nearly an hour and a half passed. It was time to call the police. What would the police do? *Oh your girlfriend is late, so you called nine-one-one. Sure, you were a cop in LA.*

The police weren't about to launch a citywide search because Barbara Nichols was late. He decided he didn't care. He picked up his cell to call them, but a solid knock sounded on his door. Luke dropped the cell and bolted for the door. It had to be her. Luke pulled the door open. His smile disappeared. In front of him stood a tall, uniformed Nevada State Trooper. "Sorry to disturb you, sir," the trooper said. "Are you familiar with a woman by the name of Barbara Nichols?"

"Yes, where is she, what happened?" Fear gripped Luke's throat.

"Your address was on her cell. Unfortunately, she was in an accident. The five-fifteen and Horizon Drive."

"An accident!" Luke gripped the edge of the door. "Where is she?"

"I'm sorry to report the accident was fatal," the trooper added. "Barbara Nichols died in the collision with a truck."

Luke was shocked. He held the door for support. His head dropped. "No, that can't be."

The trooper studied Luke. "I'm sorry, but I have to ask. Are you related to this lady? Perhaps you know how we could reach her family?"

Luke drew in a breath before looking to the trooper. "She was on her way here. I don't...I'm not familiar with her family."

"I'm sorry to bring this to you," the trooper said. "Her body will be taken to the Clark County Coroner. If you have any questions give them a call."

Luke nodded. He didn't have any words. The trooper offered a nod and turned away. Luke continued his hold on the door, he was afraid to let go. How could this be? He had just talked to her, they had plans. She was moving in. Now her body was on its way to the county morgue. How could she be gone? Luke found himself standing in the heat with the door open. He took a deep breath, stepped back and slammed the door. He sat on the couch with his head in his hands and wept. He wanted to talk to her, he wanted to see her, hold her, kiss her, help in some way, anyway, but she was dead. Their dream was dead.

She was gone and Luke knew part of him was gone too. He could see her when he closed his eyes. Agony kept him on the couch for a long hours. Finally, Luke raised his head and saw the arrangement of flowers setting on the living room table in front of him. He wiped a tear from his face and studied them. The flowers were like Barb. They were beautiful but they were no longer alive. They had been cut, they would soon fade. Luke knew he had to help. He was disappointed he couldn't remember the trooper's name that brought the news of the accident.

He couldn't even remember where the trooper said the accident occurred. He knew in order to help he needed details. He put on a fresh shirt and drove into Las Vegas on Interstate 215. He was going to the Nevada Highway Patrol Station on West Sunset in Las Vegas. He had been there before. After becoming director of security at the Silver Palace, he drove there and introduced himself to the commanding officer as well as many troopers he could find. They wore badges, and they carried guns. They were allies. There would be times when they needed him, but tonight, he needed them.

Luke exited the 215 at South Decatur and turned toward Sunset Road where the Nevada State Highway Patrol Station was located. He welcomed the chance to be around cops as he wheeled into guest parking. Cops didn't cry, they were tough, they believed in justice, and there was the unspoken Brotherhood of the Badge. Luke was no longer a police officer, but he had learned being a cop wasn't something you ever got over. Knowing he'd be walking through the sensors, Luke left his handgun in the Tesla.

Inside, Luke introduced himself to the officer at the front desk by showing his badge and ID. He was quickly traded to the watch commander. The uniformed lieutenant, a balding, robust-looking fifty-year-old man offered Luke an open hand as he led the way to the privacy of his office. "I understand you're the director of security at the Silver Palace." The lieutenant smiled.

"You've got more guns working for you than I have. How can we help you this evening?"

Luke straightened himself in his chair, leaned forward and gripped his hands together. The lieutenant read it all.

Luke steadied himself and looked directly at the lieutenant. "Barbara Nichols died in a traffic accident this afternoon. She died with her cell phone showing directions to my condo."

The lieutenant knew exactly what Luke was talking about. His question was direct, "Why is this woman of interest to you?"

Luke was candid. "She's the woman I loved. No, she's the woman I love."

The lieutenant nodded. "Sit tight. I'll be right back." He got up and left the room.

There was a police scanner on the lieutenant's desk. Luke listened to the chatter between dispatch and cars in the field. His eyes scanned the walls. A large wipe board showed deployments and scheduling. A corkboard was covered with pinned memos, announcements, and photos depicting officers at the scene of accidents. Another wall displayed a framed picture of the president, the governor, and a mix of VIPs.

The office door opened, the lieutenant returned, carrying a multi-paged report. He pushed the packet into Luke's hands.

"All you need to know is in there. Truck driver went to jail for DUI. Meth, we think. I do have to ask you to treat our report as confidential."

Luke pushed to his feet and leafed through the pages. He fought emotions and looked to the lieutenant, offering a hand. They shook again.

"I appreciate this," Luke said. "When you get downtown, stop by the Silver Palace and mention my name."

———

LUKE LAID the accident report on the passenger's seat in his Tesla and sped away from the Nevada Highway Patrol. He admitted to himself he was driving fast to nowhere. He slowed down and turned into a Walmart parking lot. He parked beneath an overheard lamp, set the brake, and looked at the report. It was as if the white, silent pages were daring him to touch. Finally, Luke grabbed the report and crushed it with both hands, growling. "You sonofabitch."

A woman with gray hair in an SUV with a big dog that didn't like Luke's voice started her car, gave him a look of contempt, and drove away. In the Telsa Luke raised his middle finger at the woman, then he began the task, unfolding the wrinkled, crumpled, torn pages of the report, trying to make them readable.

———

EIGHTEEN-YEAR-OLD TAMMY LARSON stood on the back porch of the Out of the Shadows ranch house looking at the night sky. She couldn't remember the last time she deliberately looked up at the stars, the Milky Way, the planets. There was Saturn, and then she remembered, it made her smile. Ninth-grade science class. She loved astronomy, and the beauty of it was still there, filling the sky, and then her stomach tightened. She gagged, and threw up on the porch. Not once, not twice but three times, and not quietly.

An on-duty attendant, having heard Tammy and her

aftershock gagging, arrived on the porch. She laid a hand on Tammy's shoulder. "Aftershocks," the attendant suggested. "Detox is a bitch. You okay?"

Tammy, hanging onto a post for the porch roof, managed a nod while the attendant went for a nearby hose. She turned the water on and began flushing away debris. "Some of the grass down there that's really green, is thanks to my detox. You want me to stay out here with you?"

Tammy managed another nod before she spoke. "Thanks, glad I made something greener. I'm okay."

The attendant coiled the hose, smiled and went inside. Tammy sat down on a nearby porch swing. Although, as soon as the swing moved, she stopped it. The attendant's help made Tammy think of the remarks one of the men offered before dinner. "When you use drugs, someone's going to have to clean up after you. You're going to make a mess. Think about why you're here. Someone is cleaning up after you. Why? Because they love you. We're not a cheap date. We probably cost as much as your drugs. The path you've chosen is littered with money. Someone is paying for this. Is this the best you can do with their money? We think we can make you a better deal. You know what it is? Of course you do. And we're going to help you find that dream. Dreams are much better than drugs."

———————

TAMMY COULDN'T REMEMBER what it was they put in front of her for dinner. She did hear she was one of four newbies out of the collection of twenty-six young men and women gathered in the dining room. The tables were set in squares, so you weren't looking at someone's back, you were looking at their face. She didn't eat much, but the staff waiter did insist she drink. A lot. He was polite, but insistent. Her wake-up from her transfer and sedation had come as a surprise. There were five people in her room. One male staff member and four young women, guests, she would learn they were called. The surprise was they were all on their knees and they were all praying, aloud, and not in unison. It was as if she was in a busy bus station until one of the girls noticed Tammy's eyes were open.

"Praise the Lord, she's awake."

The male staff member pushed to his feet, smiled, and laid a hand on Tammy's sheet-covered foot. "Welcome, to Out of the Shadows, Tammy."

The girls were all quickly on their feet. All offered smiles and encouragement. "Glad you're here, nice to meet you, see you at dinner, the dogs don't bite, neither does the staff." Again, they talked over one another and then even more surprising, they all left.

"Drink," the staffer encouraged. "We discourage dehydration."

Tammy, careful with her balance, dared to use the bathroom. Returning to her bed, she found a book on her bedside table, *God's Promises*. So, she was locked up with a bunch of Jesus freaks. Whose idea was this and how could she get away? Tammy laid in bed and listened. It was strangely quiet. No one invaded her space claiming they had all the answers. Worried, Tammy eventually went to the door and eased it open.

"Hi." A girl in jeans smiled as she passed. Tammy quickly closed the door.

In addition to *God's Promises*, Tammy found some of her own clothes hanging in the closet. She thanked her mother for that. A knock on her door was followed by a girl's voice announcing, "Dinner at six. Come as you are."

And Tammy did, in jeans. Before they were served, they were asked to bow their heads in prayer. "Do I have someone who feels? Yes, thank you," the male staffer said, pointing to a raised hand at another table. Tammy, like the others, bowed her head.

"Lord," an unidentified male voice somewhere from behind Tammy spoke. "Thank you for this day. Thank you for this our daily bread…and thank you, I haven't had any meth in five days."

The unidentified youth's prayer was followed by applause. Tammy included hers.

————

THIRTY-SEVEN MILES away at the intersection of Horizon Drive and Paradise Road in the city of Henderson, Luke Mitchel sat on the cement curb beneath a street lamp, elbows on his knees, staring into the shadowy nighttime street, which was littered with shrouds of wrinkled police tape, soiled scattered cotton pads, a piece of polished chrome from a headlamp, and small crystals of forgotten broken glass swept to an opposing curb. A set of headlamps approached, closing quickly on the intersection, to sweep by in a noisy flash. The collar on Luke's jacket danced in the wake from the car. The quiet returned. Luke thought about where he was. Only miles from home, but reality was even closer, and Luke knew close didn't count. The headlamps of another approaching car appeared in the distance.

SEVENTEEN

WHEN IT CAN'T GET ANY...

TAMMY WASN'T sure how she felt about coming to Out of the Shadows, but she did know sleep without meth was going to be a challenge. She took a final look at the star-filled sky and headed inside. She was surprised to find a handwritten note and a white tablet waiting on her bedside table. She picked up the note.

> *"Welcome to the new you. You're in charge of your life. It can be filled with joy, contentment, and adventure. You don't have to do it alone. The God who created all, is ready to help. Why, because He created you to find joy, contentment, and adventure. Allow us to travel along.*
>
> *The white tablet will help you sleep tonight, so will our prayers."*

Tammy swallowed the white tablet in the bathroom along with several glasses of water. She returned to the bedroom and took off her jeans. The room had no clock, but she knew it was late. It was quiet with the exception of the distant faint sound of a female weeping. Several other voices joined with the individual crying and then the quiet returned.

If those in charge were trying to make an impression it was working. Tammy was on the verge of something she had almost forgotten, Hope! Climbing into bed, Tammy was reaching for the bedside lamp when she noticed the book again.

Its title was intriguing, *God's Promises*. Tammy gave into curiosity. She picked up the book, opened it, randomly, and read...

> *And do not seek what you should eat or what you should drink, nor have an anxious mind. For all these things the nations of the world seek after, and your father knows that you need these things, but seek the Kingdom of God, and all these things shall be added to you.*

Random, or with a little help from God—Tammy wasn't sure which—but the idea that God might be involved was comforting. She closed the book and set it aside before turning off the light. Somewhere in the distance, a rooster crowded. Was it really that late, or was it really that early? Another choice. Another chance. Another day. Another run for the bathroom. Tammy made it to the toilet where she went to her knees and threw up in the bowl.

———

GREG LARSON WAS SHOCKED at what time it was. Had he and Naomi really sat and talked for hours? The place where they met unnerved Larson, but it seemed logical.

He found himself at the kitchen table in the house he and Naomi had bought nineteen years earlier.

"Let's meet where we used to talk," Naomi suggested when he called. "No one will disturb us, no one will urge us to have another drink, the music won't be too loud, and Sparky will be glad to see you."

Larson agreed. They ordered pizza and talked. He was surprised to learn the suggestion for the place in Boulder came from Naomi's housekeeper. Someone with a life-threatening drug problem had found success there. "Makes sense," Naomi argued. "If she can make this place look like home, maybe she could help with Tammy."

Larson was surprised at Naomi's remark about someone making her house look like a home. Why would Naomi no longer think of the house as her home? What woman wouldn't want to live alone in the hills above Las Vegas with five bedrooms, four baths, a man cave, an office, two fireplaces, a dining room with seating for ten, a pool, a three-car garage, and a garden with its own canopy. He always assumed Naomi would stay there after their divorce settlement. Now, he was wondering what her plans were. He knew he couldn't ask. At least, he shouldn't.

The house was secondary to what had drawn them together and that was their daughter Tammy. "Tam Marie Larson." Greg smiled after a drink from a wine cooler that came with the pizza. "I remember we tried every female name we could find in the Las Vegas telephone book. Remember those big suckers? They used to throw them in our driveway."

"I used the phone book," Naomi defended. "You used the internet. Remember you got all hung up on the names Phyliss and Shannon."

"They were two of the most popular female names," Larson defended.

"Until we met Nurse Tam Marie Hanson." Naomi smiled.

"I think it was Henson," Larson corrected.

"It was Hanson," Naomi argued. "But it wasn't her last name we chose to steal."

"I hope we got more than the name right this time," Larson suggested.

Naomi nodded in agreement. "Wait til you meet them. The gang out at Out of the Shadows. They're a little unusual, but I really felt comfortable with them when I drove away."

"Unusual in what way," Larson asked.

Naomi pushed at a pizza crust with a polished nail, then found Larson's eyes. "Kinda like cowboys, sort of holdovers from a decade ago, but sincere and friendly."

"Friendly as in, *show me the money?*"

"Yeah, but more. You'll see."

"Gotta be better than what I chose. I'm hoping you got it right. Our daughter's sleeping with them tonight."

Naomi studied her estranged husband's face. "How did we get where we are, Greg? How did we not see what was happening to Tammy?"

Larson shrugged his shoulders. "I've asked myself the same question. I like blaming you. I had a Palace to take care of. Seriously though, together we created Tammy yet somehow we both spent more time looking at ourselves than we did at her."

"I'm sorry, Greg."

"Me too," Larson assured. "Tammy fell into a pit we created. Let's make sure we don't leave her there."

"But then there's the days, weeks, and months that have to follow. It's frightening."

"I promise you won't have to do it alone."

"But we already failed once. What happens if we..." Naomi chose not to finish.

Larson reached across the table and took Naomi's hand. "If we fall down, we'll dust ourselves off, get up, and start all over again."

Naomi sniffed and forced a smile. "I hope you're right."

"Come on," Larson said, releasing Naomi's hand. "You ever know me to get it wrong?"

Sparky, their big Rottweiler, wandered into the room. The dog looked at them, then chose to lie down at Greg's feet. Larson reached down to pet the dog.

"He probably wants breakfast," Naomi suggested.

The remark made Larson glance at his watch. "Sorry, I've kept you up most of the night."

"It's a good night when we can agree on how to help our daughter."

Larson pushed to his feet and looked at the leftovers. "You want some help cleaning up."

"No, I've got this great housekeeper. Seriously, Greg, I appreciate you coming up here tonight. I couldn't do this without you."

"Nor I, without you," Larson answered as their eyes met. Their words went much further. They both knew it. Sparky pushed up into a sitting position. "I think he's saying enough for tonight. I'll give you a call tomorrow."

"Good night, Greg," Naomi answered with tears welling in her eyes.

Larson smiled, turned and walked away.

———

Luke Mitchel made the short drive home from the scene of the fatal crash. He turned the lights on, poured himself a drink in the kitchen and carried it to the bedroom. There, in the master bath, he brushed his teeth and spit in the sink, before looking at his image in the mirror. He needed a shave. That could wait until morning. He sat on the bed and pushed his shoes off. He was pulling at a sock when his cell phone gave an electronic chirp. It was a sound he programmed for calls from security at the Silver Palace. He had the phone in hand for its third ring.

"This is Luke."

"Morning, boss," KC King said in his ear. "I'm not calling with good news."

"I'm listening," Luke assured.

"Policy dictates when we have an employee death on property you have to be informed."

"Go on," Luke urged.

"Engineer by the name of Stillman. Ron Stillman."

"Right, I remember him. Smoking weed on forty-something."

"Well," KC continued. "He's not smoking anymore. He hung himself in the engineering locker room. Surveillance shows him going in about two hours ago."

"And he's dead?"

"Yeah, we're certain of that. Givens went in about twenty minutes ago, looking for a wrench for the chain on the moped used in guest parking. He found him. Called me. I called you."

"Jesus."

"I'm sure he got called too."

"I'll be in, KC."

"I'll be waiting."

WHEN GREG LARSON drove out of the hills in the Lakes District to his condo in Angel Park, just blocks off the Strip, he had the feeling he had left something valuable behind. He tried dismissing it as nostalgia, but the nagging grip it held wouldn't go away. Who wouldn't be feeling strange with a daughter in drug rehab a second time, an almost ex-wife crying for help and a live-in lover who was no longer a live-in. He was tempted to drive to the Silver Palace and get lost in it like a tourist, but tomorrow would come soon enough. Maybe he could get a couple hours sleep if Charlotte hadn't taken away all of the nighttime drugs he pilfered from her on a regular basis. He parked in the gated underground garage and took the elevator to his second-floor condo.

Opening the door to his condo, Larson paused to listen to the silence. He closed the door quietly and turned on the lights. He was beginning to understand the haunting feeling he brought with him. He was lonely and he knew the irony was he wasn't the only one alone. Naomi was alone at the Lakes, Tammy was alone somewhere out in Boulder, Charlotte was alone in her condo near Summerlin, and he was alone in Angel Park. Four people who knew one another but were nonetheless alone. Larson wondered if any of the other three felt the same. He switched off the lights in the living room and headed for his bedroom. He hoped Tammy wasn't lonely.

———

THE ENGINEERING COMPLEX at the Silver Palace was ground level at the rear of the complex. Luke didn't have any problem finding it. Two sober uniformed officers stood guard outside the door marked, *Engineering Staff Only*.

One of the officers opened the door for Luke when he approached. KC King and two more officers waited inside.

"He's in the back. Their locker room," KC announced, leading Luke across a wide room filled with wall charts of electrical and plumbing systems, drafting tables, and rows of active computers, atop desks, all displaying similar screen savers. An irony haunted Luke as he followed KC King. It was the fact Barbara's death left no body to be viewed, while an engineer who smoked pot was going to be seen by dozens.

"Ready or not," KC said as they reached the door to the engineer's locker room. He opened the door to reveal Officer Givens standing inside with a cup of coffee in hand.

"Gentlemen." Givens nodded.

Beyond Officer Givens, between two rows of metal lockers, hanging from exposed plumbing in the open ceiling, was the lifeless body of Ron Stillman. On the floor beneath iron-toed shoes the engineer wore was a puddle of urine. The inside of both coverall legs and crotch were wet-stained. Stillman's arms hung slack, palms open. Two heavy shoes pointed toward the polished cement floor which was eight inches beneath them. A small folding step ladder Stillman used to launch his death lay on its side a few feet from where the body hung. Stillman's tongue, growing gray and dry, gripped between upper and lower rows of teeth, was stuck far from the corner of his mouth. His eyes were open, staring at a floor his feet could no longer touch. He was dead, unmoving, but his lifeless body looked relaxed.

"No note found anywhere?" Luke questioned as he studied the body.

"No note found," KC answered. "Surveillance checked radio traffic. Nothing there. We took pictures, shot some video, checked his car, nothing there. He's single. Lives over on Maryland Parkway somewhere. Maybe Metro will have a look there for us."

"You called them yet?" Luke asked.

"You were my first."

"Okay," Luke suggested. "Time to dial nine-one-one. Tell them we have a probable suicide, employee, death by hanging. We'll need paramedics and Metro. Preserve the scene. Have Givens move out of here with his coffee. Tell Metro we'll preserve the video we've got. Have you looked at it?"

"No, I spoke with Gil Fraiser. He's the surveillance supervisor on duty. He looked. Found Stillman coming in from the hallway about two hours before Givens came in on his wrench hunt."

"Okay, get me what you can as soon as you can. I'll reach out to the head of engineering, HR, the Chaplin, the GM." Luke glanced at his watch. "We'll have a bunch of engineers wanting in here in another hour or so. Keep your guys in the hallway. No one in or out without your approval. No mention of this by word of mouth or radio. Any questions?"

"Yeah," KC King smiled. "Rumor has it your lady was coming to town. She get here okay."

"No," Luke answered soberly. "She died last night. Killed by a truck." He turned and walked away.

Reaching his office, Luke closed the door and sat down behind his desk. He wished he hadn't made the comment about Barbara's death to KC King, but the words came without warning. There was no one else to blame. Except maybe a drunk fucking truck driver. Maybe, Luke thought, it was his own psyche finding a way to tell all. He gave up on logic and dialed into his desktop to find a home telephone number for the head of engineering. He found it. James Matthews. He made a note of the number and dialed it.

The telephone rang four times before a male voice answered, "Hello."

"I'm calling for James Matthews," Luke asked the groggy male.

"Speaking," the man answered.

"Jim, it's Luke Mitchel from the Silver Palace. I'm sorry. It's about one of your men, Ron Stillman. He committed suicide here on property. Hung himself."

"What! Hung himself! Jesus Christ!"

"I'm sorry, Jim. The area's going to be restricted for a while. We're in…"

"You…you're the sonofabitch that jammed Ron for smoking a joint," Matthews growled, cutting Luke short. "Satisfied now, you prick."

Luke punched a button on the telephone console and the light for the call went out. He tried to calm himself, but Matthew's words had cut deep. He went back to the computer's illuminated screen in search of another number. *Human Resources*. He made a note of Ron Bergman's number and went on to the next. Chaplin, Peter Townsend. Luke added the number to his notes, thinking it might be the right time to invite God into this mess. He didn't have to look up the number for the GM. Luke took a breath to steady himself, punched the contact number for Larson's private cell, and waited, wondering how the GM might feel about his contributing to the suicide death of an engineer.

"Hello," Larson's familiar voice answered.

"Boss, it's Luke. Sorry to be calling at this hour, but…"

"It's Tammy! What's the address? I don't even fucking know it!"

"Listen to me," Luke said. "This has nothing to do with Tammy. I'm sure she's fine."

"What! Not Tammy! Jesus, Luke, what's wrong? You scared the shit out of me."

"I'm calling from the Palace. There's been a suicide. An engineer. He hung himself."

"Oh, god, no," Larson groaned, swinging his bare feet to the carpeted floor. "I'll be right in."

"Sir, there's no need to…"

"I said I'd be in, goddamn it."

A dial tone sung in Luke's ear. He carefully replaced the telephone in its multi-line cradle. Then, with a vicious growl, he swung a stiff arm across the top of his desk, sending the desktop monitor, telephone console, pens and pencils, and a variety of desktop items crashing to the floor.

"Fuckkk!" he screamed.

———

GABRIELA RODRIGUEZ, from housekeeping, was pushing a wheeled cart filled with clean sheets and towels. She was en route to the back-of-the-house elevator, passing the director of security's closed office when she heard the heavy crash inside followed by a man screaming. Gabriela paused, listened. The man's scream was followed by silence. Frightened, she hurried away. Reaching the elevator, Gabriela met two other housekeepers. She told them of the crashing sound in the closed office, followed by a man screaming. The oldest of the three dug a cell phone from her apron and called security.

Four minutes later KC King and a female officer arrived outside the closed door of Luke's office. They listened. There was no noise. KC looked at the female officer and then knocked firmly on the door. "Chief, you in there?"

When there was no answer, KC knocked again. Heavier, with a flat hand that shook the door. "Chief, it's KC. Open the door."

"Go away," Luke shouted from behind the door.

KC was worried. He was uncertain what to do. He studied the closed door for a moment then looked to the female officer. He shrugged, and they walked away.

———

GREG LARSON WASN'T SURPRISED to find a fire truck, with its red lights flashing, and a Metro police car parked near the rear entrance of the Silver Palace. He knew why they were there. He parked his Maserati in his reserved spot and hurried inside. The double doors leading into the engineering complex were just inside. Larson offered a nod to the security officer at the rear entrance and hurried to the windowed double doors. He pushed the door open to find another security officer inside.

"Sorry, sir," the young officer said with a raised hand. "Metro's inside. They said no one's allowed in."

Larson was annoyed. "You do know who the hell I am, don't you?"

"Yes, sir, I do but…"

KC King and Jim Matthews appeared from a rear

hallway into the main room of the complex. They walked to where the officer and the GM stood. "They let me get my ID out of my office and told me to get out," Matthews complained. "Who the hell do they think they are?"

"I think they know who they are," Larson suggested.

"You don't want to go in there, sir," KC King cautioned. "It's ugly. I shot some video before Metro got here. I'll send it to your office."

"This is bullshit, you know," Matthews said with a glance at the hallway leading to the locker room. "Stillman was twenty-eight. A dependable Night Watch. He was upset over that marijuana thing up on forty-eight. Grass is legal in Nevada, you know. I don't see what the hell the big deal was."

"Marijuana may be legal in Nevada," Larson said soberly, "but you're not in Nevada, mister, you're in the Silver Palace, so get rid of that liberal attitude. Your day watch team will be arriving soon, so act like the manager you are."

Three paramedics pushing a wheeled stretcher appeared from the back hallway. The body on the stretcher was covered and strapped in place.

A single near blue hand hung from beneath the sheet covering the body. Larson, KC, and Matthews stepped aside as the solemn trio passed. The officer posted at the door, pushed it open. A dry wheel on the stretcher screeched as the trio moved out into the main corridor.

LUKE KNEW he had to clean up his own mess. He had sit for a long time staring at the barren top of his empty desk. His life, he decided, was much like the top of his desk. Empty. Barbara and a life of love shared was gone. KC King knocking on his door brought him back to reality. After KC was gone Luke began gathering the mess from the floor. He was relieved to find his desktop monitor and telephone were tougher than his effort at breaking them. There was a task that came with the new day and Luke dreaded it, but he knew it had to be done. He owed Barbara. He knew the number well. Luke dialed it and awaited an answer.

"Wild River Resort and Casino," a pleasant female voice said in Luke's ear. "How may I direct your call?"

"Director of Security, please."

A moment later, Calvin Many-Coats, the savvy twenty-seven-year-old Mojave who had followed Luke's path to become the Director at the Mojaves Wild River Resort in Del Rio, Arizona, answered. "Security, this Calvin."

"Cal, it's Luke Mitchel. I've got some bad news."

"I get it," the young Mojave answered. "Barbara's not coming back after her dog. She owes me a pair of Niki's. Buster ate one of them last night."

"Barbara's dead, Calvin. Eighteen Wheeler hit her head on."

The line between the two men was quiet for a long moment, then Luke continued, "Her body is at the Clark County Coroner's office here in Vegas. I need your help in finding her family. I loved her. Thought I knew her, I didn't know much. She must have provided an emergency contact, family members, or something when she signed on. Being a friend, no matter how close, doesn't help at the coroner's office."

Again, it was quiet before Calvin spoke. "Yeah, okay, I'll have a look." The pitch in his young voice had changed.

Luke didn't know what else to say. "Thanks, Calvin. If I can help on this end, call me."

"Sure, I will."

There were no goodbyes. The call just ended. Luke promised himself he would call Calvin to see what he found, but the idea of just sending flowers to someone he never met seemed senseless. Going to Barbara's funeral was another matter. He'd be there. No matter where, no matter what time.

"Big dog is in the house," Luke heard KC King's voice on the scanner on his desk. He knew KC was talking about the GM. Luke felt guilt about not answering KC's earlier knock on his door, but he knew KC understood and although he now knew the GM was on property he was in no hurry to see him.

Proving the rumor mill in the Silver Palace was alive and well, the news that the fiancée of the director of security had died in a car crash traveled far and wide through the network of the near four thousand employees on duty. The death of an unknown loved one was alarming but coupled with the story of the director of security barricading himself in his office to scream at the walls added fuel to the fire.

Ready or not, the sun would rise. Guest occupancy numbered at five thousand six hundred and thirty-four. Breakfast orders for over three thousand rooms had already been made. Shadows on the Strip were being erased by sunlight, but the card room and slots at the Silver Palace were still active. Luke knew from his watch that the security day watch briefing was likely in progress. Mario Lopez would be providing the needed data for the day ahead. KC King and some of his crew would be staying on overtime to pick up the pieces from the tragedy in engineering. If there was a lesson to be learned from the death of others, and there were many, the biggest seemed to be...*the music played on*.

Luke looked at his closed office door. He knew he had to open it. The world was waiting on the other side. He took a deep breath, pushed out of his chair, and moved for the door.

EIGHTEEN
BET ON IT!

LUKE WENT from his office to the back-of-house elevator and pushed the down button. His plan was simple. He would have surveillance track Ron Stillman's last shift. Maybe something would foreshadow the fate his last hours would show, although having once, with the death of a police partner, considered suicide, Luke learned it was seldom a random compulsion, but more likely a thought given consideration for days or weeks.

A chime sounded as the elevator arrived. Luke was surprised when the doors parted revealing an elevator full of bare-breasted beauties in skimpy black panties and high heels. Their combined scent reached out to him. He stared in awe.

"Going down?" a young brunette with ample breasts standing at the controls, questioned with a smile.

"I think I better wait," Luke answered.

"Your loss," another voice on the elevator called out as the door closed.

A graying Black janitor with a dustpan, a broom, and an empty trash can joined Luke at the elevators as the car full of beauties disappeared behind closing doors. "Going down for dress rehearsal." The old man smiled. "Only in Vegas."

Surprises for the day hadn't ended. When Luke opened the door to surveillance, he found Candice Harmon waiting with Frick and Fratt.

"I heard you were in," Candice said without her usual smile. "I was about to call. These two claim they've got news."

Frick and Fratt were both smiling. Luke took it as a good sign. He sat down in a chair next to Candice's desk. "Let's have it," Luke urged.

Both Frick and Fratt carried video tablets. Frick glanced at his and began. "When we were briefed, you provided us the identity of the blackmailer."

"Since he is an employee with internet access, the path was there," Fratt added with a satisfied smile.

"Go on," Luke urged.

"Every email in the Silver Palace becomes part of an electronic history that, by design, points to the individual sending or receiving the email, Frick explained. "Our blackmailer sits in front of a computer with internet access all day."

"So, that's where we started," Fratt added with an enthusiastic smile.

Frick gave his partner a shut-up look before continuing. "We started with yesterday's emails and reached back, day by day. A pattern quickly emerged. The blackmailer is in partnership with his brother-in-law who is a clerk for the municipal courts in Laughlin. The two conspired to find a history on Gayle Turner. What they found isn't much. What they did with what they found violates a variety of strict laws, both county, state, and federal, governing the control of criminal records, photographs, and employment histories and much more."

"Impressive," Luke agreed. "But tell us what they found on Gayle?"

Fratt chose to answer. "She was eighteen years old when arrested for prostitution in Laughlin. She pleaded guilty and served over thirty days."

"Twenty years ago, prostitution was still a crime." Frick smiled.

Fratt resumed his dialogue. "They discovered a booking photograph of the eighteen-year-old. They had no right to the photo, but after illegally obtaining it, they transmitted the photo here, another violation of a variety of laws. Once the blackmailer had the photo, he showed it to Gayle and threatened her with exposure."

"Did Gayle knowingly conceal her arrest in Laughlin when she applied for employment here at the Silver Palace?"

"We cannot say what Gayle Turner did or did not do when she applied," Frick answered. "The data the black-mailer used was obtained illegally. If it were used here, it would be, what is the word, *tainted, illegal, compromised*."

"He's saying using it would create a significant liability for the company," Fratt added.

"Give me the bottom line," Luke said to both men. "Who's guilty of what in this electronic mess?"

Frick took the lead. "The blackmailer, as the title suggests, is criminal. He and his brother-in-law are both felons and either could be prosecuted."

Candice smiled and slapped her hands together, applauding the two. They returned her smile. Then she noticed Luke wasn't smiling. "I'm sorry," she added. It's just so…

"I understand," Luke said. "Is Carter here today?"

"Yes, position three inside," Candice answered.

Luke pushed to his feet and looked to the two men. "You did good, gentlemen, but you're not done yet. I want you to come back to my office with me." Then he looked to Candice. "I'll call you when we're ready. You get to bring Carter up to my office."

Frick elbowed Fratt. "Tell him."

Fratt nodded and looked to Luke. "While researching this, we got an alarm on a telephone number we compromised by making an active call to it."

"I'm not following you."

"The number you provided was for an escort service. We set the system so when a call was initiated from within the Silver Palace, we would be alerted."

"So," Luke questioned.

"Yesterday a call was made from the general manager's office to the Blue Moon Escort Service. We listened," Fratt confessed.

"A payment of thirty-six hundred dollars was promised for two women who would meet two Chinese investors at the Hard Rock with an agreement for services lasting until six a.m. this morning."

"And who made this call?" Luke pressed.

"It was a lady's voice. The origin of the call was the assistant of the general manager."

Luke nodded and moved for the door. "Come with me, gentlemen. Candice, we'll call you."

———

DAWN WILDER GOT her call from human resources at the Cosmo before nine a.m. "Would you be available for a meet today with the head of our Food and Beverage division? He directs our servers."

Dawn's answer was yes. She was at the Cosmo twenty-two minutes later. She dressed the part. The head server interviewed her. "When can you start?" he questioned.

"Depends on the wage and I prefer nights." Dawn was bold. Oprah had talked about it on TV, get'im up front. Don't be shy. Dawn literally held her breath.

"Eighteen and hour and no split on tips. Can you start tonight at eight?"

"I'll be here at seven." Dawn smiled.

She went away with a smile, believing her charm had found a path. *Reality* held a different answer. It was sixteen floors above Dawn in the office of the Director of Rooms. *Reality's* name was Charlotte Johnson.

Back in his office, Luke reached out to housekeeping and had three more chairs brought up. Frick and Fratt provided a thumb drive with the data from their investigation. Luke loaded it on his computer. Neither of the two men had ever been in his office. He noticed their eyes searching. They looked at the flags standing in both corners, the Stars and Stripes as well a Nevada State flag, wipe board schedules, occupancy charts, a framed LAPD Badge, a detailed drawing of the glass-walled pool under construction on the roof of the Gold Tower, a chart detailing management organization, while another displayed the chain of command in security. Frick elbowed Fratt after finding their names under the title, *Network Operations.*

"I have one final thing I need your help with, gentlemen. I need an agreement on terms."

After the chairs were delivered and Frick had sat down at Luke's computer to prepare the agreement, Luke made two calls. The first was to Mario Lopez, the day watch security supervisor. "Mario, get me two of your best and post them outside my office. I want them standing tall and proud." His second call was to Candice. "We're ready, bring Carter up."

"While we wait, gentlemen," Luke said to Frick and Fratt, "this needs to be said. What happens in this room today remains confidential. It is never, under any circumstances, to be discussed or mentioned to Gayle Turner. No record of your findings will be kept in any form outside this office. Do you agree?"

The two men answered in near unison, "yes, sir."

"In addition to that, I need to offer my sincere appreciation for what you've done. Your efforts have saved hopes, dreams, and careers. I wish I could shout it from the top of the Silver Palace, but I can't. It has to stay inside these four walls, but you know, and I know, what you two have done is extraordinary. Thank you." Luke stood and offered a hand to both men.

Candice walked with surveillance agent Ted Crater to the back-of-the-house elevator. "Any idea what the chief wants up there?" Carter questioned.

"No," Candice answered as they walked shoulder to shoulder. "He called, said find Carter, and come on up."

Carter nodded as they reached the elevator. "I think it relates to Gayle. She's the head of surveillance. Her absence can only be tolerated for so long. My money is on a reorganization. Bet on it."

A heavy knock sounded on Luke's office door. "It's open," he called out. One of the uniformed officers posted outside the door opened it, revealing Candice and a surprised-looking Ted Carter.

"Come in," Luke said without standing. Frick and Fratt were sited in chairs on the left. A single chair sat empty, facing Luke's desk, and another sat empty on the right.

"Ted," Luke said, gesturing to the chair in front of his desk, then with a look to Candice, "Over there, please."

Carter, looking uneasy and worried, exchanged a look with Frick and Fratt as he sat down facing Luke's desk. Luke leaned forward to rest his elbows on his desk as he studied Carter.

"As of this moment, Ted Carter," Luke began. "Your employment as a surveillance agent for the Silver Palace is terminated. You and your brother-in-law, who is employed as a records clerk in Laughlin, are both guilty of felonious conduct including the theft of official government records, the private use, and misuse, of corporate assets, both here and in the city of Laughlin, and blackmail."

"No, now wait a minute," Carter objected. "I have rights." He looked to Candice, then Frick and Fratt before returning to Luke's glare.

"Yes, you do," Luke agreed, holding his look on Carter. "You can try to walk out of here, but you'll be arrested and held by the Metropolitan police while I make a call to the Sheriff's Department in Laughlin to have your brother-in-law arrested. Those are my rights. Shall I go on."

"This isn't fair," Carter pleaded, again searching the faces for agreement. "This is all a misunderstanding."

"Good title," Luke agreed. "Let's go with a *misunderstanding*." He reached to his desktop and turned the printout of the agreement toward Carter.

"Sign this, and you walk out of here with a misunderstanding. Don't sign, well, then you and your brother-in-law will have to call a bondsman."

"Wait, wait, let me read this," Carter begged, gathering the paper into his hands.

"Sorry, times up," Luke warned. "Candice, call the officers in here."

Candice made a move as if she were getting up.

"Okay, okay, I'll sign it."

Luke pushed a ball point toward Carter who gathered the pen and laid the paper on the front of the desk. "You won't tell my brother-in-law about this," he pleaded.

"Sign it," Luke ordered.

Carter scrawled his signature on the bottom of the agreement. Luke pulled the paper from Carter and looked at it, then he looked to Candice again. "Bring the officers in."

"I signed it. Look at it. I agreed."

"Shut up," Luke ordered as Candice got up and opened the door. "Come in, gentlemen."

Frick and Fratt watched in awe as the two officers filled the doorway. One was Black, the other Hispanic. Both were big men in their thirties.

"I want you to escort this man down to his car. Surveillance will cover you until he drives away."

"Wait, I have things at my desk."

"Your things will come with your final check. I'm sure human resources will be in touch."

"Come on," the Black officer said, taking Carter by the arm and literally lifting him out of his chair.

Candice closed the office door as Carter, sandwiched between the two officers, was led away. Frick and Fratt sat wide-eyed and silent.

Luke drew in a deep breath and pushed back in his chair. He smiled at Candice and then at Frick and Fratt. "You know I didn't think he would sign it."

"If he didn't, I would have," Candice said, sinking into her chair.

———

BREAKFAST at the Out of the Shadows Ranch consisted of oatmeal, toast, and a choice of tea or coffee. Tammy, like others crowding the tables, forced herself to eat. She learned Carol, the thirty-something beside her, was the mother of two and a heroin addict. The younger man on her left was a valet attendant from Mandalay Bay. He was a crackhead. His parents, who lived in Oregon, had flown in, spent the night and dropped him at the ranch.

After breakfast came a yoga session and then exercises. Tammy was certain she smelled of sweat. Sweat or not, a fifteen-minute break was followed by what was posted on a wipe board in the main meeting room, *The morning mind set*. Josh Logan was the speaker. Tammy sat beside the heroin addict in the gathering of twenty-plus.

Logan, with his unshaven face and long hair, reminded Tammy of a shampoo commercial. He asked all to bow their heads in prayer before he began. Tammy was uncertain how to pray, but she bowed her head.

"The challenge today," Logan said, offering a friendly smile, "is not how long it might be until you feel good," Logan walked into the midst of the group, pushing his hands into the back pockets of his jeans, "but what you believe. Most of us believe in someone or something. Most of us, and I'm including me, believe in drugs. It doesn't matter what drug, most will make you a believer." He paused near Tammy and glanced at her. She looked to the floor not wanting to see his eyes.

"They did me," said Logan as he brushed a sweep of hair from Tammy's shoulder and moved on. A spattering of laughter came from the group.

Logan continued his walk. "Close your eyes and ask, what do I believe? We're all believers. Think of what day it is, what month, what time. There's no risk in believing that. We all agree what day it is, but what about the uncertainties, like the weather? We can see it, feel it, but it's there."

"No one can control the weather, but we can and do get ready for it. Why, because we believe in it. Well, guess what? Life is like the weather. You have to get ready for it. You have to believe. Our lives have a beginning, a middle and an end. Most believe that, but we hunger for more. That's the allure of drugs. They hide us from life. We believe in what they can do. So, it's safe to say we all believe in something, and that's where this gets messy. What do you believe? What do those you love believe? It's a puzzling question, but it's a question that has to be asked. What do you believe? Close your eyes and think about it."

Logan's voice was friendly, and he wasn't asking much. Tammy closed her eyes and asked herself the question. What do I believe? She felt tears welling in her eyes. It shocked her and so did the realization she didn't know what she believed. Her hands and feet were cold. She cupped her hands together. They were trembling. *Withdrawals*, Tammy told herself. The heroin addict beside her began to cry.

In the director of security's office at the Silver Palace, Luke sent Frick and Fratt back to their electronic hideaway in surveillance. He knew the moment would come when he and Candice would have to deal with the reality of their relationship, especially now that it was stained with Barbara's death. They sat quietly for a moment after Fratt pulled the office door closed.

Candice was the first to speak after a careful glance at Luke. "I'm sorry, Luke. Sorry for what I did, and I'm sorry for what happened to Barbara."

Luke nodded agreement. "I'm sorry too. Maybe sometime we could talk, but I'm not there yet."

Candice wiped a tear with a quick swipe of a hand and nodded in agreement.

"It's time we talk about Gayle," Luke said, leaning into his desk.

"I could hardly breathe with Carter in the room," Candice confessed.

"He's toast. He can't do anything now," Luke suggested, "but Gayle was blackmailed. She should have come to me, but she didn't. It's a vote of no confidence."

"She didn't bring it to me either," Candice countered. "She was on the verge of resigning. I knew something was wrong. I had to pull it out of her. What could she have told you? I was arrested for prostitution twenty years ago. Did either of us get anything wrong in the past twenty years? This was something a woman couldn't confess to a man."

Luke rocked back in his chair as he listened. "Okay, Gayle didn't want you to say anything about her being blackmailed. What if we tell her I ran a routine audit of who does what on the net? Carter was found with multiple violations, compounded by lying about it, and he was fired. It's almost the truth."

Candice agreed. "That would keep you out of it, and it saves my relationship with her."

"Do it. Go tell her to get back to work."

Candice stood and gave Luke a look that said much without saying a word. She left, closing the door behind her.

Luke didn't want to be alone. He knew being idle

would bring it all back. In one sense it seemed only minutes since the officer knocked on his door. In another, it seemed distant and foreign. Near unbelievable, a dream, no, a *nightmare*. Morning was yielding to afternoon. Would time change it? Could time change it? He gave thought to going on the internet and googling *grief*, but he knew defining it would be like looking at a wound. There was no place to hide. No one to explain it. No one to cry to. He looked at the calendar on his desk. He pushed Ted Carter's signed agreement aside, picked up a pen and wrote *Barabara* in blue ink on a date. He laid the pen aside and pulled open a desk drawer. There, he had stashed a collection of wrapped power pars and several bottles of water. Going down to employee dining wasn't an option. By now word of Barbara's death would have made its way to every corner of the Palace. Few had ever seen her. Eating one of the power bars and chasing it with the bottled water, Luke remembered their first visit to the Palace. A nurse had tried jumping to her death. Luke saved her from that. The thought that he had saved one woman while setting Barbara's death in motion, chilled him. Luke tossed the half-eaten energy bar into the trash.

There was occasional chatter on his scanner. He heard Mario Lopez talking about a possible pickpocket in slots. It was nothing they needed him for. Hours had passed. He hoped Metro and the coroner were gone from engineering. KC King was capable. He'd be tying up the loose ends.

Jim Matthews, the head of engineering, was more than a loose end. He was an angry man. Luke understood it. Matthews had someone, a face, to point a finger at. Someone to blame for what happened. Luke had no one. What was it the Nevada Highway Patrol Lieutenant told

him, the truck driver was going to jail for DUI. Luke
would have to aim his anger at a faceless man driving a
truck. Hell, he didn't even know what kind of truck it
was. How big, how small. How old was the man? Did the
man regret what happened? None of it mattered. None
of it could change the fact Barbara was gone. None of it
could change the fact she died trying to reach him. Luke
ran a finger over the name he had written in blue ink
and pushed out of his chair. There was a piece of business Frick and Fratt had mentioned that he needed to
follow up on. Why? Because it was his job. If he keeps
doing his job, maybe the mask it provided would help.

Luke took an elevator to the casino level. He shared it
with guests. He listened to their chatter. An older couple
were on their way to Rossi's Fine Italian Diner in the
Silver Palaces Arcade for a late lunch. A younger couple
planned to visit the Bellagio to take pictures before
crossing the street to Paris, where one of them won
three hundred dollars there playing Twenty-One the
night before. Luke listened to their talk as it mixed with
a musical version of *Tie a Yellow Ribbon Around the Old
Oak Tree*, playing on the elevator's speaker. The music
made him smile. He who put the playlist together. She
was divorced and talkative. He had shared a table with
her in employee dining. The elevator reached the casino
level. Luke was the last off. The brief encounter assured
him the world was still out there. Part of it had died, no,
part of him had died, but life wasn't gone. It was in front
of him. As he exited the elevator, those waiting pushed
in. Most were new arrivals headed for their rooms.
Others passed by and headed for the arcade where they
would find an array of restaurants, open cafés, Mariachi
bands, jewelry stores and the Old Navy.

The casino was active, wasn't it always? There were

those among the check-ins who couldn't walk past the Twenty-One tables without trying their luck. An excited shout from one of the tables proved Luke right.

He found comfort in seeing familiar faces dealing, behind the heavy glass at the cash cage and at the busy front desk. Luke walked the perimeter of the card room, feeding on the background music, the voices, the laughter, and the electronic clinking from slots, until he reached sunlight near the front door. There he stepped out of the way of a valet attendant pushing a wheeled cart full of luggage, and several guests carrying their own bags. Finally, he was through the double glass doors and into the sunshine.

The Strip had its own sounds, and a helicopter slapped the air above. Traffic on the divided Boulevard was busy with buses, trucks carrying signs for massages and an assortment of glossy limousines, new and old EVs, SUVs, pickups, and cars of every color. The sidewalk was crowned with people staring at the towers lining the Strip with colorful towering videos and flashing lights. Many with phones held high were taking pictures. Some strolled, others hurried, while others just stood and stared. Luke had seen it before, but it always looked different. One hundred thousand visitors came and went every day. They brought their money and the hope they would leave with more, but then there was the real world. Today, the real world for Luke was the Star Bucks sidewalk café in front of the Silver Palace. Its umbrellas and sidewalk tables provided an escape from the casino and Luke liked to sit and watch the tourists. They provided a private preview. They were beautiful, young, old, flashy, and dull. Luke went to the service counter and ordered his usual—a grande iced Americano with several pumps of caramel syrup. The attractive barista put the drink in front of him with a smile.

The café was busy. Drink in hand, Luke looked for a vacant table. He gave up looking for a table, deciding to settle for a chair at an occupied table. What he found surprised him. He recognized the woman, although he couldn't remember her name. She was an attractive brunette, his age, and although she had the Vegas look, it wasn't over the top. He remembered she claimed to be a freelance writer for the Las Vegas Sun. He was surprised at who shared her table. Her companion, maybe thirty, was dressed for sale. Wearing spiked heels, a short dark skirt that covered little of her thighs, a deep cut blouse showing the swell of her breasts and impeccable makeup, assured Luke his guess at her occupation was accurate.

The two women had yet to see Luke. Their attention was on a middle-aged Asian man who approached their table.

The man spoke with the woman Luke had met before. He watched as an introduction was made to the young woman. The man liked what he saw. He nodded and the young beauty got up, took his arm and they walked together toward the entrance of the Silver Palace. Luke approached the table, where the brunette waited.

"May I?" he questioned, gesturing to the chair emptied by the girl.

The brunette was surprised, but offered a quick smile. "Of course. I remember you. Please, join me."

Luke sat down. "I didn't want to interrupt. I thought maybe your companion would be returning."

"Just a couple in town for some fun, I guess," the brunette answered, showing her anxiety.

Luke set his coffee down and gathered his phone

from beneath his jacket. He looked to the brunette. "Excuse me, while I call Cloud Nine Escorts." He punched in the number. The brunette turned stone-faced and stiffened in her chair. Luke held the phone to his ear as a cell phone in the woman's purse atop the table began ringing. "Aren't you going to answer?" Luke questioned, matching her sober look.

The brunette bolted to her feet, reached, and grabbed her purse. "Fuck you," she growled and marched away.

Luke ignored the disapproving looks from nearby tables. He pushed his cell beneath his jacket and sipped his coffee. Luke's retreat to the Starbucks sidewalk café where he hoped just to get lost in the crowd, turned into business. Not just business but sex hidden behind the ruse, it was simply an attractive escort providing companionship for a guest. Luke didn't allow the fleeting thought that Barbara died coming to have sex with him. He pushed out of his chair, tossed his coffee into the trash, and headed inside. He needed to go to surveillance and have them isolate the video of the guest with the girl and his encounter with the now-identified *Madam* of Cloud Nine Escorts.

Luke was aware of the fact Jackie Fallon, the GM's assistant, had called Cloud Nine earlier to arrange companionship for two Silver Palace investors visiting from Hong Kong. Finding the line between prostitution and just having fun in Vegas was becoming more of a challenge every day.

EPILOGUE

LUKE WAS HEADING for the elevators at the back of card room when his cell phone began vibrating. He pulled it from beneath his jacket and looked at the caller ID. It was Jackie Fallon in the GM's office.

"Yes, Jackie," Luke said into his phone continuing his walk to the elevators.

"Luke," Jackie answered in his ear. "The GM would like to speak with you. Can you stop by?"

Luke thought the alleged reporter, who was really the force behind Cloud Nine, had called the GM to complain about him. "Yes," Luke answered. "Be there in a couple minutes."

He noticed, crossing the card room and into the back of the house, that many familiar faces he saw didn't speak to him. Luke guessed it was a case of their not knowing what to say. They knew he was tainted by death. It was easier to say nothing than it was to say something about his loss. He felt guilty. He should have stayed away. Said nothing. Now, he was on his way to see a man who wouldn't avoid talking, and Luke didn't want to talk. Not only that, he was on his way to the GM's office, unshaven and wearing the same clothes he had on yesterday.

———

JACKIE FALLON OFFERED Luke a brief smile when he stepped into her office. "I'll let him know you're here," she said, gathering up her telephone.

Luke didn't bother to sit down. He looked at the GM's closed door. It was obvious Jackie was among those who didn't know what to say.

"Sir," she said into her telephone. "Luke Mitchel is here."

Luke heard the GM's voice on the phone. Jackie looked to him and nodded. Luke reached for the door.

Greg Larson pushed out of the chair behind his desk as Luke entered. "Luke, close the door."

Luke closed the door and crossed to a chair in front of Larson's desk. Before Luke sat down, Larson extended a hand, and Luke accepted it.

"Sorry to hear about the loss of your fiancée," Larson said as they shook. Larson's grip was warm and firm. "Sit down, let's talk."

Luke sat down. Larson resumed his seat behind his wide ornate desk. "Been a shit day, hasn't it?" he suggested, studying Luke.

Luke nodded in agreement.

"I expected to find you in engineering when I came in this morning. You weren't there."

"I was in surveillance. We were looking at Stillman's moves before he went into engineering."

"Matthews told me you jammed Stillman the other

day for smoking on duty. He's blaming you for the man's suicide."

Luke didn't like Larson's accusatory tone. "I didn't jam anyone. Stillman was found on surveillance video going into a blind spot in a stairway where he smoked weed and ground out the butt on the stairs."

"I got no word on that," Larson countered.

"You canceled our daily briefing," Luke defended.

"True, but I'm concerned about getting things second-hand. Such as a surveillance agent being fired and escorted off property this morning. And that came just after Stillman hung himself. There's a lot of shit happening, Luke. A young housekeeper found dead in a stairway. The chase and arrest of a server involved in her death. Metro on property. Then, a female server is caught holding while another housekeeper bites it with a stash of dope in her car. Two dead, lots of cops, and a guy fired. I can't answer all the questions I'm getting. We're all sorry for your personal loss, but you've got to get a handle on it, Luke. This is the Silver Palace, we can't allow shit like this to be happening."

"Sounds like Matthews did a sales job on you," Luke suggested.

"Yeah, he's pissed. I couldn't defend you because I had no idea what the fuck happened. You want some time off, you know, get some rest? Find your *True North*."

Luke was angry. "You want a resignation. I'll provide it."

"Hell, no," Larson answered, leaning into his desk. "We've been through a lot of together. You have my trust and confidence. I've asked a lot of you, and you've deliv-ered. But I have to run this great big fucking bus filled with demands, shadows, and fears. The more the world pulls back the curtain on us the more we chance losing our asses. I'm on your side, Luke, all I'm asking is you help me pull this mess out of the fire before we both get burned."

"Got it," Luke answered.

He left without speaking to Jackie Fallon. He wanted in his car and away from this place. Gayle Turner, Candice Harmon, Ron Matthews, and Greg Larson could all kiss his ass. He had done his best. He was being blamed for shit where blame didn't fit. It was the Vegas curse. If you lost, it was your own fault. He was almost to the elevator when his cell vibrated again. He was annoyed, he didn't want to talk, what the hell was he going to be blamed for now, but he gathered the phone from his belt and looked at caller ID. It was Charlotte Johnson. What could she want? He pushed a button for the elevator and answered her call. "Hi, Charlotte, what's up?" He knew the help he asked for Dawn Wilder had somehow turned into a pile of crap.

"Luke, I'm at Kings and Queens," Charlotte said in his ear. "That's only four blocks from you. I need to see you. Just give the Matre Dee my name when you get here."

"You want me there now?"

"Yes, please. Remember, you owe me."

"I remember," Luke answered. "Give me ten. I'll be there."

Luke got to his car without speaking to anyone. He found relief when he drove onto the Strip and became just another car sandwiched in the crush of cars, cabs, and buses. He glanced at what he could see of the Silver Palace in his rearview mirror. He surrendered his car to a valet at the rear of the Kings and Queens Restaurant. He suspected what Charlotte wanted was the latest on Greg Larson. Maybe she would fill in the blanks on what had him on edge. Women, you couldn't live without them, but it was often harder to live with them. He remembered the phrase from some lounge act he'd seen, but it fit, and it was painful.

Luke found the Matre Dee in the shadowed lounge and asked for Charlotte. "This way, sir."

He was surprised. Charlotte was waiting, but she wasn't alone. A gray-haired man in a suit and tie sat with her.

"Luke, thanks for coming." Charlotte smiled as she and the gray hair pushed to their feet. "This is Howard Fisher, head of our human resources department. Please, sit down. Would you like a drink?"

A server appeared as they sat down. She was young, shapely and dressed in heels, snug dark shorts with a K&Q emblem on her hip and a form-fitting blouse that added to her Vegas persona. Her dark hair was pulled back in a smooth bun which amplified her dark eyes and lashes. Luke looked at the girl. He wondered if she had finished high school. "I'd welcome a Jack and Diet Coke, please."

The girl gave Luke a smile from glossy lips and turned away. Luke turned his attention to Charlotte and the gray hair. His surprise was turning to suspicion.

He gave his attention to Charlotte. He was wary of the suit and tie. "Charlotte, how can I help?"

"By listening to Howard," Charlotte answered with a glance at the man.

"Luke," the gray hair began. "For most, Vegas is a big crowded town full of nosey people in a hurry. For those of us who live and work here, it's a small town full of competitive professionals who not only know one another but cooperate. In short, Luke, we know who you are, we've seen your work, and we know what you've done. From our perspective, you're what is known as a leader of the pack."

Luke's drink arrived. The girl added another smile as she sat it in front of Luke. The gray hair and Luke watched as the girl marched away. The gray hair continued. "In short, Luke, on behalf of our general manager, we would be pleased to have you consider joining our team as Director of Risk Management. You would be in charge of Resort and Casino security as well the assessment of liabilities and hazards in all our operations. For your experience, resume, talents and proven skills, we are prepared to offer a salary that is not only negotiable, but far above what you are currently earning."

Luke picked up his drink. He thought it strange, but he wished Barbara was there. He would share the news with her. He smiled at Charlotte. He knew who had planted the seed, a second time. Luke tasted his drink and looked to the gray hair. "I'm flattered. May I think about it and get back to you."

"Of course," the gray hair agreed. "Perhaps, seventy-two hours and we must ask our offer remain confidential."

Luke nodded and pushed to his feet. Charlotte and the gray hair followed his lead. Luke offered a hand across the table to Charlotte. "Always good to see you, lady."

"Likewise," Charlotte agreed as they shook hands. "We look forward to hearing from you."

Luke shook hands with the *gray hair*, smiled and headed for the door.

"Holy shit!" he mumbled to himself as he walked out into the sunshine.

He drove the 215 to neighboring Henderson, thankful it was a multilane Interstate that required little more than moving with the flow of traffic. Luke's thoughts were on the offer. He was learning there was another dimension to the Vegas experience other than luck. It was friendship. Charlotte Johnson, a beautiful Black woman who turned heads in Las Vegas was much more than a friend and business associate. She was an ally. She had been key to him becoming director of security at the Silver Palace. Now, there was little doubt she was the moving force behind the offer he'd just listened to. Was the gray hair really talking about him? Ironically, the offer came only minutes after Greg Larson, the GM of the Silver Palace, had taken a big bite off of his ass. Vegas, life there was different, not only different, it was exciting.

City streets took him there. He didn't understand the compulsion, but that didn't matter. No one else would know. He wouldn't have to explain, probably couldn't explain. He parked in a Walgreens parking lot and walked to the intersection. Traffic was light. The afternoon heat was high. Reaching the intersection, Luke stood and studied it. The traces of the accident he had seen before were gone now. He sat down on the warm cement curb to look at the stretch of asphalt.

"Barbara," he said in a near whisper as a passing car blew its horn.

The man in the dark sports coat sitting on the curb on the corner of the intersection looked unusual. Cars flashing by ruffled his collar and his hair. Luke Mitchel didn't seem to care. Another passing car sounded its horn.

A LOOK AT: VEGAS ODDS (THE VEGAS TRILOGY BOOK 3)

In Las Vegas, the odds are never in your favor...especially when millions are on the line.

Luke Mitchell, Director of Security at the opulent Silver Palace Casino, faces his toughest challenge yet. A mysterious spike in the casino's losses has him hunting for thieves among the 10,000-strong staff, all while juggling high-stakes demands from the General Manager. When a notorious high roller, Prince Zayan Omar, arrives for a weekend of lavish gambling, Luke's team shifts into overdrive. But after a string of jaw-dropping wins, the Prince is found dead in his suite.

With $38 million in the casino's cage, a grieving oil baron demanding answers, and a sudden widow brandishing a surprise marriage certificate, the stakes have never been higher. As the Silver Palace teeters on the brink of scandal, Luke must unravel a web of deceit, greed, and betrayal while ensuring justice for the Prince and the casino.

Is the Prince's death a tragic accident, or a carefully orchestrated play? And can Luke protect the casino—and himself—from the dark forces circling ever closer?

Step behind the curtain and into the shadowy world of Sin City's elite in this gripping police procedural. *Vegas Odds* is a pulse-pounding tale of mystery, power, and the relentless pursuit of truth in a city built on secrets.

AVAILABLE MARCH 2025

ABOUT THE AUTHOR

Dallas Barnes, a former Director of Security & Surveillance in Las Vegas as well as a Los Angeles Police Homicide Detective, is the author of twelve novels. Vegas Gold is the first novel in the series based on his experiences while serving as Director of Security & Surveillance in Resort & Casino environments, including those listed below...

MGM Grand Signature—Las Vegas, NV
Hyatt Regency Resort & Casino—Lake Las Vegas, NV
Fantasy Springs Resort & Casino—Cabazon, CA
Agua Caliente Casino & Resort—Palm Springs, CA
Augustine Casino—Coachella, CA
Morongo Resort & Casino—Cabazon, CA
Blue Water Resort & Casino—Parker, AZ

www.ingramcontent.com/pod-product-compliance
Lightning Source LLC
Chambersburg PA
CBHW010728250626
47155CB00011B/3596